To John

Happy 80th birthday

# Becoming Someone

## An identity 'Annethology'

Anne Goodwin

Inspired
Quill

Published by Inspired Quill: November 2018

First Edition

Contact the author through her website: annegoodwin.weebly.com

Chief Editor: Sara-Jayne Slack
Cover Design: Paper & Sage Designs
Typesetting: BB eBooks
Typeset in Adobe Garamond Pro

Paperback ISBN: 978-1-908600-77-6
eBook ISBN: 978-1-908600-78-3
Print Edition

Printed in the United Kingdom
1 2 3 4 5 6 7 8 9 10

**Inspired Quill Publishing, UK**
**Business Reg. No. 7592847**
www.inspired-quill.com

# Praise for *Underneath*

*A dark and disturbing tale of a man who appears ordinary on the surface, but is deeply damaged. Clever and chilling; [Underneath] is a story that will stay with you long after you've finished reading.*

– Sanjida Kay,
author of *Bone by Bone*

*[Underneath] is a compelling, insightful and brave novel of doomed, twisted romance driven by a sustained and unsettling voice.*

– Ashley Stokes,
author of *The Syllabus of Errors*

*It's a quiet novel that gradually unpicks the past to discover what lies behind the protagonist's façade. Obviously drawing on her experience as a clinical psychologist, Anne Goodwin takes what could have been a dry case study and builds it into a compelling read.*

– Mary Mayfield,
*Our Book Reviews*

*Intelligent, insightful writing which takes you beneath the surface of life in many, many ways.*

– Pamela Robertson,
*Books, Life and Everything*

*As different from* Sugar and Snails *as chalk and cheese, Anne Goodwin turns to the dark side in her new novel,* Underneath. *Dark, twisted and compelling,* Underneath *is filled with tension and intrigue.*

– Michelle,
*The Book Magnet*

# Praise for *Sugar & Snails*

*An absorbing, clever and heartening debut novel.*

– Alison Moore,
author of Booker-shortlisted *The Lighthouse*

*This secret tantalisingly grips the reader, gradually being pieced together bit by bit, so intrinsically and poignantly mapped out that I truly cannot praise this novel highly enough.*

– Isabelle on *The Contemporary Small Press*

*Fiction delivered by a writer who knows not only how to craft her words but also what those words should be communicating.*

– Dr Suzanne Conboy-Hill in *The Psychologist*

*A probing debut novel and, like its protagonist, not what it first seems.*

– Gavin Weston,
author of *Harmattan*

*I loved this book. Sugar and Snails is beautifully written and a truly impressive debut by Anne Goodwin. It reminded me a little of Claire Messud's The Woman Upstairs. The character of Di, at first frustrating, grows more endearing as you begin to understand her. Her friend Venus and lover Simon are well-drawn; there as foils to Di's story. A beautiful and gripping read.*

– Fleur Smithwick,
author of *How to make a Friend*

*Sugar and Snails is a brave and bold emotional roller-coaster of a read. Anne Goodwin's prose is at once sensitive, invigorating and inspired. I was hooked from the start and in bits by the end. Very much to be recommended.*

– Rebecca Root,
actor and voice teacher

*For Norah Colvin and Charli Mills*

# Contents

# Stranded in the Dark

# Madonna and Child

THE WHINE OF the bin lorry had her hurtling out of bed, leaving the door to the flat ajar as she dashed, barefoot, downstairs. Gagging at the stench from the partly-open lid, she grabbed the handle of the wheelie bin and lugged it across the cracked paving to the street. But the refuse lorry was already turning the corner, leaving behind a cluster of emptied bins belonging to the more organised tenants of the apartment block. "Fuck!"

From across the road, an au pair en route from the posh houses to the shops appraised her coldly. The Betty Boop T-shirt she wore as a nightdress barely covered her buttocks and her hair was always a nightmare first thing. Gemma gave the au pair the finger and trundled the wheelie bin to its parking-place by the back door, the rough paving damp beneath her feet.

Whatever she did, however hard she tried, it was never enough. This was only a small disappointment, but brick by brick her small disappointments and failures massed into a substantial wall. And her day hadn't even started.

Why didn't her neighbours help out more? Was it beyond them to drag *her* bin around to the front along with their own? After all, a bin-load of shitty nappies languishing by the back door until the next collection would offend them as much as Gemma. But they'd do anything to get back at her for the noise.

Now the stairwell was uncannily quiet. Had the door to her flat slammed shut? Clad in nothing but a T-shirt, and with a hungry baby on the other side, she'd be fucked if it had. Gemma took the stairs two at a time.

The door stood open, and silence reigned within. Brilliant – but also rather weird. Weird too was another kind of absence: being snubbed by the bin-men added only a tiny brick – the smallest piece of Lego instead of a chunk of breezeblock – to the wall. Most days felt like running a marathon while taking an exam, with a hangover and no time for training or revision. Today Gemma felt almost normal, the teenager she would have been if she hadn't been caught out. Her mother used to nag her about the benefits of a good night's sleep, but she hadn't bothered to teach her how to achieve such a thing on her own with a baby. Gemma calculated the hours of slumber: the bin lorry usually came around half-nine and Milly had finally got off to sleep a little after three. Six solid hours of zzz!

Tiptoeing into the bed-sitting-room, a new feeling swept over her, colonising the space left by the departure of fatigue, frustration and rage. Asleep in the cot, Milly was like a doll fresh from the factory, only more perfect. A surge of love tempted Gemma to gather up the baby and smother her with kisses, but she resisted. Milly must be exhausted after several hours howling before Gemma had finally got her quiet. No point disturbing her now.

Easing open the wardrobe door, Gemma recalled her pride at primary school, gaining top marks in a test. Deep down, she'd always believed she'd get it right eventually with Milly. At last, her persistence had paid off.

She selected an outfit for Milly to wear later – a proper old-fashioned baby-dress with frills and bows and layers of petticoats she'd been saving for a christening that had never happened – and laid it on the bed. For herself, she chose a black miniskirt and low-cut glittery top she'd last worn at the school Christmas party. She had to lift the clotheshorse off the bath and dump it in the hallway to use the shower, and then it was only a rubber hose shoved onto the taps that released a mere trickle of water, but it felt so good she screamed. A proper mother at last!

Admiring her reflection in the wardrobe mirror as Milly slept on, the doorbell rang. She closed the door to the bed-sitting-room before answering. The postman – Dylan Iversen from school – handed her a heap of junk mail he could easily have slipped through the letterbox. "I thought you must be out. Quiet as a morgue in here."

"Milly's having her morning nap."

"Makes a change. I usually hear her screaming from the bottom of the stairs."

Another brick. Gemma crushed it. *I'm her mother and those sneering old biddies at the bus stop can mind their own business.* "She's got a strong pair of lungs."

As Dylan turned to go, Gemma noticed the butterfly tattoo on his neck. Did he have that at school? It looked so pretty and cheerful, she called him back, "I was gonna put the kettle on."

"Thanks. I could murder a coffee."

Gemma tamped down a flutter of anxiety as he stepped into the flat. She and Milly weren't used to visitors. She hoped he was too preoccupied with setting down his bulky mailbag to notice her grey underwear amid the damp babygros as she bundled the clotheshorse back into the bathroom, then ushered him into the kitchen.

"Awesome having your own place," said Dylan.

Filling the kettle, Gemma shrugged. Up until then the flat had felt more Milly's than hers. Squeezing past him to get the semi-skimmed from the fridge, she imagined the place seeming small and shabby to someone who still lived in a proper house with his parents.

"You look nice," said Dylan. "Going out?"

"Nowhere special. I might take Milly down the shops later."

"Mind if I tag along?"

"I thought you were working."

"I get off at two."

Was he taking the piss? They'd flirted a bit at school, but a lad with a butterfly tattoo wouldn't want to saddle himself with a girl with a baby. Even if she did have her own place. She handed him a mug.

"Why not get a babysitter and we'll go down the pub. I could beat you at pool."

"I've no money for the babysitters."

"Can't you ask your mum?"

Gemma grabbed the dishcloth and scrubbed at the worktop. "Milly's my responsibility."

"We'll go for a walk then. The three of us. This afternoon."

"If you want." Gemma imagined his hands beside hers on the pram. She brushed the hope away. "Don't blame me if you're bored. Everything's ten times slower with a baby."

"I know that. I've been changing nappies for my sister's kids since I was twelve. I probably know more about babies than you do." Putting down his mug, Dylan edged towards the door. "I could show you if you like."

"She's sleeping."

"Let's check." Finger pressed theatrically to his lips, Dylan tiptoed into the tiny lobby. With only three doors to choose between, the main door marked by the letterbox and the bathroom door wide open, it was obvious where he'd find Milly.

Torn between irritation at his presumption and relief at someone else taking control, Gemma followed. As before, Milly lay on her back, saturated with sleep. Pride flushed her cheeks as she imagined Dylan whispering, *Good as gold. How do you do it?* Yet Dylan frowned as he edged towards the cot. She had to admit that, with the curtains blocking the daylight, the baby looked a bit dull. Gemma indicated the dress on the bed. "I'll put that on her when we go out."

Grimacing, Dylan touched Milly's cheek. Then he leant right over the cot and put his own cheek against her face. As if expecting a sleeping child to kiss him. So much for being experienced with babies.

He turned to her briefly, his expression unrecognisable, as if he hadn't asked her out five minutes before. Gemma made a clown face like she used at school to entertain her friends, but it was wasted on Dylan. He bent over the cot again and pressed his mouth against Milly's.

"What the fuck are you up to?" Had she invited a paedophile into her home?

Turning his head aside, Dylan took a gulp of air before clamping his mouth back on Milly's. Fortunately, there wasn't a whimper of complaint from Milly, but that didn't stop Gemma from tugging at Dylan's arm. "Leave her alone, you bastard!"

Shaking her off, Dylan became even more aggressive towards the baby. Throwing the Jemima Puddleduck quilt on the floor, he yanked her from her cot by the ankles and slapped her back. Gemma rushed at him, trying to squeeze between this monster and her child.

Dylan screamed at her, but she couldn't make out the words. Something about not crying, but what kind of pervert would enjoy making a baby cry? Everything was confused. Laying her back in the cot, Dylan looked close to tears himself.

As Dylan pushed her backwards towards the bed, Gemma feared his next move would be to rape her. She kicked out, hoping for the groin area. Dylan sprang back and reached into his pocket for his phone. Sitting on the bed, propped against the wall, Gemma planned her next move. While he was preoccupied, could she make a dash for the door? But she couldn't leave without Milly, and she couldn't get to the cot without attracting Dylan's attention.

Her head felt heavy, as if she'd been drugged.

Dylan finished his call. "Would you like to hold her till they come?" In contrast to his previous behaviour, his voice was gentle. His movements too, as he scooped Milly from her cot and laid her in her mother's arms.

Gemma stroked the baby's cold grey cheek. So still. So quiet. So perfect. Like she'd been the last time Gemma put her down, not long after three that morning. This was her daughter. She was a mother. It had been a struggle for the two of them, but now it was fine. Peace and harmony: Madonna and child.

# After Icarus

H E CRUISES THROUGH the troposphere, parting the clouds with his arms like a swimmer. Effortless: his body as light as a bride's veil. He could go on like this for ever. Not going anywhere in particular. Just going.

Far below, the regular people are fussing about their homes and jobs and families, erecting the petty obstacles that make their world go round. Here in the realm of birds – whose chatter is only of the latest workout for wings, and the juiciness of slugs – he truly belongs.

ON THE FIRST Tuesday of the month, I call in at the surgery for my prescription. Today there is a new lady on the reception. Her frizzy hair is the colour of a robin's breast. She looks at my form and says, You can't have your prescription until you've seen the doctor for a medication review.

So I go, Okay, and take a seat in the waiting area among

the out-of-date magazines.

And she calls across, You can't see him now. There are no more appointments left today.

So I go, Okay, give me one for tomorrow.

And she shakes her head and says, You can't make an appointment at this time of day. You have to ring up between half-past eight and half-past nine in the morning.

So I go, Thank you, miss, and head back home.

LATCHING ONTO A thermal, he is carried through the blue, the air caressing his cheek like a lover. It's all so easy for those few lucky enough to have discovered how arms can be made to function as wings.

Over the houses of the regular people he goes. The obstructive people, the no-you-can't-have-it people who, unlike him, will never experience the exhilaration of flight.

IF YOU WANT to know something about me: well, I've got two eyes, a nose and a mouth. I live in this city and my name is … No, let's leave that for now, shall we?

Before getting dressed in the mornings, I drink tea with a dash of milk and two sugars out of my RSPB mug. Then I have two slices of wholemeal toast with lemon marmalade and a second mug of tea.

After breakfast this morning, I go out to the phone box to call the doctor's. There aren't so many public phones around these days, so it's a bit of a walk.

I'm sorry, says the receptionist, we can only do appointments between eight-thirty and nine-thirty. It's after ten now.

What am I going to do? I've run out of medication.

I'm sorry, she says again. You'll have to ring back tomorrow morning.

Are you the new lady? The one with red hair? The old receptionist wouldn't make things so difficult.

Ring up tomorrow. She puts the phone down.

HE JOINS A swarm of swallows on their farewell tour of the Home Counties prior to moving south for the winter. He feels snug in the middle of the party as they fly over their favourite haunts. Every so often one of them breaks away from the group and swoops down to perch momentarily on a selected rooftop.

What's going on?

The swallows flanking him cock their heads and giggle. Didn't you know? We've taken on the job of shitting on the homes of all the red-haired receptionists in the world.

I'M HAVING TROUBLE sleeping at night. Strange noises come from next door, as if the neighbours are building a machine to send microwaves through the wall. I don't feel safe enough to sleep until it gets light and then I don't wake up again until nearly noon. Too late to phone the GP's surgery.

After breakfast – or maybe I should call it lunch – I collect my post from the doormat. There is only a leaflet from the supermarket advertising this month's promotions. I take it to the dining table and study it carefully. There's a special offer on aluminium foil. It must be a sign. I go straight out and buy ten rolls for the price of eight. I spend the next couple of days making my place safe. I roll out the foil and stick the sheets onto my bedroom walls like wallpaper. That should stop the microwaves coming through from next door.

I'm so busy I don't notice the time, and maybe I forget to go to bed, I'm not sure. At some point someone, probably my neighbour, calls through the letterbox, Stop that banging. Which is a bit much, given his behaviour, don't you think?

SPARROWHAWK, GOSHAWK, HONEY buzzard, kestrel.
  Sea eagle, red kite, black-shouldered kite, osprey.
  Golden eagle, griffon vulture, bearded vulture, falcon.
  Toucan, pelican, Peter Pan, Superman.
  Can he fly? Corsican.

THE NOISES FROM next door have multiplied. Banging and shouting at odd times in the night. In the daytime, a strange whirring sound, like machinery. People whispering, plotting. The foil gives me some protection, but for how long? Can it hold out until the birds come?

Perhaps I should make a fire in the garden to attract their attention. But it isn't safe outside. Can't trust anyone. Not even you. At least I had the sense not to tell you my name.

I've no more bread, so I make do with marmalade and crackers for breakfast. If they run out, I'm sure the birds will forgive me if I break into the nuts and seeds I've stored up for winter.

At night, I hear the birds coming.

COME, SAY THE sunbirds, we will take you to visit our mother, Aurora.

He soars through the atmosphere, rising higher than he ever dreamt possible. Fireworks spangle into Technicolor above his head. It's beautiful, he says. I could stay here for ever.

You must fly higher, say the sunbirds. Our mother is waiting.

As he rises, heat cuddles his soul like his grandmother's kitchen on baking day. Below, the earth is as dull as an old tennis ball. People can't hurt him when they're reduced to the size of fleas.

To his right, a rocket bursts into stars, peppering his flying arm with flaming saltpetre. Ouch, he says.

The sunbirds laugh. Wimp!

High above, Aurora sits on her throne, combing her golden hair. Come children, she calls.

Swaddled by the heat, he can barely move his wings.

Mother, he's getting tired, say the sunbirds.

Fire infiltrates his body with every breath. Hot stings his eyes. He cannot go on.

Aurora lets down a braid of her hair. Catch hold, she says, and I will pull you up to our home.

The golden rope swings before his eyes. Inebriated with heat, he reaches out, misses. Reaches out. Misses.

Clumpo! Mongol! Idiot!

Shhh, says their mother. You should respect our guest.

Summoning his last atom of earthly cool, he fixes his gaze on his lifeline to the sun and reaches out once more. He catches it with his right, squeezes tight. He wrinkles his nose at the smell of smouldering flesh as he feels himself pulled heavenwards.

Hold tight, calls Aurora.

The pain shoots into his armpit. Gasping, he lets go of the hair-rope and goes falling, tumbling, somersaulting, crashing. Down to earth.

Never mind, Aurora tells her children. I'll find you a better playmate.


A POLICEMAN STANDS in my bedroom along with one of the doctors from the surgery.

Sorry about your front door, he says.

How did you know about the microwaves? I ask. How did you know to come?

Your neighbours were concerned about the noise. And they thought they could smell fire. Let me see your hand.

Did the birds say when they'd be coming?

Not to me, says the doctor. But why not come to the hospital? There are lots of birds around there.


GROUNDED NOW, HIS arms ache with nostalgia. Down here among the regular people, his movements are clumsy, like an astronaut adapting to gravity all over again. But it doesn't matter. This is only a resting point on his migration route to the sun.

Be patient, the voices tell him, you will rise again.

# Ghost Girl

THE OTHER CHILDREN threw rocks at me, but that was all right when Mama was there to wipe away my tears. They called me Ghost Girl but she called me Pure. She said *they* were ignorant, *I* was special. People like me brought good luck.

Each evening, when the sun was done with blinding and burning, Mama and I sat outside our hut. With a stick, she scraped shapes in the dirt, and I copied her. Little by little I learned my letters. One day I'd know enough to read a book.

When I grew tired, I lay with my head in Mama's lap staring at the stars while she told me stories. In Mama's stories, the warthog always outwitted the lion. He might have been small and ugly, but he had the better brain.

Mama warned me never to venture alone into the forest. The medicine man would get me, she said. But, with Mama gone and the neighbours wrapped in superstition, how else would I fetch the firewood to cook my food?

Now the doctor says I'm special, so special people walk miles for a lock of my hair. The doctor says my body can cure anything from malaria to leprosy. But I'd rather be back with the village children throwing rocks.

The doctor earns himself a goat for the clippings from my fingernails, an ox for a single toe. One day, if the offer's good enough, he'll sacrifice my beating heart.

# Pre-Raphaelite Muse

A T FIRST, I laughed at what he claimed to see. In me, a girl like any other! Why flee my playmates in the sun to stand statue-still for hours? I did not care for dukes and lords with their vaunted galleries. Let them hang another's likeness on their walls. Freed from school and chores, I was content to race my friends, to scrape my knees, to shout and laugh and dance.

He courted me. Just once, he pleaded, try it once and see. He placed my arm, he raised my chin, but what of it? He'd never peer beneath my bones to catch the secrets of my soul.

Once became twice, three times; still the hunger his, the power of yes or no all mine. Until, past counting, friends stopped calling me to play. I did not mind, so fulfilled I felt indoors, the object of his gaze. What lover would regard me so intently? What glass reflect such light? What mother display such devotion? I did not tire of standing still for hours while he sought my essence in his paints.

I never dreamt my features would come to bore him. I never dreamt I'd grow beyond the shape he so admired. When I did there was no returning to the girl I'd been before he found me. There was nothing left beneath my bones.

Starved of his attention I'd become a spectre. I could not see myself unless he saw me too. When he chose another muse I thought I'd drown, Ophelia-like, singing in a river of flowers.

# Had To Be You

I FLICK THE indicator, dog-leg the gear lever down to second and ease the car round the corner into the terrace. While my sensible side scopes the margins for a place to park, another part of me is already soaking in a perfumed bath, a glass of wine by the soap dish, Mozart on the CD player and the sweet smell of oven-baked lasagne wafting up the stairs.

Sometimes, I like to imagine the street's original inhabitants. Prim Edwardians who'd never have dreamt of an indoor bathroom or a motor at the kerbside, yet couldn't last a day without a maid to hold the house together. A century on, the servant bells are purely ornamental, but we can all get territorial over the stretch of road alongside our bay windows. Even I, house-sitting while the owners are abroad, want to stake a claim on my few feet of tarmac. So it's a little jarring when I see the hatchback in my parking space, even if it is such a pretty duck-egg blue.

As I edge nearer, I notice someone in the driving seat, so I slow right down and give them a look that might nudge them to move on. They give me a look back that says *I'm not budging for anyone, girl*, and, I realise, too late, it's not just any old car, not just any old driver, it's you. And you've certainly clocked me. Your gaze zips through laminated glass and pressed steel, peels away layers of lycra and organic cotton, till I'm raw and helpless as a baby, bound by your desire. Goodbye bubble-bath and Beaujolais. Goodbye servant bells. Goodbye me.

You incline your head towards a gap between a white Transit and a blood-red roadster a little farther down the terrace on the left. Fear fizzes through my stomach and I don't stop to argue. I line up my car against the van and wiggle the gear-stick into reverse.

I'm not wonderful at parking at the best of times, and my first attempt leaves the wheels a couple of feet from the kerb. I hear a car door slam as I weave back into position alongside the white van. Through the rear-view mirror I see you looming in the road, arms akimbo, your face a strange amalgam of adulation and hate.

I think of how hard I've worked to get away from you, the homes I've fled, the jobs. I don't dare look back as I let the car nose beyond the Transit, like I'm giving a horse its head. I let it lunge past a battered mini and a pair of motorbikes, and soon we're careering to the end of the terrace, scooting up the back alley and hurtling onto the main road. I drive like my life depends on it, my sanity, my self.

My hands feed the wheel back and forth between them,

my feet ease the pedals up and down. My eyes monitor the mirror for the merest hint of blue metal, while my mind repeats: *My stalker's back and there's nowhere to hide.* The radio rumbles, but I can't say if it's dialogue or an instrumental. There's not much that can penetrate the buzzing in my brain.

Out of nowhere, an angry horn bears down on me. I'm at a roundabout, and it's not the first I've navigated, judging by the distance out of town, but it's the first that's reached my consciousness so far. I screech to a halt as a juggernaut roars across from the right. There's a race-track smell of cooked latex. I've never burned rubber before.

I pull in at an industrial estate a few hundred yards along the road. The car park is deserted apart from a learner rehearsing three-point turns. As I kill the engine, my body starts to tremble, every muscle and sinew rattling out the feelings that reel across the years. I'm shivering at the school gates, abandoned and forlorn, waiting and waiting long after my classmates have been claimed. I'm cowering beneath my iron bed, assailed by storming voices, willing myself as small and lifeless as a doll.

After a while, I wipe my eyes with the back of my hand and lean across to grab my handbag from the passenger foot-well. At times like this I wish I smoked. A pack of cigarettes is more dependable than a phone.

The screen lights up with an image of a dancing lemur. You'd think me sentimental but, even in freeze-frame, the cuddly black and white sifaka seems buoyed up with the magic of his own existence. Leaping through the forest, long furry arms raised towards the sky, glad to be alive. I tasted that joy those two years I spent in Madagascar, despite the deprivations, the poverty. I felt safe, knowing you wouldn't follow me that far. Two years of heady freedom until you turned up in Arrivals at Heathrow, ready to resume our bizarre relationship where we'd left off.

I thumb the green phone icon, although there's no one I can call. The police might be sympathetic initially, but their manners tend to melt away when we get to the crunch: "Do you know the identity of your stalker, Ms Lytton?"

You bought me this phone, as you no doubt recall. I bet you've logged every present you've sent me, every letter, every bunch of flowers, every card. The phone came by recorded delivery to the flat I rented above the chip shop. When I threw it in the trash it was like I'd ripped out your heart. I held out for three days, although the guilt induced the world's worst migraine, but when I heard the bin-lorry rolling up the alley at seven the next morning, I crumbled. I sprang out of bed and went down in my nightie, fished out the phone from among the mouldy potato peelings and empty yoghurt pots moments before the truck caught the wheelie bin in its maw.

How did you find me this time? How? I've laboured so hard to cover my tracks. No one you know knows where I live now. No one knows where I work. I suppose when you're determined, you find a way.

I changed the number, of course, opened up the back and slid in a fresh SIM card. I told myself I'd be a fool to turn down the offer of a top-of-the-range phone. A fool as well to keep it: nothing you gave me ever felt genuinely my own.

I touch the contacts icon and scroll down the list of names. Who can I call who hasn't heard it all before? In the beginning, friends would listen patiently, murmuring empathically in all the right places. They'd offer opinions, advice or a bed for the night. They'd pick apart your personality, analyse your motivations, compare your behaviour with stalkers in books. But, as the years went by, they grew weary. My friends had relationship issues of their own: self-absorbed husbands; stroppy teenage children; ailing mothers greedy for their time. Now, if I mention you, they're brusque and dismissive. They think I should be over you by now.

I go to the photo gallery and thumb through snaps of autumn trees and seaside sunsets all the way back to the start. To the picture you'd set as wallpaper when you sent me the phone. I'm sure you'll remember, it's that old birthday photo where I'm sitting on your lap, your arms wrapped around me like you'd never let me go. I stare at our expressions, searching for some sense within the torment. Was that love in your eyes or possession? Fear or devotion in mine?

The sky is leaching its light as the learner-driver exits the car park. Time to make up my mind what I'm going to do tonight. Should I stay away: check into a travel lodge and go to work tomorrow in today's stale clothes? Should I try for home: sneak down the back alley, scale the yard wall and break in like a thief through the kitchen window? Even if I phoned a friend, I'd be no nearer a solution.

"She just wants to talk to you," Jane would tell me. "Can't you spare a few minutes of your precious time?"

"You've got to stand up to her," Sal would say. "If you don't want her in your life, tell her to leave you alone."

Appease or confront you: they're equally impossible. Much more straightforward to scramble in unsuitable shoes over a seven-foot wall without a ladder. Much gentler to smash a window and trigger the alarm.

My phone beeps and a message stamps itself across the photo, warning me the battery's low. My thumb jumps to the dustbin icon and the screen flashes back: *Delete image? Yes? No?* I'm still hovering when the screen blacks out.

Perhaps I won't have to see you this evening. Perhaps you've given up and gone home. Renounced your claim on me after all these years. Given me the greatest gift of all and let me go.

Turning the key in the ignition, the engine purrs. As I drive, I fix my mind on the road, earnest as a learner, no headspace in reserve to fret about what I'll do if you're still parked outside my door.

The street lights are limbering up as I trundle down the terrace past the duck-egg blue hatchback on the right. I reverse into the space between the white van and the red roadster, no longer caring if I'm too far from the kerb. In the twilight, I can't see what you're up to, but my teeth are chattering as I walk across the road. I focus on the green front door like an athlete at the finishing line, kidding myself sanctuary could soon be mine.

With every step I'm amazed you don't accost me, and a little confused. I should keep centred on the soothing green door, but I can't help it, I have to check on you. You've reclined the seat and pushed it back, stretched yourself out behind the wheel. Your eyes are closed and your mouth hangs loose and, through the window, I fancy I hear you snore.

I could steal indoors without you knowing, run my belated bath and warm up my meal. These walls are so thick I could even risk the Mozart, so long as I kept the volume low. I could leave you in the street and you'd be none the wiser, festering in your car while I'm tucked up cosy in bed. Yet when I see your grey hair splayed across the head rest, when I trace the shape of your nose that's the exact spit of mine, I can't do it. To hell with my ambitions for a life of my own, you're a lonely old woman and I'm all you've got.

It isn't love I feel as I crouch down and tap on the window, but it's the nearest I've known. There's a familiar comfort in duty and resignation, in opting out of a battle I'm programmed to lose.

You come to with a jolt but you recover quickly. You wipe the drool from your chin and wind down the window. "Oh, Alice," you say, "I thought I'd never see you again."

I open your door and offer you my arm. "Come in and have a drink, Mum," I say. "You're an awfully long way from home."

# My Father's Love

WHEN I WAS a baby in my cradle, or so the story goes, my father gathered up his love for me and fashioned a chalice of burnished gold. He swaddled the chalice in a skein of silk shipped all the way from China and bedded it down in a drawer in his wardrobe where he used to store his cufflinks and bowties. He locked the drawer with a silver key which he dangled from a string around his neck, beneath his shirt, inches from his heart. When it was done, my father smiled, stood back and watched me grow.

I was about five when my father told me the story of the golden chalice: old enough to write my name and do up the buttons on my dress but still too young to venture to the sweet shop alone. "May I see it?" The prospect of the chalice nestling in its silken shroud sent my body tingling from the ribbon in my hair to the buckle on my shoes. "Wait a while," said my father. "Small hands and sticky fingers could rub away the sheen."

That summer I fell sick, and no doctor could fathom the cause or cure. My mother carried me, in sweat-stained pyjamas, into her bed. "Don't tell your father," she said, taking a tiny key from her purse. She unlocked the drawer in the mahogany wardrobe and unfurled a bundle of turquoise silk. The sun, streaming through the latticed window, bounced off the golden goblet to light up my cheeks. "You can touch it if you like," she said, but I shook my head and banished my hands beneath the quilt where they could do no harm.

As soon as I was well again, I went to visit my friend. We poured pretend tea from a plastic teapot and served it to our dolls. "When you were a baby," I said, "did your father melt down his love to make you a cup of gold?" My friend shook her pigtails. Her envy warmed my heart.

MY FATHER WAS a handsome man, tall and dark. He carried a brown leather briefcase and wore crisp white shirts with spotted bowties. He left for work while I was still asleep and came home long after I'd said my prayers. On Sundays, after church, he'd play cricket on the green with lots of other fathers, dressed neck to toe in white. Sometimes, I'd go along in the afternoon with my mother to hand out cucumber sandwiches and watch her pour real tea.

When we moved to a bigger house, the mahogany wardrobe came too, and the chalice, tucked up snug inside its drawer. I moved to a bigger school and found a new friend, a tomboy who preferred climbing trees and roller-skating to playing house. One day, too wet to roam outside, she took me upstairs to her room. I gazed around at the crumpled sheets and dog-eared books and jumbled toys. "When I was a baby," I said, "my father made me a golden chalice. What did your father make for you?"

The girl held out a hollowed lump of garish pottery, roughly made and chipped at the rim. With its flat base, long stem and cup without a handle, it was a crude imitation of a father's love. It froze my heart that she should have so little and I so much.

My friend tossed the goblet into the air and caught it in her hands. Laughing, she made to throw it across the room to me.

"Don't!" I cried. "It'll smash to pieces if it falls."

My friend narrowed her eyes and grew dimples in her cheeks. "If we break it, he'll make me another, bigger and better and yet more beautiful."

Tears punched the backs of my eyes. "But it's your father's love! Once it's damaged you can never get it back."

"My father's love isn't locked up in this pot." She spread her hands, as if to encompass, not just that higgledy-piggledy room, but the whole world: "It's here, there, everywhere. In all I have and everything I do."

I could've slapped her, except that my parents had taught me right from wrong. So I ran all the way home to my mother and vowed never to make another friend.

MY BODY CHANGED, tiny buds of womanhood blooming on my chest. It was no longer enough to picture my father's love draped in silk in the drawer in his wardrobe; I needed to feel the heft of it in my hands. I asked politely, I bargained and I wheedled, but still my father said: "Not yet!" I raged and stormed and screamed, but he wouldn't grant me a single glimpse. He turned his back on me, rustling his newspaper until he settled on the obituary column towards the back.

One day when I was alone in the house, I took the extra key from my mother's purse and crept up to their room. The key turned smoothly in the lock and I slid open the wooden drawer. Inside it smelled of old leather and starch from generations past. The blue-green silk lay ruffled, like the lining of a coffin, but otherwise the drawer was empty: no gold, nor even brass or copper; no goblet, nor even an egg-cup or a spoon. I searched through racks of shirts, his cricket bag and briefcase, but my father's love had gone.

I FINISHED SCHOOL and went to college, where I shared a flat with girls who liked to dance and flirt. We lived off macaroni cheese, cheap coffee and cider, and finished off our essays in the hour before dawn. Young men would knock at our door with guitars and roll-ups, or rendezvous outside the library to escort us to the pub. There were one or two I fancied, and yet more claimed a fondness for me, but when I asked if they could prove their love they didn't have a clue. They tried to woo me with champagne suppers and bedtime gymnastics but I'd been raised to hope for more.

The night before my graduation, my dreams oozed parental pride. I watched them watching misty-eyed as their only daughter mounted the stage in cap and gown. Yet when the Chancellor called my name and placed the scroll in my clammy hands and I scanned the rows of relatives for my father's smile, I could make out nothing but the bland masks of strangers. As I stepped back down, the tassel of the mortarboard tapping my ponytail, I spotted my mother waving from the crowd. I squinted at the seat to the left of her, the seat to the right, but I couldn't see my father. Instead, resplendent on a shimmering cloth, sat the golden chalice of his love.

MY STUDENT DAYS were over, but I didn't want to settle down. I craved new sights and sounds, a life on the move. I wandered the world, taking short-term jobs to pay my way. In every new country, in every new town, I'd zoom in on the museum. Inside, I'd march past bandaged bodies in hieroglyphed sarcophagi. I'd bypass buttons and buckles of ancient bronze and bone. I'd boycott fig-leafed Olympians and goddesses with stumpy arms. I was seeking out the one particular artefact that would make me feel at home.

Sometimes my quest led to me to the Christian reliquary; sometimes to the regimental silver and the spoils of war. Other times I'd end my search in rooms replete with tableware and cooking pots requisitioned from the palaces of princes or the hovels of the poor. In every place I visited I could count on finding a gilded goblet behind a pane of gleaming glass. There I'd stand, feasting on the memory of my father's love, until an attendant tapped me on the shoulder to say it was time to leave.

WHEN MY MOTHER took ill I swapped the itinerant life for an office nine-to-five. I watched my colleagues acquire mortgages and babies, but I couldn't follow suit. The mothers smelled of milk and talcum powder, and yearning without end. The fathers spoke of nappy rash and four o'clock feeds. They kept photos of their red-faced offspring beside the phones on their desks. I contrived to be on my lunch break when they brought in their infants for the others to ooh and aah.

When my mother died, I moved back home to cook and clean for my father. He was handsome still, with a shock of snowy hair, but when he went to the cricket club, it was to keep the score and not to bat or bowl. My father wasn't given to chitchat but, on winter evenings, we'd sit at the fireside in companionable proximity, or so I like to think. He still enjoyed his paper with the obituaries at the back, and I'd do the crossword or knit and purl a cosy cardigan for him or for me. Now and then we'd watch the television; he liked the occasional detective drama and I was partial to the travelogues. Some evenings, he'd hobble upstairs to fetch a parcel bound in turquoise cloth, and unwrap it on his lap. I knew better then than to comment or let him know I'd noticed, but it pleased me to watch, through downcast eyes, as my father took a scrap of moleskin and polished his love.

He's dead now, and the house is mine and everything in it. His bowties and cricket whites have gone to charity but, otherwise, things are much as they were when I was a girl. My father's love stays locked in the drawer of his mahogany wardrobe, and I keep both keys close to me, hanging between my breasts from a string around my neck. I take out the chalice from time to time to shine it. But not often. A daughter's sentiments will cling to her fingertips whether she wants them to or not, and I can't let bitterness tarnish the sheen of my father's love.

# Shaggy Dog Story

I SIT, ALONG with Rufus, and we wait. Every day we wait. Yet each day's waiting has a texture of its own.

Sunday's is the hardest wait. On Sundays we sit together in the wingback chair, our limbs entangled like tights in the washing machine, to wait for death.

On Mondays, our triumph over the weekend perks us up somewhat. After I empty the remains of our microwaved meal into the pedal bin, we retire to the chair beside the window, to await the young ladies from Queen Elizabeth High School. Visiting the elderly and housebound; we never had that when I was a lass. The teachers call it Community Service but, to the students, it's their opportunity to fleece me at poker. They cheat, those girls from Queen Elizabeth's in their smart blazers and hitched-up skirts. They look at my cards, and how could they not, when my hands, as supple as boxing gloves, refuse to marshal the cards into a fan? By the time they go back to school, I'm five quid and a packet of

Penguins poorer.

Tuesdays we wait for the bath lady. Fridays too. It used to be three days a week but I lost one bath to The Cuts. When the supervisor came to tell me, there were tears in her eyes. I shook my head and looked serious, but it was a lot of fuss about nothing. Sunday night in the tub was good enough when we were kids, and that was with all day and every day running around the backstreets, playing hopscotch and piggy-in-the-middle. Just taking my zimmer from the toilet to the kitchen to the bedroom to the wingback chair beside the window can't produce much of a sweat, can it? A splash of water on my face of a morning and a wipe *down there* with a damp flannel ought to suffice at my age. It's not as if there's any pleasure in it, anyway, with that hoist like a crane on a bloody building site, and the bath lady doing her best to look anywhere but at my gnarled body. But it's not for me to say, is it? And the bath lady lends focus to Tuesday's wait.

Today, however, is Wednesday: the best day of the week. Wednesdays are when we wait for the vicar lady – or one of her do-gooding helpers – to ring the doorbell and escort us down to the communal lounge for a paper plate of pie and peas and a couple of rounds of bingo. All it costs us is to join in with the croaking hymns while the vicar lady tinkles away on the piano. My mouth is watering already as I sit here, bent and twisted as the trees in the windswept park beyond the window. Rufus waits with me, his body wrapped around mine like ivy. I hum a few bars of *All Things Bright and Beautiful* and Rufus joins in with his funny doggie whine. I laugh and squeeze his body tight to my chest like a hot water bottle, and he growls and licks my face. You daft dog, I say, and bury my nose in the teddy-bear fur of his neck. He has a sour smell, like the sludge of fallen leaves in the winter gutter.

Along with the poker and the bingo and the pie and peas, Rufus is my saviour. Never had time for pets before, too busy with a house and a husband and a market stall to see to. But when the work stops and you find yourself suddenly alone, you need something to share the waiting with you. Companionship. Something to cuddle and push out the thoughts that echo in your head like footsteps in an empty room.

While loyal to me, Rufus can be standoffish with some of my visitors. When the home-helps come round, or the district nurse or the warden or the bath lady, he goes and lies under my bed, out of the way. He can sense when someone doesn't approve of his ways. Whenever Kim – that's the young home-help who looks anorexic – finds a hair on the carpet with too much colour to be mine, she wrinkles her nose at me accusingly. I blame the Queen Elizabeth girls. Their hair always has far more colour than is good for them. Then, when Shirley – the district nurse who married one of the doctors – hints there's a funny smell, I accuse the home-helps of being too lazy to clean properly.

Rufus feels more at home with Monday's and Wednesday's visitors. When the Queen Elizabeth girls come, he barks and wags his tail and jumps up to lick their faces until one of them takes him for a runaround in the park to burn off some of that adrenalin. He's more sedate with Marjorie, the vicar lady. I think he perceives the dog collar as the mark of a kindred spirit.

Today, when the doorbell goes, I feel Rufus tense in my arms. Under all his layers, the shaggy hair and the warm skin and the play-pen cage of his ribs, his heart seems to miss a beat. And then he turns his head to look at me, and almost smiles. You daft dog, I say.

He springs off the chair and runs in circles round the room, while I clamp my arthritic fingers around the zimmer and edge towards the door.

"Sorry I'm a bit late," says Marjorie. "Are you ready?"

Of course I'm ready. What else have I to do but wait? "If you wouldn't mind getting my handbag? It's over by my chair."

Marjorie squeezes past me to get the bag. The lead is lying on the floor nearby. "Is Rufus coming?"

"Of course," I say. "He wouldn't miss it for the world."

Marjorie picks up the dog's lead. She reaches out and presses the clip at the end as if attaching it to a phantom collar. Then she strides back towards me at the door, my white handbag in her left hand and the brown leather strap dangling from her right. Meanwhile, Rufus dances around the wingback chair, unfettered.

I giggle.

"What is it?"

I point at the empty lead, then at Rufus. "He's over there, by the window."

Marjorie flings down the lead. It lies on the carpet, coiled like a snake. "I give up."

Rufus and I hold our breath, me leaning on my zimmer by the door, he slouching low on the floor, his back legs tucked under the wingback chair. We wait.

Marjorie's neck above her dog collar has turned bishop's purple. "I'm sorry, it's just that …" She bends down and picks up the lead, turns back towards the window. "Come on, Rufus. Good dog."

As we make our way out into the corridor, me shuffling with the zimmer, she encumbered with my bulging handbag and an excited dog, Marjorie apologises again. "I didn't mean to offend you, but a dog like Rufus, a *special* kind of dog – not everyone sees him as clearly as you do." She presses the down-button and we stand there, two women and a dog, waiting for the lift. "You do understand?"

"You're saying he's not real?"

"No, of course not." Marjorie's neck colours again. "He's real to you. That's what matters."

The lift goes ping and the metallic doors slide apart. Marjorie keeps her finger pressed on the button while I hobble inside. Rufus rests his body against Marjorie's legs as the doors close on us. He barks nervously as the floor shudders and we begin our descent. "It's okay, Rufus." Marjorie pats the air above an invisible head.

I laugh. "You do look daft."

"Pardon?"

"Pretending you're stroking a dog. Like a kid with an imaginary friend."

Marjorie looks forlorn, like a market stall in the rain. "I was only doing it for you."

Does she think I've completely lost my marbles? How could I manage with a real dog – horrible smelly thing – with my arthritis? Besides, they don't allow pets in these places. Health and safety, isn't it? I'd have to be completely off my trolley to think Rufus was a real dog.

She winds the lead around her hand, looking, not at me, not at Rufus, but solemnly at the floor. I start to hum.

The floor shudders, the lift pings and the doors slide open. We stumble into the vestibule: one vexed lady vicar, one whimsical old widow and one fantasy man's-best-friend.

Wednesday's waiting is over. Time at last for our bingo, hymns and pie and peas.

# Tattoos and Rubber Gloves

O N THE DAY of the funeral, Elsa vowed that the end of Albert's life wouldn't presage the withering of hers. It wasn't that she didn't miss him, didn't feel the ache of his loss with the dawn of each new day, but she'd learnt, long ago, that life was not to be squandered. She had a duty to carry on.

She decided to seek out some voluntary work; something to take her out of the house and out of herself. She imagined perching on a low stool reading stories to tousle-haired children or in the office of a charity putting the filing system to rights. But those kind of jobs required typed applications, security checks and references, even for volunteers, and Elsa hadn't the patience to track down the employers who'd praised her work twenty years before.

Eventually, she found a few hours a week at the old folks' luncheon club in the church hall round the corner from where she got her hair done: Tuesdays and Fridays, ten till half past two. The work provided colleagues, a sense of purpose, and a greater appreciation of the intervening days when she was responsible to no-one but herself.

The luncheon club was managed, in the loosest sense of the word, by a young man in his mid-thirties who might have been handsome had he not succumbed to the unfortunate fashion of ridding himself of his hair before nature did it for him, and adorning his arms with tattoos. Gavin seemed tickled to recruit someone who was older than half the punters, and he didn't object when Elsa said she'd happily wait on tables and chop onions until her eyes streamed, but she wasn't prepared to roll up her sleeves and plunge her hands into a bowl of greasy dishwater. He'd teased her for it mercilessly however, bringing her gifts of rubber gloves in unlikely colours when he wasn't goading her to admire a new piece of artwork on his arm. "You could've bought us a dishwasher with all the money you've frittered away," she told him. Gavin only laughed.

Not everyone found it amusing. Ferrying stacks of dirty plates to the kitchen, Elsa had overheard Joan mutter to Margaret that *some people* considered themselves far too lah-di-dah to assist with the washing up. Elsa didn't care what they thought of her, although she'd have loved to see their jaws drop had she revealed that, as a child in Berlin, they'd had servants to deal with that kind of thing. But she had no desire to spark their curiosity about her background. Elsa was of a generation that preferred to keep the personal to themselves.

She felt the volunteers badgered the proper old people, those who came twice a week for their meat and two veg.

Gavin insisted that the club was as much about social interaction as nutrition, and expected the volunteers to nudge the quieter members to join in. Chloe, young enough to be their granddaughter, quizzed the old folk about outdoor privies and learning to write with chalk on slates. Elsa tried to divert them onto grown-up subjects, like the work they used to do, or travel. Yet few of the attendees had had anything that could be termed a career, and their travels, whether to Blackpool, Benidorm or Bermuda, had been in search of sun instead of culture, so she tended to make do with asking about their grandchildren while stifling a yawn.

What made Elsa continue with her voluntary job was her unexpected friendship with Chloe. Amidst Gavin's ribbing and Joan and Margaret's grumbling, she relished the way the younger woman seemed to look up to her, soliciting her advice on all sorts of matters from how to get a chocolate stain out of a T-shirt to her son's education. Childless herself, Elsa was initially reluctant to express an opinion on William's development but, when what was asked of her was so straightforward and the child so endearing, she couldn't resist. Hosting mother and son for tea the other week, pouring over her holiday photos for the boy's school project on volcanoes, she hadn't missed Albert for the entire afternoon.

So when Chloe asked at the beginning of Tuesday's shift if she'd help with another project, Elsa readily agreed. As she peeled potatoes for the mash and apples for the crumble, as she listened yet again to the saga of Mrs Sanderson's hip replacement and half-smiled at Gavin's jokes, she looked forward to browsing through another of her photo albums with Chloe and William. Her travelling days were far behind her, but the memories remained strong.

Collecting the tea and coffee cups with Chloe at the end of the meal, Elsa broached the subject of William's project.

"History this time," said Chloe. "The Holocaust."

Elsa shook her head as dregs of coffee from an undrained cup splashed onto her shoe. "I'm sorry. Albert and I never fancied those concentration camp tours."

"It wouldn't be my idea of a holiday either," said Chloe. She inclined her head towards Elsa's feet. "Shall I get a cloth?"

Elsa glanced down, bewildered by the brown stain creeping across her burgundy court shoe. She blinked hard. Somehow she'd expected to find her feet clad in heavy wooden clogs. "Tell William I'm sorry I can't help him this time."

Chloe took the cups from Elsa's hands and stacked them on the trolley. "Of course you can. Don't worry about photos, he can get them from the internet. But you'll have memories …" Chloe blushed. "I suppose you'd be only a child in the war, but you'd have heard the grown-ups talking. Especially when the news broke about what happened to the Jews."

"It was not good manners to talk. Even more, it was not polite to ask."

Chloe stared at her strangely, her head cocked to the side. Elsa had surprised herself with the harshness of her tone, but it wasn't only that. It was the accent, much parodied in the post-war years, she thought she'd shed along with her maiden name.

"I keep forgetting you're German."

Elsa turned to walk away, but Chloe laid a restraining hand on her shoulder. "It would be ever so interesting for William to learn about it from the other side." Chloe looked so sure of herself, so confident of obtaining whatever she needed for her child.

"Interesting is not polite." Elsa grabbed the trolley and rattled it away towards the kitchen.

Albert would have liked children; she hadn't been blind to the yearning in his eyes as he bounced his nephew on his knee. But he hadn't pressed her. He hadn't pressed her to tell him what became of mothers denied the power to keep their children safe.

Margaret and Joan stood with their backs to her at the far end of the kitchen, tackling a mountain of dirty crockery. At the sound of the trolley, Joan spun round, splashing soapsuds onto the rubber floor. "The second shift's arrived. Come on, Elsa, get those sleeves rolled up!"

Elsa parked the trolley alongside the stainless-steel draining board. "Wouldn't that be interesting?"

Margaret's expression was not dissimilar to the one she used with Mr Hepworth, who didn't know which way was up half the time. "I've never heard it called that before."

Joan laughed. "Well, if you've spent a lifetime avoiding it you probably would find washing-up a novelty."

The heat in Elsa's cheeks came from more than the steam rising from the sinks. She fumbled with the button on the cuff of her blouse. They wanted interesting? She'd give them interesting. It wasn't only William who could use a lesson on the Holocaust.

"All right ladies?" Gavin beamed from the doorway. His bald head shone in the artificial light and his T-shirt, with no more than a flap for sleeves, exposed the graffiti that ran down his arms from his shoulders to his knuckles.

The mass of inked skin made Elsa's stomach churn. "Stupid boy! You'll be saddled with those damn tattoos for the rest of your life."

Gavin rolled his eyes, stepping aside as Chloe entered the kitchen, concern written across her face. Elsa could've slapped it. The young woman's sympathy couldn't give her back her childhood.

She clutched the cuff of her blouse, as if to read her pulse through the fabric. Albert had urged her to wear short sleeves in the summer heat, but Elsa had no desire to offer herself as a prop in a history lesson or as an object of pity.

Joan and Margaret muttered in the background. Chloe gazed at Elsa with puppy eyes. "Has anything upset you?" said Gavin.

Elsa laughed; she'd left her capacity for tears along with her family in the camp. "I'm sorry." She focused on her fingers as they secured the button on her sleeve. "This job isn't right for me."

"Nonsense!" said Gavin. "You're my star worker."

She edged past them to the recess where they hung their coats. She hadn't felt so old and raw since back then, when the guards pushed her mother one way and her the other. As she slipped her cold arms through the sleeves of her mac, it hit her, as if for the first time, that her husband was dead.

# No Through Road

# Across the Table

"NOPE, SORRY, I don't recognise you."

It's not until I hear your words, until they solidify and sink inside me, that I realise how much I'd relied on a warmer welcome. As if the miles I've travelled and the money I've spent, along with the time I've wasted dreaming, would earn me something, if only a grudging prize for effort. But the world's not fair, I know that. That's one thing you taught me.

They warned me you might deny it, just as they warned me you might try to deflect me as you're doing now, with that sheepish smile that reminds me of my son. The smile that declares you no worse than the lovable rogue who steals from my purse only to buy me a present. Rebuttal and mind games; they warned me, but it doesn't make it any less of a shock. I gasp, and through air tinged with stale cigarettes and disinfectant, rage seeps into my soul. The man who has monopolised my mind for a quarter century doesn't remember me? The man whose shadow has followed me through marriage, childbirth and divorce doesn't see who I am? I want to kick back my chair, reach across the table and throttle you.

The chaplain shoots me a glance; I can't decide if it's meant to console or constrain, but it grounds me. *Focus on the concrete. Articulate the external. Name what you can see.* Techniques from the therapy group that saved my life.

Table. Chairs. Walls. Window. Hands. Shirt. Men. *How many men?* Only three: one standing; one sitting across from me; another seated quietly at my side.

A stainless-steel rectangle with bolt-down legs. Three metal-framed chairs with wooden seats not styled for lingering. Four walls stained institutional beige. A single barred window positioned so near the ceiling only strips of cloud show through. Your hands flat on the table as per instructions; mine on my lap in white-knuckled fists. Your shirt, pale blue, your number stamped on the breast pocket; mine, starched white and buttoned to the chin. A uniformed figure immobile by the door. Man at my side channelling another kind of restraint. Man sitting across the table: that shirt, your thinning hair, sallow skin and smoker's teeth embodying your debasement, yet you retain the power to menace my mind.

Prison officer. Chaplain. The man who ruled and ruined my life. You *chose* me for Christ's sake! How dare you fail to recognise me now?

I stretch out my legs beneath the table, careful not to tangle them with yours. "I guess I've grown up a bit since then."

You shake your head. "It's more than that. Your story. I can't make it fit."

So I go over again how you dragged me into the bushes, how you bound my hands and gagged me. You listen, and even nod occasionally, like a counsellor would.

"I'm sorry," you say. "I'd help you if I could but that wasn't me."

Twelve men paraded in jeans and T-shirts, a spot-the-difference of criminal clones. Identical clothes and identical haircuts, but you were the only one who made my stomach churn.

The police thanked me for my contribution but they had enough for a conviction without me. The other girls' evidence was stronger, more robust. I felt I'd failed, somehow, but my mother was relieved. With exams looming, she thought I should concentrate on my schoolwork instead of testifying in court.

Up in my bedroom, books splayed across my desk; when I should have been rehearsing Shakespearian soliloquies, I reviewed my teenage tragedy till every detail was scorched on my brain. I resolved to remember each moment, to keep it fresh and vital till I could confront the man who'd torn my childhood from me. My belief in the future, too. It took years of persistence and persuasion to get this meeting. I wasn't counting on an apology, only that you'd acknowledge the damage you'd done.

The bandstand. The playing field. The woods. Your arm against my jugular. Your hand across my mouth.

Twigs snarling my hair. The smell of beer and leaf mould. The taste of blood and sweat. The searing pain.

"I suppose when you've done so many, you might forget the odd one."

"No, no, the way you said it happened, it wasn't my style."

I inhale deeply, ready to rattle off my story once more. But the familiar words regroup themselves and stick in my throat. I'm caught in an anxiety dream; a crucial exam where I know the answer to the question yet can't transfer it to the page.

"I've no incentive to lie to you. It's not as if I've anything more to lose."

The chaplain reaches for my hand but I pull away, wrap my arms around my chest and curl into myself. I'm in another room, at another table, another man holding my hand. My mother's standing by the sink and crying. *You wouldn't want Uncle Jim put away, now would you?* She won't say who's upset her most but I don't think it's him.

He squeezes my hand, like he did the day my mother introduced him, when he promised to treat me like one of his own. *Course she wouldn't. Got herself a bit confused, that's all.*

"I'm sorry you've had a wasted journey." Your frown draws attention to a scar cutting through your eyebrow I hadn't noticed before.

I push back the chair and turn away. At the door, the prison officer springs into action with a rattling of keys. The chaplain mumbles something, but no words get through to me.

I've read the testimonies of women who've confronted the men who raped them. Some met their assailant with forgiveness, others to scan his face for guilt. They write about closure; they write about release from the resentment that can erode what dregs of dignity their attacker left behind. Must I receive so little? Must I leave with less than I had when I arrived?

The chaplain invites me to his office for a debrief, but I shrug him off. A female officer leads me down the corridor and out the front door.

The breeze brushes my cheek. The traffic murmurs in my ears. The light seems sharp, despite the clouds, but still too blunt to point the way from here. I cross the paved courtyard to the low wall that marks the boundary between the prison and the facade of freedom beyond.

Squatting on the wall, my feet still on prison territory, I hug my bag. It's not much consolation, but it's all I've got. I ought to kickstart my grounding exercise, but there's too much out here to name. Or maybe I don't want to be grounded. Maybe I'd rather float away.

I run through a checklist of emotions; another therapy trick. It's not the negative feelings we should be wary of, but the absence of any feelings at all.

Not sad, not scared, not shocked. Not disgusted, despairing, disappointed. Not anxious, angry or afraid. The adjectives I want don't figure on the list they gave us. I'm seeking something grander, four syllables at least. Liberated. Vindicated. Authenticated. Fancy words, alien, but I'm going to make them mine.

I came for the truth and you've provided it. Showed me what I took as truth was false. It's time to confront the real culprit. Or the person who covered his tracks.

I uncoil myself from my bag, dive within for my phone. I thumb through my contacts and tap the icon beside my mother's name. On hearing the ringtone, I nod towards the prison walls and mouth my thanks.

# Bugsy the Bear's
## *Danse Macabre*

ONCE THE NURSES shuffle out with their instruments of torture, there's a moment of calm before the ghouls and vampires wake up. Bugsy the Bear materialises first. She stands guard at the foot of the bed, one hand jiggling my temperature chart and the other beckoning to the troupe. The spirits shimmy out from under the bed, contorting their gruesome bodies in a parody of dance.

Oh, I know what you're thinking: it's only a cuddly teddy bear. Who could be jollier; who could bestow more comfort on a dying man? Well let me tell you that this particular Bugsy is a right harridan who hasn't been jolly for nigh on thirty years. And yes, I do realise it's more a male name. That's only one of a whole litany of failings for which my daughter rebukes me.

She springs onto the bed to recite her complaints,

enunciating carefully as if to a foreigner, emphasising each crime against fatherhood with a different scowl. She's perched where my right leg used to be and, every time she wriggles her arse, the pain shoots into my phantom toes.

I press the button on the morphine pump and the ache floats off to the outer edge. But I ought to have known the drug would have the opposite effect on Bugsy. She swells like a balloon – fat but still not jolly – to loom above me, screaming in my face like she's softening up a detainee for interrogation: YOU MISSED MY THIRTEENTH BIRTHDAY PARTY!

I watch a chorus line of red-eyed goblins beat their breasts and tear at their clothes. I'm in no fit state to protest that she didn't need me to sit in the theatre with a bunch of just-turned teens to watch a load of anorexics prance about in tutus. She needed a taxi to ferry them there and back and I provided the wherewithal for that. Bugsy has harboured this grievance all her adult life and she's not going to let it go just because her old dad is about to croak.

She pokes me in the chest. I'VE A GOOD MIND TO BOYCOTT YOUR FUNERAL. She's so illogical, so like the child she used to be that I giggle. Sometimes the morphine gets you that way, as if nothing matters. Then it all turns topsy-turvy and it matters, it bloody does.

I remember her grabbing my hands and placing her tiny feet on top of mine. *Dance me, Daddy! Dance me!* I couldn't dance her now and she wouldn't condescend to let me try.

Give me another chance, I say. I'll be a better father, I promise.

After some consideration, she offers me a deal: All right,

then. Name one of the friends who came to that party. Anyone will do. Better still, prove you know *my* real name. You wouldn't be much of a father if you only recognised your daughter by her nickname.

Of course I could tell you my daughter's name, same as I could tell you the date of my wedding anniversary. But under stress, taking account of the strained circumstances, things can slip.

There's no clue in her nickname; she wasn't born when Bugsy Malone came out. My mother watched it half a dozen times at the cinema. So what? Yet before her forgetfulness congealed into full-blown dementia, my old mum had a strategy that was surprisingly helpful: *If you can't remember something, rummage through the alphabet till you find it.*

I've hardly got going when the system throws up Beattie: not my daughter, but my wife. Look, there she is, leaning against the basin with the elbow-push taps. Can I rely on her to slip our daughter's name into the conversation? Or to deflect the talk to something safer?

Beattie is decked out in a naval uniform, with the skirt hitched up well above her knees. Is Beattie really her name or something the morphine's dreamed up? She winks as if posing for a saucy seaside postcard as she raises a glass for a toast: *To your wife and mistress – may we never meet!*

The wraiths and shades take up the refrain: *To his wives and mistresses – may they never meet!*

Mistress? Isn't that rather outdated in this age of anything goes?

My wife hiccups, as if she's raised too many toasts already. Will they ever meet? It wouldn't be appropriate at a child's birthday party. Perhaps at the funeral then?

Sensation returns to my phantom limb. At first it's an itch I'm unable to scratch because there's nothing there. Why does the bit I've lost cause more trouble than the stump left behind?

Charlotte's ballet teacher of all people, scoffs my wife. Not very imaginative.

C for Charlotte: Bugsy the Bear has a proper girl's name! I'd have got there by myself if she hadn't interfered. The joy of it makes me forget the creeping pain for an entire minute.

No wonder you were so obliging, says Beattie. Ferrying the child back and forth to her dancing class.

So you knew? Is that why you invited her to the party, to smoke out our secret?

My wife laughs: I invited her because I thought she was a lonely spinster with no social life. And because Charlotte doted on her. You put a stop to that.

I follow my wife's gaze towards the drip-stand. A figure hovers behind it, muttering to herself as she tries and fails to rise onto her points. Is this shadow the reason I messed up my daughter's thirteenth birthday, and perhaps the rest of her life? I feel as little for her now as for any of the other spectres, but if I could bring to mind her name I might understand why I caused my family such pain.

I've got as far as R, and still no joy, when the door opens and a little girl waltzes in, a flesh-and-blood little girl in a green dress with her hair held up in ribbons. The spooks move apart as she comes forward to plant a kiss on my cheek. "Hello Granddad."

Bugsy the Bear and my naval officer wife and my

spinster mistress and all the other demons are siphoned back under the bed, and even my phantom limb stops howling, as my granddaughter lays a homemade get-well card on the white coverlet.

Behind the child stands a woman, sophisticated now and glamorous, but with a hint of the girl with the teddy bear nickname who used to love to dance on my feet. "Don't I get a kiss?" says Charlotte.

It's a tremendous comfort to have them here. I mustn't spoil the moment by looking ahead to when they've gone, to when Bugsy the Bear summons her friends from under the bed to dance me back to purgatory.

# A Place of Safety

WHEN SHE SAW the mess they'd made of the flat, the woman posing as a social worker was quick to act. A glance at the figurines in fragments in the fireplace, the disembowelled television, the trail of blood-red ink across the floor, and she'd whipped out her phone. "Go and pack a bag," she said. "I'm taking you to a place of safety."

I could see they'd sent a smart one. No need to explain how they drugged me. She cottoned on to the seriousness of the situation right away.

I take a Tesco's bag-for-life to the bedroom. I pull open my underwear drawer and shove some bras and knickers into the bag. Long time since they were white.

I snatch my hairbrush from the dressing-table; select a half-empty bottle of eau-de-toilette. My ID badge frowns at me from among the clutter. Won't need that at the safe house.

I don't mind leaving my name behind. I can easily get

another. And that photo will be redundant once I get my new disguise. But my job? That's quite a wrench.

I loved the library: pushing my trolley across the wrinkly carpet; stamping books; collecting fines. I used to blend in so well among the lowered eyes and voices, the battalions of shelves, the musty smell of books stained by greasy thumbs and coffee cups. Boring librarian: the secret agent's perfect cover. They called me a dinosaur, but that was fine by me.

They threw out half the books and brought in music and films. Cassettes, CDs, videos, then DVDs, all demanding a different kind of shelving, waist level, opening up the room to scrutiny. I kept my head down and went about my work.

They retired the pink cardex and put the catalogue onto microfiche, then computers. They replaced the carousel of tickets with barcodes and scanners. The new system wasn't easy to learn, but I moved with the times.

Relations shifted between staff and public. They were customers now. So what were we? Shop assistants? Perhaps I'd merged too well with my confected identity. When the system shifted, it hurt.

I turn away and slip a cotton blouse from its hanger. I lay it on the bed and start to fold it, sleeves tucked in to the back. Then I realise it's only going to get crumpled in my bag-for-life and throw it in.

The customers wanted email, and chatter. And the internet. All the information you'd ever want at the click of a mouse; they called it a librarian's dream. Instant connections from Aachen to Zwedru; shrinking the world while expanding our minds.

"Did I startle you?" The woman posing as a social worker hovers in the doorway. "I was wondering if you were ready."

I wait for my breathing to return to normal. If I can't trust her, who can I trust?

I let her take the bag. I let her lead me out to her car. There's no one around to jeer and spit as she drives me down the terrace and onto the high street. Past Tesco's. Past the Post Office. Approaching the library I'm hyperventilating again. I was fine when it was books, but the internet leaves no hiding place.

The woman posing as a social worker takes the turn-off to the hospital. I'd expected something more elaborate. Perhaps a plane journey, a blindfolded drive through forests to the hideout. This is almost on my doorstep. Ingenious!

We park outside a low-rise building. I recognise this place. I remember its cosy library: a few hundred paperbacks in a reclaimed linen-cupboard. I remember the kindness of the personnel there and the pills that make you feel safe.

# Communal Shower

WITH FROZEN FINGERS, I claw at the buttons down the spine of Esther's dress. Arms crossed in silent protest, she clutches her collar, rimmed with soot from our travels. My daughter is indignant at the prospect of swapping silk, however soiled, for the rough jackets and trousers people wear here.

My thoughts drift, as so often lately, to the Rosenbergs. How could they abandon their friends, their factory, their fine collection of contemporary art? What made them believe the ranting of a madman? When did they surrender hope?

At thirteen, Esther is shy undressing among strangers. Shamed by the loss of her thick dark hair. Shivering, I wrap my arms around her nakedness, squeeze her budding breasts against my own. "You needn't put on that ugly uniform," I tell her. "But won't it be lovely, after such a journey, to finally take a shower?"

# Habeas Corpus

A FTER FIVE WEEKS and a day, they bound a rope around his wrists, put a sack over his head and bundled him into the boot of a car. His body shook and sweated and loosened in all the wrong places, yet he was determined to hold on to his mind right to the end. If he couldn't die nobly or bravely, if he couldn't die for some worthwhile cause, at least he could go honestly. With gratitude for all that had made him who he was and with his sense of self intact.

Sacks of grain lay alongside him in the boot. He imagined them being put there for his comfort, like he'd imagined they cared on the odd occasion the food was still hot when they slid the tin plate across the dirt floor.

The sacks stopped him from rolling over too far, but they didn't prevent his body bouncing against the lid of the boot as the car bumped along the track. There were no tarred roads in these parts. Inside the dusty hood, he sneezed, and his ribcage grumbled.

Yet he'd had a good life. A career that let him roam the world, and a secure foundation to set out from. The steely love of his parents, the very different love of Hassan, and the others before him. Too late to let them know how much he'd loved them back.

He must have passed out. The stillness roused him, a sudden unrattling of his bones. The ache in his head, in his back, announced he was not yet dead.

He thought of his father, mounting his bike amid the crowd streaming from the shipyard as the siren announced the shift's end. It was the first photograph he'd ever sold, and he thought of his mother's shriek as she opened the *Clydebank Post.* Of reaching out for his camera to complete the circle with an image of her laughter and tears.

The boot creaked open. They hustled him out. He tried to stand but they kicked him down. The ground was hard and cold, with a gritty covering of sand. He heard talk and bitter laughter, its meaning muffled by the obscure dialect and the hood. He coughed and felt a boot in his kidneys.

He thought of his brother, his lopsided smile as he posed on the church steps, a girl in white lace on his arm.

A scuffle in the sand and something pressed against his temple. Even through the hessian he recognized the metallic chill. He heard the revolver click.

His life not yet over. His determination to live to the end. He thought of Hassan, the pleasure in his half-closed eyes as he smoked his early-morning cigarette.

His executioner shuffled. Tested the rope around his wrists. Moved back. Car doors slammed. The engine revved and it all became clear. The love and buzz and satisfactions of his life could not compensate for how it was to end. Dragged behind that car at forty miles an hour, skin flayed and bones splintered. Thirty-seven years of connections and commitments whittled down to a trail of scrappy body parts on a dirt road in a neglected land.

He had no thoughts. No memories. No pictures of better times to steer him through his final moments.

The thud of an object tossed from the car. Another door slammed. The car moved off. He braced himself for the jerk of the rope around his wrists that would pull him with it. That bullet would've been so sweet.

He lay on the ground, unable to move beyond an involuntary shaking from head to toe. The car whined into the distance.


HE LAY UNTIL he stopped shivering, until he dared to move. First, he jiggled his wrists. His shackles fell away, scaring him more until he realised their final act hadn't been to attach a tow-rope, but to set him free. He ripped off the stinking hood. Blinked at the moonlight, ran his hand across the fuzz on his chin, on his head. He patted his body, torso arms legs; apart from a few sticky damp patches, he seemed intact.

They'd left him on a dirt road between fields of grain. Above, stars dotted a navy-blue sky. Beside him, his backpack. Far on the horizon, the lights of a small town.

Still unsteady, he rose to his feet. Slipped off his jeans and emptied out the contents of his jockeys. He cleaned his buttocks and thighs as best he could, finishing off with grit from the road. He slung the jockeys into the ditch, rubbed his hands in the dirt and stepped back into his jeans. Then he picked up his backpack and began walking towards the lights.

THE TRACK SEEMED endless, the town sloping away like a mirage. He stumbled along regardless, accompanied by an ache that migrated around his body, leaping from toe to shoulder, from neck to knee with a vigour no other part of him possessed. His eyes stung and dust caked his throat. When he tripped over a stone, he eased himself down by the roadside. His fingers still stank of shit.

Remembering his backpack, he slipped it off his shoulders and scrabbled inside. It would've contained a bottle of water the night they picked him up outside the Astoria; the expats never left base without a half-litre of imported *eau minérale*. He found his camera and a cashmere sweater of indeterminate colour, but the water was gone.

They'd used the Nikon to take his photograph, that day's newspaper in his hand. The flash an assault after days in the gloom. Like the locals, he wondered if the camera stole his soul.

He held the sweater to his cheek; its gentle weave served only to mock him. He pulled it over his head, only now registering the chill of the night.

Once a week, with his camera, holding up the newspaper. The images would still be on the memory card, unless they'd wiped them. He felt defiled, like a woman with her rapist's seed taking root inside her.

The photographs. The lukewarm stew, carrot and lamb

flotsam in a sea of grease. The fatigue, the boredom, the hypervigilance. Trying to guess from a tone of voice, from the weight of a footfall, from the smell of the air how his captors envisaged his disposal. Sitting on his arse and marking off the days in bundles of scratches on the wall.

On the whole, they treated him well.

They treated him badly.

It was nothing. It had been a terrible ordeal.

He'd coped valiantly. He'd been a coward. It was over now. He'd never be free.

There was no point dwelling on those five weeks and a day. He had to move forward, get his body to the town somehow and from there to the safety of his flat. He hauled himself up, shuffled on his backpack and limped towards life.


HIS TRAINERS SCRAPED along the surface of the road. *Dinna scuff your shoes, Dougie*, his mother used to say.

He raised his head, looked up at the sky. A proper rural night, stars sharp as diamonds.

As a boy, he'd shared a bedroom with his wee brother. When he grew tall enough, he'd climbed a ladder and painted the ceiling navy-blue. Then he'd climbed back up again and stuck on a galaxy of fluorescent stars. He'd done it as a surprise for Frazer's tenth birthday. That boy was now a headmaster with children of his own.

He'd kept himself going in captivity with thoughts of home. All the homes he'd ever lived in, from his parents' ex-council semi-detached with the raspberries in the back garden to his current apartment with a view of the mosque from the balcony. It was his own space he now longed for: turning his key in the front door; the plastic-flower scent of cleaning fluid in the bathroom; the freedom to choose what and when to eat, whether to eat at all. The ritual of his old-fashioned stove-top espresso maker; his own photographs on the walls.

His trainers scraped along the track. The lights of the town like dust in his eyes. Or diamonds.


AT THE HOSPITAL, they inspected him, x-rayed him, prodded and injected him. Cleaned him up and dressed his wounds. They fed him and watered him and let him sleep a while.

A woman arrived from the Foreign Office, asked him questions he couldn't answer. *How many were they? Tall or short, fat or thin, dark or light and what was their shoe size?* If it were an interview, he wouldn't have got the job.

Cameras flashed around his bed. *This way, Dougie, smile now! How's it feel to be free?* He knew most of them by sight at least; all the media crowd drank at the Astoria. He cracked jokes about being on the other side of the lens.

They brought more food, changed his dressings, let him sleep some more. They let him take a shower and put on clean clothes that weren't his. They gave him a razor, let him shave his face but not his head. The woman from the Foreign Office said it wouldn't look right on TV.

They filmed him phoning his parents. His mother sobbed and said *Thank God* and told him his niece had passed her piano grade three. His father said the snow had arrived in the Cairngorms. He ate some more and slept some more and had his dressings changed.

He did a longer interview for the BBC. *How did they treat you, Mr Leckie? Have you any idea why they picked on you?* The woman from the Foreign Office prompted him through an earpiece. He thought of his flat with the clanking air-conditioning, the sweet smell of cleaning fluid and the espresso pot idling by the stove. He tried to give them the answers they needed, but his tongue clogged his mouth.

Food and sleep and more dressing of the wounds. When he said he'd like to go home, the people from the Foreign Office drove him to the airport and put him on a plane to Glasgow.

HE WAS WHISKED through Arrivals to a party at the working men's club. There were glittery banners proclaiming *Welcome home Dougie* and more cameras to record it. There were people he'd hardly seen in twenty years: his parents' neighbours and former workmates; old school pals and sundry hangers-on. His brother had come over with his family from Edinburgh; parents and children granted a day off school. Frazer grabbed him in a bear hug. "You look a right daft gowk with hair."

When it was over, he went with his parents in a taxi back to Bruce Street. He lay down in the bed he'd slept in as a boy. It was the guest room now, little used apart from a week in the summer when Frazer's girls came to stay. The astronaut wallpaper had been replaced with dancing Barbies, but the fluorescent stars still twinkled in a ceiling of navy-blue.

He'd marked off his five weeks and a day in clusters of

lines scraped on the stone wall with the edge of a spoon. Now the hours and days went by unchecked. His parents went to the supermarket and came home to watch television. He lay on his back upstairs staring at the ceiling he'd painted as a boy. At night when his parents slept, he watched old soaps in the front room, or shivered outside among the raspberry canes, a cigarette burning itself out in his hand.

His mother brought him tea and fig rolls, bowls of tomato soup from a tin. She fetched the phone when his old school pals rang, or his brother, and made excuses when he couldn't talk. His father invited him to play cards, to come to the club for a pint and a game of darts. He brought him books from the library, memoirs of men who'd been kidnapped for much longer than five weeks and a day and bounced back into life.

His mind turned over the questions he'd been asked on his release, looking for the answers that evaded him at the time. *Why did they take you? Why did they let you go?* He didn't know, and the Foreign Office had lost interest. His story was old news.

There were other questions, simple ones a bairn could answer. *How did they treat you? How did you cope?* He even stumbled over those.

His parents had always been supportive, tolerant of a way of life they didn't understand. They didn't argue with his choice of degree, even though photography seemed more a hobby than a step towards a job with a pension. They didn't flinch when he invited young men to stay over at New Year. They didn't grumble when he set off to earn his living in a war zone, with nothing more than what he could carry on his back. But now he'd pushed them to the limit. Spending his days staring at an ersatz sky, how could they tolerate something even *he* didn't want or understand?

After five days or weeks or months, his brother came from Edinburgh and sat on the other bed. "Hey, skiver!"

His gaze stayed fixed on the ceiling.

"What's the matter with you?" said Frazer.

"Nothing."

"You're wasting your life away."

"I'm fine here with mum and dad."

Frazer laughed. "You were desperate to get away when we were kids."

"Maybe I was wrong."

"You're going to stare at stick-on stars for the rest of your days?"

"So what if I do?"

Frazer moved across to his brother's bed. "Do you mind when you did that ceiling? I thought it was the sky from the Arabian nights."

He almost smiled.

"I thought, that's my big brother," said Frazer. "He can do anything."

"Aye well, perhaps I could back then."


AT NIGHT HE used to lie with his hands on the quilt, staring at the ceiling until he could be sure his wee brother was asleep. Then, without making a sound, he unfastened the drawstring of his own pyjama bottoms. He took hold of his sex and, as it swelled, he felt the power and promise of being Douglas Leckie. The adventure his life would bring.

It was partly out of pity that he'd painted the navy-blue sky of the Arabian nights. Other discoveries, other pleasures, he'd been able to share with his wee brother. But Frazer would have to wait a few more years for this. Yet he'd wanted the boy to have something, something exciting in the bedroom, but right for a child.

Although what he did while his brother slept was secret, there was no shame in the act. Even when he climaxed to the image of Ewan Campbell, rather than his auburn-haired sister Lorna, he knew what he did was good. Although nothing could be said to his family, it was their love, their belief in him, that let it happen. The act was a celebration of belongingness and solitude. It was taking custody of his body and leaving childhood behind.

THE MAN THAT child became no longer existed, the man who craved adventure because his place in the world was secure. Dougie had been mourning that man since he was taken from outside the Astoria and hustled into a car. He'd wanted to lie, nursing his grief indefinitely. But not even a prize-winning photograph can genuinely stop time.

He picked up his camera and aimed it at his big toe. He framed the shot, clicked the shutter and moved on to the next, capturing his body piece by piece through the lens. Feet, knees, belly, groin. Fingers, elbows, chin, chest. He played with different lenses, angles, speeds and focal lengths. Mounting the Nikon on a tripod and setting the timer, he took back ownership of his nose, his ears, the top of his head.

There would never be an answer to the what and the

why. He'd have to learn to live without one. He'd have to learn to live.

THERE WAS A leanness, a lightness, about Douglas Leckie as he stood in line with his single carry-on bag. His clothes were more suited to a warmer climate and, with his hair and beard newly shorn, his face took on a somewhat gaunt appearance. But it didn't matter. There was no one around to ask questions, except as part of the standard check-in procedure. No cameras to record his departure, save the one buried in his own bag.

No matter how many airports he'd been to, they still delivered the thrill he'd felt as a wee boy, off with his family to the Costas for their fortnight in the sun. The queues, the waiting around had never bothered him. The airport was where life's adventures began.

The stewardesses pushed the trolleys down the aisle. They offered him chicken or fish, tea or coffee, wine or a soft drink or beer. Douglas savoured the choice.

If ever he felt unsure, if those questions started up in his head, he thought first of the stars on his boyhood bedroom ceiling. Then he pictured his flat, smelt its cleanliness, tasted the bitter coffee from his stove-top espresso maker.

There were several empty seats on the flight. The Foreign Office still advised against non-essential travel to the area. Douglas was able to stretch out across the row and doze until the pilot announced the preparations for landing.

When the fasten-seat-belt sign was switched off, Douglas took out his phone and scrolled through the address book for Hassan's number. He thought of his espresso maker, the gentle breeze on the balcony, the green and blue striped sheets on the bed. He smiled, switched off his phone and returned it to his pocket. First, he needed to reclaim his space alone. There'd be plenty of time tomorrow to find Hassan.

# The Arrangement

I N THE FIVE years they'd been together, she'd only once caused Clinton to lose his smile. It was early on, when they were still dancing around the fine detail of the arrangement, and Julia had poked her nose where it didn't belong. As soon as she heard herself laugh – more of a hiccup, really, serving to emphasise rather than disguise her anxiety – she regretted it. For three days her texts went unanswered, leaving her to lounge beside the pool drinking *piña coladas* and feigning absorption in a trashy paperback. Finally, on the day before she was due to fly home, he turned up as she was helping herself to slices of papaya and pineapple from the breakfast buffet, holding the answer to her question by the hand.

His cute little girl was rendered cuter still by her fussy party dress, all lace and bows with layers of scratchy net fanning out the skirt. Her hair was moulded in intricate cornrows and, sweet as she looked, Julia felt sad that a child so small should be capable of sitting still for the time it would take to construct such an elaborate hairstyle.

Julia had whisked her off to the hotel shop while Clinton lingered on the terrace fiddling with his phone. She'd been disappointed when, told she could choose whatever she wanted, the child had gone for a *white* doll. Julia didn't know how to suggest something different without making her more solemn and serious than she already appeared.

If Julia wondered why Clinton never brought the girl along again, she didn't say so. She'd learnt her lesson. If she wanted to keep him, she'd have to curb her curiosity about Clinton the family man.

Later, Julia came not only to *accept* the existence of Clinton's wife and child, but to regard them as the cornerstone of the arrangement. Some of her compatriots, or so she'd heard, had been seduced into long-distance affairs with men who were after a ticket to a new life in the UK. A foreign husband, or a husband of any kind, was the last thing Julia wanted.

Working twelve-hour days with weekends devoted to catching up on sleep and laundry, Julia didn't have *time* for a partner. Besides, she was hellish to live with; if she was wedded to anything, it was to doing as she pleased.

Did she feel guilty? Not when men had bought themselves access to the bodies of nubile young women since trade was conducted in salt and seashells. Julia had money, money she'd worked hard for; surely she was entitled to dispose of it how she chose? She didn't see it as paying for sex, but helping to redress the imbalance between rich and poor economies. She bought him clothes, gave him cash to pay for their lobster bisque and *Cuba libre*s, and never asked for the change. In her head, that little bit extra was her contribution to the college fund that would free Clinton's daughter from a future of drudgery like her mother's.

Julia didn't need to meet his wife to know all about her. Women's lives followed a similar pattern throughout the Third World. Small and self-effacing, a new baby the instant the last one was weaned. Old before her time, too busy looking after other people to attend to her own appearance. She pictured her stirring a pot of stew over a wood fire, smoke stinging eyes that had never been enhanced with mascara. She envisioned her handwashing his T-shirts with a block of green soap under a tap dribbling water that was only ever lukewarm. Julia pitied Clinton's wife, but the arrangement did not *cause* her oppression. On the contrary, Julia was convinced it eased her burden.

But it wasn't the spectre of his wife that had made Clinton's face cloud over that morning as, loosely wrapped in hotel bath-robes, they drank coffee on the balcony of Julia's room. Was it the decision itself that upset him, or that she'd fixed it without consulting him?

She'd had no thoughts of such an arrangement on her first trip to the resort five years earlier. Ironically, the holiday had been Debra's idea; Julia had preferred museums to beaches. She'd never had any desire to visit the Caribbean.

It was sheer chance that Clinton's boat and not some other had taken them to the secluded snorkelling spot on the other side of the reef. It was his smile, and his dreadlocks swinging as he turned his head, that had seduced her, and the firmness of his grip as he hauled her back into the boat. Even so, she hadn't expected to go beyond the flirtatious banter that was almost *de rigueur* between the local men and single female tourists.

Debra had been furious. The arrangement had cost Julia that friendship but, by then, she was tired of sharing with a woman who left bits of dental floss in the plughole. She was tired of the protracted negotiations over the selection of the right holiday, the right hotel. Now she was free to return to the same resort, the same hotel, even the same room if it were available, two or three times a year. The same handsome hulk to escort her from bar to beach. No overlap between her work life and her holidays, apart from a photograph on her desk and the right to drop his name into water-cooler conversations to show her colleagues she wasn't some fusty old maid.

Nor did he do so badly. The arrangement wasn't only financial; Julia kept herself trim and she'd always looked good with a tan. So why did he hesitate when she told him she'd decided to stay a week longer?

He brought the heel of his hand to his forehead. "Dat great, Julia, but next week, shame, I carn see you so much. Gotta take out da boat."

"I realise that," she said, although she hadn't. He spent so much of each day in her company, she'd forgotten he had a job. "But we could meet up at night."

Her cup rattled in the saucer as she placed it on the wrought-iron table. Gazing beyond the balustrade, beyond the bougainvillea in the gardens, beyond the beach to where the waves frothed like meringue above the reef, she wondered if she might have misunderstood the terms of the arrangement. She'd never asked herself why Clinton needed to clarify her dates so far in advance. Why sometimes he'd email to ask her to swap one week for another. She'd assumed he was juggling childcare, his wife's antenatal appointments.

*If he can cheat on his wife, he can cheat on you, Julia.* When Debra had tried to warn her, she'd dismissed it as sour grapes.

CLINTON WAS GLAD his mouth wasn't full of coffee, for he'd surely have spewed it down his front. For a beat he was speechless; she'd never before shown any inclination to postpone her flight home.

He couldn't deny that he was fond of Julia. Their arrangement would have been intolerable if he were not. He liked the way she tucked her hair behind her ear when she laughed, how she always forgot to rub that last dollop of sunscreen into the bridge of her nose. He liked watching her dress in the evenings, choosing her outfit with care even if they were only going to a reggae party in a shack by the shore. But after two weeks, his pleasure in her company was waning. Only a couple more hours, he'd told himself, to endure her opinions on global inequalities, to laugh at her inane jokes. Breakfast, a farewell kiss at the security gate, then a glorious interlude of freedom: a solitary coffee to clear his head before picking up the next.

It had begun, as they all did, with a boat trip. Clinton

remembered it clearly because it was the other one who'd caught his eye, Julia seeming too aloof. But it was Julia who, after cocktails in the hotel bar, had ordered another drink for her friend and led him up to their room.

For five years, the arrangement seemed to suit her. No histrionics on departure, no wrangling – apart from one occasion – for a bigger part in his life. He wondered if growing older unsettled her, igniting a fear of running out of time. Clinton had seen her passport; he knew she'd not been honest about her age.

He told her he'd be working next week and, when she still seemed dejected, he lifted her hand to his lips. She smiled then, the way his daughter did when trying to act older than her years.

It would take more than a kiss to solve the problem. Clinton was skilled in the seduction and the swagger, but he wasn't a fixer. Could he salvage something, or was it time to let Julia go? Could he juggle two women, pretending to be busy with the boat? But in such a small resort there was a high risk of bumping into one when his arm was around the other. If he didn't deal with this correctly, they'd lose them both.

THE COMPUTER SCREEN went black. The blades of the ceiling fan slurred to a stop. Without the buzz of the fridge in the back room, the silence of the shop was suffocating. Selecting a brochure from the pile on the counter, Leticia fanned her face with an image of white bodies roasting on a palm-fringed beach. With only the stilled fan as her witness, she tugged at the collar of her cotton blouse and blew down her cleavage. She did not dare remove her stilettos lest her feet swell so much she'd never get them on again. First impressions were vital in her industry and, with her salon-sculpted hair, her crisp white blouse with *Leticia's Travels* embroidered in blue above the breast pocket, with her navy skirt, her heels and American tan pantyhose, she certainly looked professional. Sometimes, stuck behind a desk in the sweltering heat, she envied her husband's beach-bum uniform of vest, shorts and flip-flops, but not much. Leticia was proud to be the brains behind the business.

Seven years they'd been in operation; Suki still in nappies when they'd picked up the keys. Now the pickney could read and write, and run errands to the market. By the time their daughter joined the family firm, they'd be so established her husband could go back to full-time ferrying tourists across the reef.

Her friends were unimpressed initially. They thought a degree in tourism should have earned her a post with one of the major airlines or, failing that, a desk in an office with air con and a generator to kick in when the electricity failed. Of course, they were unaware of the arrangement, but they should have known Leticia well enough to realise she'd never kowtow to some bossman.

Leticia had been online when the current died, scheduling texts to be sent from her husband's phone. She could do them from her own cell, no problem, but it was less fiddly on the computer with the larger keyboard and screen. Changeover day meant extra work, and extra tension, for Leticia. Today's change was further complicated by the similarities in the two women's names. She could ensure his texts told of his grief at Julia's leaving and his excitement at Judy's arrival but might he, dispatching one and greeting the other in the flesh, muddle their names?

Leticia rose to her feet the moment she detected movement at the door. She wasn't surprised to see the white woman but she was shocked at the sight of her companion. It had never been part of the arrangement for Clinton to bring one of his women to mission control.

He greeted her like a cousin or the wife of a friend. "How dat no-good husband of your?"

"Getting into mischief I don' doubt." Leticia did not say, *You tell me! I staring him right in da face.* "And who your glamorous friend?"

When Clinton introduced them, Leticia did not say, *You look ten years older in da flesh!* She did not say, *Nobody told you girl don' go wearing da hotpants with those thighs?* She did not say, this time to her husband, *What mess you got we into now?* Instead, she asked Julia if she needed assistance with her travel arrangements.

Julia looked like she'd been hit on the head by a falling coconut. Clinton spoke on her behalf. "Well you see, my friend here, she so relax and content on our little island she decide stay an extra week."

Leticia could tell from the slope of her reddened shoulders that Julia realised Clinton was not enthused by the idea. But what did he expect *her* to do about it? Pretend Immigration wouldn't allow it? Claim there wasn't a single vacant room in the resort? "Madam," she said, "I see you got sense."

"Oh, call me Julia, please," said Julia.

"You seen da east side of da island, Madam Julia?"

"No, I haven't been out that way at all."

There was no time for pity. She had to spirit Julia away from the resort before Judy checked into her hotel. Theatrically, Leticia kissed the tips of her fingers. "Oh but you should, Julia Madam!"

Grinning, Clinton nodded his assent. Leticia loved how the movement made his dreads bounce. Damp seeped between her legs, and it wasn't sweat. Beyond the boost to their income, the arrangement gave their sex life an extra edge.

"What would you recommend?" Julia blinked back tears.

Leticia was surprised she caved in so easily. "I know da perfect place for you, right on da beach." Leticia unlocked her desk drawer and brought out a brochure. "Too small to have a website." The white woman would consider that quaint.

As Julia scanned the pamphlet, Leticia stole a glance at the racks of client files at the back of the drawer. Paper was cumbersome but, with the electricity supply so erratic, a spreadsheet posed too much of a risk. As she drew the woman's attention to the rustic features of the guesthouse on the east of the island, her thoughts raced ahead to tidying up the files, disposing of those that had lingered in the system too long.

"So, you tempted, Madam Julia?" Beaming, Leticia touched, for the first and last time, the white woman's bare arm. "Shall I make da arrangement?"

# The Invention of Harmony

F ROM THE SWEEP of her skirts and the smell of
rosemary, Sister Perpetua was clear that it was the
abbess who had come to relieve her. Who else would enter
another nun's cell without knocking? After three days of
silence, the older woman's words drummed on her ears.

"You may rise."

Sister Perpetua peeled herself from the flagstones. Now
her limbs had permission to move, she noticed how they
ached.

"You may sit on the cot."

Fearing she might faint if required to remain standing,
Sister Perpetua was glad to perch on her straw pallet while
the abbess towered above her.

"Have you repented, My Child?"

She had prayed night and day to the Blessed Virgin, but
she still didn't know whether God or the Devil had kindled
the fire in her throat. She stared at her toes, red and swollen

with chilblains. "I don't know what came over me, Reverend Mother."

"The ague, My Child. God often sends some pestilence to test us during Lent. Even Sister Benedictus cried out last night…" The abbess shivered. "Now you've recovered from your fever, I'll send a novice with some gruel. You may join us for Vespers."

Sister Perpetua nodded. If the abbess considered her ready, she would gladly take her place in the choir stalls.

At the door, the abbess hesitated. "I've spoken to the bishop. And the bishop has spoken to the archbishop. So I have it on the highest authority. Plainchant is plainchant and always will be. Each voice at the exact same pitch at precisely the same time."

EVERY DAY SHE thanked God for choosing her for the cloistered life. Every year, as another Visiting Day was measured by yet another of her cousin Elisabet's confinements, she rejoiced in having escaped the yoke of marriage. Such freedom in the toll of the bells marking the time to work, to pray, to study. Such contentment in the rhythms of resignation.

Yet, alone in her tiny cell, waiting for the novice to bring her the sustenance necessary to resume her duties, Sister Perpetua had a thought so unwelcome it made her dizzy. That the familiar routines might not be supportive, but smothering. She shook her head, as if to expunge the dregs of malaria the abbess had diagnosed. Her memory of the other morning in the chapel was cloudy, yet she was convinced her fever had been not cause, but consequence, of her crying out. Her voice had soared above the others, taken wing and floated up to the rafters, not in sickness, but in ecstasy.

With a tap at the door, the novice crept in, bearing a wooden bowl like a blessed chalice. Sister Perpetua wanted to grab the food and gobble it down, but that would be disrespectful to both God and her growling stomach. She bent her head to say grace, before taking the bowl and dismissing the girl.

The girl did not move. "Sister Augusta said I must wait for the bowl."

Francesca was one of the more troublesome novices. With her tortured questions and her childish tantrums, she was slow to adapt to a life of poverty, chastity and obedience. The Sisters had begun to wonder if she'd ever take her vows.

But that wasn't Sister Perpetua's problem. She turned her attention to the porridge, spooning it slowly into her mouth, her heart swelling with God's beneficence as it warmed her insides.

"Will you be coming to Vespers?" said Francesca.

Sister Perpetua thought of Sister Augusta in her kitchen, stirring a cauldron of gruel. Counting the wooden bowls stacked on the shelves and ensuring, like the Good Shepherd with his sheep, none would go astray.

"Will you …? Will you sing again?"

Sister Perpetua put down her spoon. She stared hard at the girl, unsure which of them was most afraid. What would become of Francesca if she couldn't take her vows? Would she be cast out to fend for herself?

"I do hope you'll sing," said Francesca. "The other morning, you were like an angel. It was the most beautiful sound I've ever heard."

Sister Perpetua's mouth went dry, despite the watery gruel. The abbess was right. What God wanted was plainsong: all of them chanting together, hardly varying the notes and no single voice distinguishing itself from the others. If ever she was tempted to let it happen again, she would picture her cousin, sweating and screaming, pushing out a baby from between her legs, glistening with blood and slime. But first she must point Francesca along the path of abnegation. "Return to the kitchen," she said, "and inform Sister Augusta that you have broken the rule forbidding conversation in the dormitories."

MANY YEARS LATER, when they gathered around the abbess's body in the Lady Chapel, the nuns found comfort in the knowledge that their chant of *Requiem aeternam dona eis* would've been heard in Heaven as a single voice. Sister Perpetua prayed also for the soul of her cousin, Elisabet, recently called to God by the birth of her twelfth child.

They elected a new abbess, and the days settled down as before, the nuns shuffling quietly between the dormitory cells and the *lavatorium*, the refectory and the abbey. Only the seasons altered, and even Francesca's failure to take her vows seemed part of God's plan.

Sister Perpetua was weeding between the onions when the postulant arrived to call her to an assembly in the chapter house. Rubbing her hip as she hobbled along the cloister, she was convinced the pope must've died for the abbess to interrupt the morning's work. So she was relieved it was merely a choirmaster sent by the bishop. Yet, once reassured His Holiness had not been taken from them, she found the purpose of the meeting equally disturbing.

Sister Perpetua repeatedly thanked God that, while her body was failing, He'd left her mind as sharp as ever. Yet she couldn't comprehend what the choirmaster meant by this new method of singing the offices. Different people singing different words and melodies all jumbled up together? Such a clash of voices could only be the work of the Devil.

Sister Perpetua wasn't alone in her confusion. Sister Catalina could hardly suppress her giggles.

"What is it, Sister Catalina?" said the abbess.

"Forgive me, Reverend Mother, but it reminds me of Francesca's ranting."

The choirmaster beamed. "Where is this Sister Francesca? Perhaps she could explain it more clearly than I can."

A coughing and shifting of habits filled the gap before the abbess spoke. "Francesca isn't one of the sisters. Merely one of God's unfortunates in the infirmary."

Poor Francesca. Her father should have given her to a husband instead of confining her to the convent. Sister Perpetua had visited her from time to time until Sister Catalina reported that her presence unsettled her charge, left the girl screaming and tugging at her chains.

"Imagine the various voices blending together," said the choirmaster. "Like the separate sections of the convent, each relying on the others, working in partnership to create an organism that pays greater homage to God's glory than any individual component, no matter how magnified, could ever do alone."

The nuns flanking Sister Perpetua on the wooden bench nodded. As she wriggled her toes, crumbs of soil rubbed against the leather insoles of her sandals. There was no point her toiling in the herb garden unless Sister Augusta peeled and chopped and boiled the produce for the table. Similarly, she'd be as naked as a baby without the sisters from the sewing room to clothe her. The community's effectiveness depended on the nuns' dedication to their distinct tasks. Yet she had been blind to their differences, as if their grey scapulas and bland food screened all else. As if she hadn't noticed how the devotions altered with the Hours, from Matins through to Compline. Sister Perpetua's heart thumped against her ribcage and, in her throat, her vocal cords quivered.

"I know it sounds strange," said the choirmaster, "but once I teach you your parts, you'll understand. After all, it was a nun, like you, who invented harmony."

The Sisters shook their heads, not trusting they'd heard him correctly. God would not choose a nun to introduce so radical a change. But they brushed the conundrum aside as they turned as one to Sister Perpetua.

Did she cry out? Or did she only imagine her voice rising to the heavens and hovering there among the angels before crashing back to earth? The nuns at either side of her broke the worst of her fall, but they couldn't prevent the belt of pain tightening around her chest until it stopped her heart. They couldn't silence the devilish cacophony, nor shield her from the terrifying visions of the lives she might have had: rattling her chains like poor Francesca in the infirmary or writhing in agony like her dear cousin, Elisabet, as she brought forth child after mewling child.

Despite decades of prayer and mortification, she was going to meet her maker unprepared. She thought she'd dedicated her life to Him but, when God had called her to be His instrument, she had turned away in fear.

# Tobacco and Testosterone

H E'D SET OUT to find the blue mosque, but he must have taken a wrong turning, veered right instead of left somewhere, because now he was lost within a mash of alleyways devoid of street signs. He'd tried asking for directions, homing in on men in European dress who might speak English, but without luck. Did they walk on because they genuinely couldn't understand him or because they couldn't be arsed to help?

The narrow lanes amplified the heat, sniping it from stone wall to cobbled wynd and back again, catching him in the crossfire. Sweat traced rivulets down his back while the searing sun reminded him constantly of his bald patch. Had Maureen come along, she'd have ensured he wore a hat. But she'd opted to remain in the resort, with a guard at the gate and round-the-clock buffet serving both local and European cuisine. Part of him wished he'd stayed there too.

The holiday was a gift from their children; *our three*

*gorgeous girls* as Maureen intoned at the slightest opportunity, though the youngest was over thirty with girls of her own. Despite being presented in honour of his retirement, Roy had known he'd have no say in where they pitched up. Even so, he was surprised Maureen plumped for Morocco. If it had been a lifetime's ambition to go there, she'd been extremely adept at keeping it to herself.

There'd been talk of *our three gorgeous girls* joining them but, in the end, only the middle one, Hayley, could find the time. Or the funds. She seemed to have money to burn: when Roy proved unable to lounge in the sun for more than five minutes without complaining of boredom, she'd collared the rep to book him a city break. While relieved to escape the sanitised splendour of the resort, Roy felt as if it were Hayley and Maureen who were the parents and he the child, banished to his room for fidgeting.

The alley shunted to the right, opening out into a small square, where nothing matched the picture in his guidebook. Laundry stretched between the upper windows like paper chains at Christmas. A man sat on a stool aside a dark doorway, leathered hands clasped across his belly. His throat parched, and his left heel throbbing with the beginnings of a blister, Roy resolved to abandon his search for the mosque and ask for directions back to his hotel or, better still, a taxi to deliver him there.

The man smiled as Roy approached, revealing a set of gums interrupted by a single brown-stained tooth. "As-salam'alaikum."

Roy recognised the words, but he couldn't contort his tongue around the customary reply. "Taxi?" he asked instead.

"Aiwa." Grinning, the man gestured towards the open doorway.

Thinking it unlikely the rectangle of solid black concealed the office of a taxi firm, Roy asked again. "Taxi?"

This time, in addition to smiling and pointing, the man mimed bringing a cup to his lips. He nodded vigorously as Roy peered into the gloom. Patting the pocket of the lightweight travel trousers where he kept his passport, Roy inched into the shadows.

Twenty or so men in traditional Arab dress, the loose long-sleeved full-length nightshirt-affair that brought to mind Wee Willie Winkie. Clustered around low tables, cross-legged or lounging on cushions, they paused their chat and card and board games, to examine the intruder. Had he gate-crashed some private club?

As he pondered whether to bolt or brazen it out, a waiter sidled up to him, his long apron stiff with grease. The other men resumed their play as the waiter escorted Roy to a vacant table, fortunately one at a more regular height.

Roy assumed the waiter had disappeared to fetch a menu, but he returned almost immediately to set down a small straight-sided glass of amber liquid. It wasn't until the heat shocked his fingertips that he smelled the mint and realised this wasn't lager. He gazed around sheepishly but no-one appeared to care.

Was it the absence of alcohol or of women that made this place so much calmer than the pubs back home? Certainly there was none of the posturing he'd come to expect. In his youth, he'd known bars where women weren't welcome, where fathers taught their sons to hold their ale and a layer of sawdust absorbed what their stomachs couldn't tolerate. He'd left such places behind when he was courting Maureen and hadn't missed them until this moment. Now it struck him that, when he'd envisioned initiating his son into the rites of manhood, one of those bars had formed a constant backdrop: the air thick with tobacco and testosterone, relics of an era in which everyone knew their place and stayed there.

His mind had screened the father-son scenarios with the allure of a soft-focused TV commercial. A gentle rivalry over their allegiance to opposing football teams. Buying the lad his first razor and showing him how to use it. Advising him to carry a condom. An argument over his first tattoo. As the waiter crept up again, Roy shook the regrets from his head.

"Shisha?"

When the waiter indicated a nearby table, where two men hunched over a backgammon board, Roy took it for an invitation to join the game. Until he noticed the water-pipe bubbling on the floor. Roy nodded. They had these in England now, but he'd never tried one. His marriage had been a smoke-free zone since the birth of their first grandchild.

He wondered what they were up to back at the resort. In fact, it didn't take much wondering: they'd be lying by the pool cultivating their tans and, if the rep wasn't around to remind her it could offend the locals, Hayley would have removed her bikini top. He'd blushed the first time, but Maureen had laughed, saying her breasts had cost enough, she might as well flaunt them.

Watching the waiter assemble the water-pipe with the solemnity of a priest, Roy imagined Hayley by his side. *She'd* bombard the man with questions, ignoring any signs of unease on his part. She'd be loud, brash, comfortable in her skin. She'd be an embarrassment.

The waiter placed a glass flask on the floor, half filled it with water and screwed an elaborate metal cylinder into the opening. This he crowned with a ceramic bowl, into which he crumbled tobacco, and covered it with a perforated metal plate. Summoning a boy to bring a tray of glowing charcoal, he took a pair of tongs and added the fuel.

Roy wondered if the holiday would have been easier if their other daughters had accompanied them. When Louise and Zoe had given their apologies, or perhaps excuses, he'd hinted to Maureen they might be better off as a couple, without any of their *gorgeous girls*. She'd soon put him in his place. "You want me to tell Hayley she's not welcome? When she's been out of our lives for so long?"

He'd worried Maureen would be disappointed. That, after such a lengthy estrangement, they wouldn't bond as she'd hoped. As things turned out, the disappointment was entirely his: Maureen and Hayley got along all too well.

The waiter inserted a hose into a slot at the side of the contraption and passed Roy the mouthpiece. The water in the flask frothed as the cool smoke began to permeate his lungs.

He'd never forget her ringing the doorbell as they settled down to the evening news. Not a word in fifteen years apart from that one postcard to let them know she was alive. All those years swinging between blaming themselves and blaming each other; between fury at, and fear for, their child.

Then there she was in their front room without warning or apology. There she was sipping tea from the best china with new breasts and a new name. Squeezing Maureen's hand to stop her from crying, while relishing the fuss she'd brought back to the family home.

"The prodigal son returns!" He'd meant to lighten the mood and, indeed, Hayley's glossed lips had shaped themselves into a smile. But Maureen had flashed him a look rife with decades of accusations and he'd realised, as the newsreader babbled in the background about some faraway catastrophe, that his views no longer counted. On the brink of retirement, he'd got the message that it wasn't only at work his contribution was no longer required.

Maureen complained he'd been too hard on the boy, criticising when he should have encouraged. But their middle child seemed determined to avoid doing anything that merited encouragement. Roy wondered if he'd actually been too soft; his own father would have thrashed it out of the lad the day he came down for breakfast in his sister's dress.

If only they'd found a place like this for a proper heart-to-heart. If only the boy had stuck around long enough for Roy to teach him the skills he'd need to be a man. How not to get a girl pregnant. How to wield a razor without nicking his chin. By running away before he'd finished school, his son had made a mug of him. By returning, Hayley had done the same.

She'd offered no explanation, at least not to him.

Perhaps she'd confided in her mother. Perhaps she thought a skirt and heels and boob job explanation enough.

His gaze lingered now on the men in their alien clothes, his ears struggling to attune themselves to the rhythms of their speech. Their talk was a succession of throat clearings, but that was the least of what he failed to understand. Men in gowns that looked like dresses. Sons returning to their childhood homes as girls. A father's inability to navigate a foreign city. The whereabouts of the blue mosque.

Savouring the tobacco through the water-pipe, Roy watched the bubbles tumbling in the flask. He thought of his youngest grandchild, three months old and blowing raspberries. Perhaps it was a reflex, something all kids did, but he couldn't imagine any other baby looking so cute.

What was he trying to prove by fleeing his family? By clinging to authority he no longer possessed? "You've got to accept folk as they are, not as you think they should be," Maureen insisted. That was all very well, but he craved acceptance too.

The man at the next table caught his gaze. Before Roy could look away, he raised his glass and smiled.

He'd lost a part of himself when he lost his son, but no amount of sulking would bring him back. Perhaps here, where everything was topsy-turvy, he might discover a part of himself that could adapt to gaining an extra daughter. He didn't have to approve of her choices. Only concede her right to choose for herself.

He raised his glass to salute the man at the next table. A man so different to Roy in culture, language and dress. But wouldn't they drink to the same objectives? Wouldn't they toast their families' health?

There'd be no shame in returning to the resort a day early. Challenging his daughter to a game of snooker or a few lengths of the pool.

# No Way Back

# In Praise of Female Parts

REMEMBER THOSE SUNDAYS when we used to sleep past lunchtime? It used to drive our mothers wild. These days, I wake up long before the night has done with strutting its stuff and lie motionless in the dark, waiting for my brain to figure out where I am. Then I remember my clitoris, and laugh.

At school they showed us how to put a condom on a cucumber. You turned to me and said, *Urgh! Could you imagine taking a thing like that inside you? It's worse than a fucking tampon.* That night, babysitting for your shrimp of a brother, we opened your mum's book with the photos of hippies holding a mirror up to their cunts, and learned how to do it for ourselves. Along with that first Oh-oh-oh, we discovered that the little pearl hidden away next to our piss-hole had a proper name, and a purpose. We were so full of ourselves back then.

Some women here like to trade their dreams at

breakfast, dreams in which they're constantly on the go. Swimming the Channel or climbing Everest or running the London Marathon; but the dreams they like best are the ones where they're flying. They can look down from the sky on all the poor sods who have to trundle around on two legs, and feel smug. Or so they make out.

Remember how we tittered over the chapter on lesbians? It looked as if that girl-on-girl stuff had been written specially for us. It turned out we were only killing time till the boys we half-fancied caught up: you for Toby to be introduced to the wonders of deodorant; me for the goth at the gymkhana to prove himself capable of jumping a clear-round.

These early mornings, before my brain cottons on to where it is, I believe I can feel my clitoris. If I concentrate hard enough, I swear there's some sensation there. I feel it in the pool, too, sometimes; it's like being tickled by a ghost. I don't say anything, but I see the physio smile.

You'll come and visit, won't you? Everyone here is nearly as old as my mum, and I get so bored. I know you'll want to go around with your other friends, but you could spare an afternoon, couldn't you? Please!

I've never dreamt of flying. In my dreams, I'm galloping through a forest on a piebald stallion. I've removed my hat to feel my hair streaming a banner at my back. I'm naked, and riding bareback, and each time a hoof hits the ground, my clitoris tingles. I hold tight with my knees and jiggle my arse to rub myself against the horse. And then I come, right down to my toes. As I say, it's just a dream, but when they turn me over in the night they think I've wet myself and have to change the sheets.

You'll want time with Toby, too; isn't it weird about sweat being an aphrodisiac? I suppose you've moved on from those cucumber-condom lessons now. Did you need your mum's book, or does it jigsaw together when you're in love? Like in the songs?

In my dream, the forest closes in on us, but we don't slow our pace. We thunder through the cracks between the trees and I lean right and left to dodge the lower branches. Still woozy from my orgasm, I can't duck quickly enough and the forest claws at my body, leaving an autograph of blood across my breasts. Far far away in the background I hear my mum screaming, *Slow down! You'll break your bloody neck.*

Will you try to get a job for the holidays? Maybe you could come and work at the unit. Wouldn't that be weird? You'd need a car to get out here. Would your mum lend you hers?

When it gets lighter, I flick my eyes sideways to squint at the clock. It's not long then till the day staff come on duty. After their handover, one of them will come into my room and squeeze past the equipment to open the curtains. *How did you sleep?* she'll say. *Shall I turn you or are you ready to get up?*

Remember how we used to think we were so streetwise? Confident of handling any calamity that could befall a teenager, right through from a disastrous haircut the day before a party to our parents looking solemn and announcing they were getting divorced.

Like I said, my day starts differently these days. I wake

early and lie motionless in the dark, waiting for the day staff to come and move me. I lie here, thinking about the old days. Then I remember my clitoris, and weep.

# A Smell of Paint

TODAY MY DAUGHTER is coming home. At last. Her brother has gone to bring her here to the house of her childhood to paint pictures and be mothered back to herself.

Left behind, I shuffle from room to room, arranging curtains, fluffing up cushions, nudging pictures into position on the walls. I'd like to fill the space with the scent of baking: flapjacks and sultana scones and a rich Victoria sponge. Then we might play at cafés again: she, with a tea towel wrapped around her waist, clutching a spiral-bound notebook; me at the table in a dressing-up-box hat and my little finger extended as I sip from a doll's tea cup. Instead, I drift out to the garden to pluck daffodils for her room. Custard-yellow daffodils and double-cream daffodils and icing-sugar-white daffodils with a cheddar-red trumpet in the middle. Perhaps they'll move her to paint.

Not thinking – surely, not needing to think after twenty-two years of mothering – I take the flowers up to the apple-green bedroom at the back. I push open the door and stop short, drops of water shooting out of the vase onto my hand. It's not *her* bathrobe that lies slumped across the duvet, but mine. Not *her* impressionist prints that clothe the walls, but mine. Not *her* lipsticks and lotions that litter the dressing table, leaving barely a gap for the vase, but mine. For a moment I'm disorientated, not by the incongruity of finding my things in her room, but by how right it feels. As if this was how it was meant to be. Mother inside daughter, like Russian dolls.

I wipe my hand on my skirt and step across the landing to the master bedroom, Ellen's room now. When we heard she was finally coming home I thought, Why not? Why not forgo the bay window and the en-suite to give Ellen a room where she might paint? It's ten years since I had need of a double bed and now Joe spends so much time at his girlfriend's I'll rarely even have to share the second bathroom.

Going from my room – Ellen's old room – at the back to the double bedroom at the front is like leaving January for July. The light is so much better at the front of the house. It beams on Ellen's old teddy bears lined up along the headboard of what used to be my bed. It glows on the virgin surface of the dressing table, awaiting my daughter's lipsticks and lotions and bijouterie. It shines on the easel standing sentinel in the bay window. An artist craves light more than anything. More than food. More than sex. More than life.

I place the daffodils on the dressing table and go and stand by the easel in the window. The view from here isn't as pretty as the view out the back, especially not since I had half the front lawn paved over to accommodate the extra car. But Ellen won't mind. She doesn't do views. These days, she prefers a modernistic form of still-life, a twenty-first-century take on those bowls of oranges and pheasants ready for the pot.

From the moment she could grip a fat wax crayon in her dimpled fist, Ellen loved to make pictures. Since the days of jagged squiggles across the eternal computer paper I salvaged from work she has been absorbed by drawing, painting, colouring, sketching. Totally self-contained, which was a boon when Joe came along. To look at him now with those butcher-boy biceps it's hard to believe he was such a sickly little thing. Needing so much attention. An ordinary three-year-old would have struggled, but all I had to say to Ellen was "You do me a nice drawing while I change the baby," and she'd sit quietly at the table with her tongue tucked into the corner of her mouth, scribbling away as if her life depended on it. I could have left her like that for hours.

Joe's biceps came in handy when it came to switching rooms, transporting bedding and clothes and knickknacks between mine and hers. I couldn't have managed to emulsion the walls without him to drag the furniture into the middle of the room. Covering over the brooding cherry-red I've lived with since not long after Pete left. Replacing it with a more subtle apricot. No artist wants light streaming in through the windows only for it to be swallowed by the walls.

I was grateful for Joe's help. But he made me wait for it. Wait till Thursday half-day closing before he could spare the time. Too busy with his girlfriend in the evenings. That's why it was all such a rush. If I'm honest, there's still a whiff of paint in the air. I wonder if she'll notice. I wonder if she'll mind. I shouldn't worry; no artist would complain about a smell of paint.

She was never one to grumble, to criticise, to make a mockery of mothering with a slap of words across the face. Only that once; and then, poor love, so sadly off target. "You've always blamed me that you didn't finish university," she said, and I was stunned, aghast, first that she could think that and second that she couldn't do the maths. I know she's an artist, but a shopkeeper's daughter should at least be able to count.

I was twenty-two when I had her, the same age as she is now. I could have got my degree if I'd been determined enough, if I could have tolerated living away from Pete and his father's butcher shop. Far from blaming her for ruining my chances I'm sorry I didn't conceive sooner. Seems ironic now, the way he let me down in the end, but I was in love and desperate for his child.

Ellen's circumstances were different, with no boyfriend to drag her back at weekends, but she didn't take to university either. It isn't easy to go from a small town like ours to a big city campus buzzing with young people and ideas. A small town where everyone knows each other, where there are still shops that close for a half-day on a Thursday, where the rituals of butchering are passed down from father to son, father to son, and the craft-shop-cum-tea-shop puts a teenager's artwork on display.

"Come home," I said. Just as I didn't need a degree to be a mother, she didn't need one to paint. "Come home." I could've looked after her.

The truth is, I suppose, it didn't feel like home anymore; not after he left.

"That's a lovely picture," Pete used to say. "Is that for Mummy or for Daddy?"

"It's for both of you," she'd say. "For Mummy *and* Daddy."

He bought her oils and acrylics in metal tubes. He bought her a wooden palette where she could set out all those colours with the fancy names: vermillion; burnt umber; cobalt blue. He bought her huge boards and sealed them with white primer. He bought her giant sketchpads with pages thick as greetings cards. He led her to believe she could have everything she wanted. Everything but two parents at home.

Joe was all right as long as Pete picked him up a couple of times a week to play football, but Ellen was inconsolable. Enough tears for a hot shower; cold shower's what he should have had but it was too late then. "I hate him," she said. "How can he not love you anymore? You're the most beautiful woman in the world."

She looked for comfort where she always had, in her art. And I was to be her muse. Sketchbook at the ready, she'd study me cooking or ironing or watching TV. She said she was planning to paint my portrait. A *beautiful* portrait. She would show him, she said.

What could I do? She seemed happy enough. At least she had a purpose, instead of sitting around moping. Or playing those mindless computer games her brother favoured.

And what mother wouldn't be flattered to have her preteen daughter obsessing on her beauty? But after a while, it got irritating. I'd be trying to catch a quiet half-hour to read a magazine while Joe was off with his dad, or I'd be cursing as I struggled to unblock a sink, and I'd look up and find her staring at me, pencil in hand. "For heaven's sake, can't you go out and play like normal kids?" It was hard enough coping with being dumped without having to double up as artist's model.

Unlike Joe, she refused to stay overnight at her dad's new place. But she would visit in the early evening once a week after school. She always took a picture to show him and, of course, it had to be a picture of me. Yet she was never satisfied with the quality. The night before a visit I could hardly get her to bed. Fretting over her painting. Wanting to add that final touch.

It didn't do me justice, she said. Of course it didn't. She may have had talent, but she was only twelve. But at twelve you don't know you're 'only'. You think you can save the world.

Pete rang me at work one morning. "We're going to have to talk about Ellen."

"There's nothing I can do," I said. "You're the one who left."

"She's not eating," he said.

"She's turned vegetarian. We both have. Can't stomach any more of your meat."

"It's not only meat she's refusing."

"Must be the atmosphere at your place. That woman poisoning her appetite."

He tried to fix up family meetings at the children's clinic. If it hadn't been so cruel it would have been funny, the way he tried to shift his guilt onto her. As if by making out that she was crazy, he could come across as the doting father. Ellen told him what to do with his family meetings.

After that, she wouldn't even go to her dad's for tea. What could I do? She was old enough to know her own mind. And giving up that burden left her so much more relaxed. It helped me relax, too, when she swapped the portraits for still-life. A vase of daffodils. A bowl of fruit. A jug of clotted cream so realistic you wanted to reach into the painting and spoon it onto a scone.

She seemed contented enough. We were more like friends than mother and daughter. In the evenings, while Joe played upstairs on his computer, I'd put on some old Beatles records, and we'd curl up together on the sofa with the photo album.

If only she hadn't pushed herself into going away. If only she'd allowed herself to come home when university didn't work out.

The social worker at Prince Edward's must have been reading the same pop-psychology book as Pete. She tried to cajole us into meeting with her as a family; not just Ellen and me, but Joe and Pete as well. Ellen wasn't having it. "He's not my family anymore. He gave that up when I was twelve years old."

Then the stupid social worker took to quizzing me. Senseless questions about when he left. "What did you do to remind her that her dad still loved her?"

I stared at her nasty pinched face, her stupid staring

eyes. I didn't know what to say.

And then my lovely daughter spoke up. "It wasn't my mother who left."

She abandoned the daffodils. Fruit would rot in the bowl before she would bring herself to paint it. Instead she spent hours in the kitchen concocting bizarre meals: turnip and custard; chargrilled potato sprinkled with hundreds and thousands. Not to eat, of course, but to paint. I didn't pretend to understand it; I've never been able to fathom modern art.

THE SOUND OF a car turning into the cul-de-sac. A tank of a car with a big butcher-boy engine. I creep back behind the velvet curtain. I want to see the relief on her face when she finally comes home.

The 4x4 pulls up by the front door on what used to be part of the lawn. Joe cuts the engine. I wait for the passenger door to open, for her to rush out, searching for her mother, as if she were five years old again and I was meeting her from school. I wait. I can't see inside the car from this angle. I imagine them gathering up the paraphernalia of the journey, the soft-drink cans and CDs. I imagine them finishing off a brother-and-sister conversation before being reunited with their mother. When they still don't emerge, I imagine – and with the thought my legs start to shake and I have to grab hold of the easel for support – my son sitting in the driver's seat wondering how to break it to me that he's come home alone.

Oh, relief! The door opens and my daughter steps onto the block paving. She wrinkles her nose at the forgotten smell of home. She shivers in the pale sunshine and reaches back into the 4x4 for her padded jacket. She pulls it across her scraggy shoulders, pokes her bony arms through the sleeves. She looks around and up towards the bay window. My heart is thumping against my chest as I step back out of view.

The car door slams. Brother and sister walk towards the front door. I tiptoe nearer the window to watch them: a hale-and-hearty nineteen-year-old man dragging the suitcase of his shrunken sister.

I hear the doorbell ring. Joe has forgotten his key again. I should go down. I turn from the window and look around the room. A room with apricot walls and a big window to encourage the light. The room where that skeletal girl was conceived. And her sturdy brother. We had no need of light for that.

Nor will Ellen make use of the light in this room. A light like this would send her scurrying into the shadows. She hasn't come back to the house of her childhood to paint pictures to hang in the gallery on the high street where the shops still close on a Thursday afternoon.

The doorbell again. That young man has no patience. I should go down. My daughter has come home. At last.

I breathe in the sickly smell of paint. It almost chokes me.

# Cracks

THAT LONG JAGGED one above the dressing table mimics the coast of Amalfi with its inlets, fjords and bays. Locked in its folds are her memories of bougainvillea and majolica domes, of whitewashed houses clinging to cliffs. The scent of lemon blossom, and sunscreen mixed with sea salt; the taste of barbecued fish and their first night as husband and wife.

The short straight one above the window reminds her of the scar from her Caesarean. Neat as the list of baby names they dreamt up in tribute to the place he was conceived.

The large one, branching through the middle, mirrors the map of a family across the generations. Charting Vittorio's – or Angelo's or Pascal's – connections to the couple who made him and the couples who made them.

She should be too busy to lie in bed studying the cracks in the ceiling. The long jagged one above the dressing table evoking the honeymoon where he cheated on her the first time. The short straight one above the window recalling the Caesarean scar from the baby they began when he promised it wouldn't happen again. The big one fanning out like a tree conjuring his other family, his secret second wife whose babies emerge from her body screaming with life.

One day she will rise from her bed and drape old sheets across the surfaces. She will shroud the bed, the dressing table, and the rocking chair where she should have sat nursing their boy. One day she will climb a ladder and paint the ceiling. But not yet. Not until she can be sure the cracks will not show through.

# How's Your Sister?

WHENEVER I CATCH up with friends, we always end up chewing over the same old topics: how our dream jobs gave way to marking time till retirement; how those gorgeous hunks, who we lost our hearts to, matured into middle-aged bores; how our angelic children transmogrified into grunting adolescents. Once we've dealt with those old chestnuts we'll move on to analysing, depending on the season, *The Great British Bake Off* or *I'm a Celebrity Get Me Out Of Here*. And finally, they might ask about my sister.

*SO HOW'S SHE doing these days?*
    *She's doing fine.*
    *Helluva thing to come to terms with.*
    *She's happy enough.*
    *What was it again?*
    *Cancer.*
    *What she must have gone through. Puts all our grumbles in*

*perspective.*

*You could say that.*

*Well, pass on my regards when you see her next.*

*Sure.*

*SO HOW'S SHE doing these days?*

"Why don't you go round?" says my mother. "You could see for yourself."

I don't exactly tell Mum I won't go. I tell her about the latest reorganisation at work; four middle managers having to reapply for three posts. I tell her I'm thinking of asking my GP for HRT. I tell her about the endless negotiations with the builders about the loft conversion, and the infernal dust.

"You should see what your sister's had done to her place. New kitchen units at exactly the right height."

My husband and I had this fantasy of creating a teenage den in the loft, sealing off the noise and hormones from the rest of the house. Instead, we've got builder's grime in the salt cellar.

"You can't be too busy to drive ten miles," says my mother. "It's not like it's the other end of the country."

It's not.

"You didn't even send her a Get Well card."

I didn't.

Selfish cow, me.

*SHE'S DOING FINE.*

Or so my mother tells me. But she's always looked for the silver lining where Vicky's concerned. "You should be pleased for her."

I search and search for a part of me that can be pleased for my sister. It should be in me somewhere, even if it's not where I want it, like dust in the salt cellar. She's living her own life: I must be pleased.

"At least it's put an end to all that waiting. All that fighting. She's happy now."

I believe in empowerment. I believe in a woman's right to choose. Lots of us are opting for cosmetic surgery these days. Lots of us are dissatisfied with our bodies. Who wouldn't fix herself if she got the chance?

"I hate to say this," says my mother, "but you've always been jealous."

*HELLUVA THING TO come to terms with.*

Even if it's what you've always wanted? "You know what Vicky told me last week? She said, 'I used to feel trapped in the wrong body. Now I feel complete.'"

All her life, my sister needed to be less in order to be more. She was like that exercise in English class: précis. They gave us a passage and we had to chop bits out without losing the meaning. Cutting through the crap. I used to enjoy it.

Weren't we all like that at school, to a degree? Didn't we compete as much for the pounds lost as for the marks gained when the homework was returned? It's even worse these days, with the size zero supermodels and such pressure on children to succeed.

So my sister was like the rest of us. Just that bit more dramatic in her desire to be less. Just that bit more determined.

"You're always saying a woman has the right to do things her own way," says my mother. "You should be proud of her."

And I am. Surely I am.

*SHE'S HAPPY ENOUGH.*

Or so my mother keeps insisting, banging on about it like she's hammering a wonky nail into a particularly stubborn wall. Persuading me? Persuading herself?

"All that stuff your dad and I pushed on her when she was little. Thinking she enjoyed it. Ballet lessons. Tap. That bike with the basket on the front we got her for Christmas. When all she wanted was to sit in a wheelchair and let her legs wither away. Remember when she fell off the shed roof and broke her leg?"

Jumped. I said so then and got slapped for it. They said I begrudged her the box of chocolates for being brave at the hospital. Jumped, not fell.

"Now she tells me breaking her leg was the high point of her childhood." My mother's voice quavers. "Poor little mite. She must have felt so lonely. So misunderstood."

"You just treated her normal." My voice comes out unnaturally loud. Better calm down.

*WHAT WAS IT again?*

She told us, didn't she? Warned us. In her own way. Gave us twenty years to get used to the idea. Or block it out of our minds.

Her twenty-first birthday. Didn't want a party. Didn't want a fuss. Just her and me and Mum and Dad and an ordinary lunch at home for her coming-of-age. Coming out. Sharing her ambitions for the future. Ambitions of never having to walk or dance or ride a bike again.

"Why?" I'd asked her. Back then, when the mere idea of it killed our appetite for lunch. Back then, when we thought *the idea* was all we needed to get our heads round. A crazy dream that could never be realised. No doctor would perform the operation, no matter how much she claimed to want it.

Mum sat at the kitchen table, tearing crumbs off a paper napkin. "You've got lovely legs, Vicky. How could you hate them?"

"They're a lot better than mine." Thick ankles were my own worst feature. "Why don't we do a swap?"

"Why don't you take me seriously?" said my sister.

"I'm trying to. I just don't understand. How can you imagine losing your legs is going to make you happy? Is it something sexual?"

Dad was warming up the bolognese sauce on the hob. Tears ran down his nose and into the pan. I'd never seen him cry before.

I'll never forget the look my sister gave me. It was as if I were offering her a gift of used tampons. As if I'd just shat on her dinner plate. As if *I* were the one who was going against the groove.


CANCER. THAT'S THE line we're taking for now.

"What am I going to tell people?" my mother asked, when she found out it was really going to happen.

"I don't know," said my sister. "Tell them it's none of

their business."

"I'll have to tell them something. I'll say it was cancer."

No, I've never heard of cancer of the legs, either, but that's not to say it doesn't exist. Or some form of cancer that means you have to have your legs chopped off above the knee and the flaps of skin sewn together across the stumps and spend the rest of your life in a wheelchair.

When my mother told me, I said, "Cancer of the brain, more like. It's a psychiatrist she needs, not a surgeon."

"She's seen a psychiatrist," said Mum. "Told her there's nothing he can do for her. Anyway, he can hardly call a halt to the operation. Not now it's got to this stage."

That psychiatrist needs his head looked at, too.

*WHAT SHE MUST have gone through.*

Sat up all night with her legs in a bath of dry ice. Sat screaming along with the night-owl radio phone-in while the blisters and blackness spread from her toes to her thighs. Knocking back the vodka while her legs turned to stone and she couldn't have run away even if she'd wanted to. Passing in and out of consciousness. In and out of sanity. "Takes a certain kind of courage, that," says Mum. "Must have been agony. And all on her own, poor love."

At least she didn't pressgang mum into sitting there with her. Holding her hand and whispering words of encouragement while she sacrificed her perfectly functional legs.

After that night the surgeon had no choice. Once the frostbite had taken over, her legs were as good as lost anyway. It was either chop them off or watch them turn to gangrene. She must have felt some kind of triumph as she hauled herself out of the bath and reached for the phone.

No longer having more body than she believed in. No more struggling to be taken seriously as an amputee-in-waiting. No more having to strap her leg up and hop around like someone playing Long John Silver in a pantomime. It made us laugh when she was little.

*PUTS ALL OUR grumbles in perspective.*

*You could say that.* Or you could ask why my mother's scared to go to bed for the nightmares and my dad's on antidepressants. Ask why I haven't been able to bring myself to tell my kids, even if they are self-absorbed teenagers who wouldn't give a monkey's. Ask why I feel I've lost my sister, not just her legs.

*PASS ON MY regards when you see her next.*

If, when, whatever, maybe.

Selfish cow, me.

# Stepping into Dan's Shoes

THEY CALLED ME in for interview on the day Dan was deported. It was rotten timing but, as Kate said, he'd left a vacancy and it was her job to fill it.

They ribbed me about my shiny brogues and funeral suit borrowed from my brother. Ours wasn't the kind of work where you'd turn up in collar and tie at nine. But we were all relieved to have something to laugh about that day, even Kate. Took our minds off what they'd done to Dan.

Dan wasn't his real name, of course. His real name was a spew of letters glimpsed now and then on the manila envelopes that housed his pay slip or other dispatches from HQ. Dan didn't ask us to twist our tongues round the mismatched syllables. He'd been Dan so long I don't think even *he* remembered how to pronounce the name his mother gave him.

I was the only one outside Kate's office, waiting. They hadn't bothered to open up the post to applicants from outside. As Kate said, that job had always had my name on it and the entire team was rooting for me. It's just that no-one expected me to step into Dan's shoes so soon.

Dan was as practical and unassuming as his footwear: worn-out trainers in the cabin, thick-soled boots to stomp across the moors. A pair of steel-capped workboots or wellies for the heavy jobs, such as chopping down rhododendrons or replacing a gate. He'd have raised an eyebrow at my polished shoes with their tracks of gimlet holes running through the leather.

Walking into Kate's office, my fancy shoes pinched my toes. My collar bit into my neck like a noose. Sweating in my brother's woollen suit, I relished my discomfort, as if, in some magical way, I could share Dan's load.

I hadn't been nervous about the interview until, seated across the desk from Kate, and Tony from HQ, my heart began to pound. I felt overdressed and alien in my city clothes, I wished, like them, I'd worn my everyday work gear of cargo pants and polo shirt with the logo of the reserve across the chest. When Tony launched into his first question, I could hardly hear for the buzzing in my ears.

I reminded myself I had nothing to worry about: if I phrased my answers as Dan would have done, I couldn't go far wrong. For six years I'd been his deputy, six years immersed in his wisdom on everything from the nesting patterns of lapwings to the myriad species of moss. I aped his methods and strategies on everything from constructing a stile to brewing a mid-morning cuppa. I might not have been sure of my own skills, but I'd always been sure of Dan.

Kate nodded in encouragement as I staggered over my

replies. She'd told me the interview was a mere formality, but what if Tony didn't see it that way?

*What would you do, and what would you not do, if you got a report of a bunch of kids camping in the reserve, pumping out music into the night?* Don't ask me about that, Tony. Today of all days, please don't ask me that.

What Dan had done was to tramp over there to talk to them, to tell them it wasn't allowed. Most people, confronted by his calm authority, would have packed up and gone home. But this lot were determined to party, whatever the rules might say.

When I arrived as back up, I thought it was all over and done. From the verge, where I pulled up behind a police car, there wasn't a sound except the hooting of owl. I didn't need the moon's light to guide my steps to the lakeside; I knew that track like I knew the path to my own front door.

The kids were loading their gear into wheelbarrows, disappointed but resigned. But there's always someone who won't take a telling, someone with a grievance they won't let go. And the police, well, they've got to act like they're impartial, even though they'd rather take our side.

A guy with waist-length dreadlocks was shouting, pointing from a giant speaker back to Dan. "It's malicious damage. Any fool knows not to tamper with the connections."

Under an awning, a network of wires meandered between a generator, mixer and amplifier. I could see the temptation. Grinning, I turned to Dan, "You didn't, did you?"

"Five hundred quid's equipment ruined," said

Dreadlocks.

"Should've left it safe at home then," said one of the cops.

"It's criminal damage. You've gotta arrest him. I know my rights."

"More bloody paperwork," said the other cop. He could hardly get his words out for laughing as he asked Dan to accompany him to the station.

I was laughing too, thinking how it would make for some jammy overtime, but Dan looked shit scared. I thought he was shamming it to appease Dreadlocks when I told the cops he liked two sugars in his tea.

WE ALL WENT down the pub after my interview, after Tony told me I'd got Dan's job. We went through the motions, but it was more of a wake than a celebration, given what had happened to Dan. Nobody blamed me; even had I known he'd overstayed his visa, I couldn't have prevented the cops from taking him in. Although they'd never meant to charge him, they'd had their forms to fill and, when they found he wasn't legal, they couldn't let him go.

For months we lived in limbo: Dan at the detention centre; me up here covering his job. Every day I'd find a new way to miss him: another pair of eyes to distinguish the heath and common spotted orchids; another pair of hands to hammer in a stake. But I consoled myself the lawyers were fighting his corner. He'd given so much to this country, surely he'd be coming back?

Until officialdom returned its verdict, they couldn't advertise his post. But when Kate requested I submit an application, it meant Dan had a deportation date.

My workmates lined up the pints on the table and I poured them down my neck. Although nothing could blot out the thought of Dan being frogmarched onto that plane. But tomorrow, swapping these brogues for walking boots, I'll remember him, and every day after until I retire.

# Telling the Parents

T HE OTHER NIGHT I sat my parents down and told them. I reckoned they were ready; I reckoned I had the whole thing sussed.

Mum's skin turned blotchy round the throat and her eyes welled with tears. "What did we do wrong, Adam?" You know how it is with mums, first to take the rap for anything.

I pushed the kitchen roll across the table. I'd known this would be tricky and I'd come prepared.

Dad raised his mug and put it down again. Like he couldn't trust his hand to stay steady enough to transport it to his lips. "I always felt there were summat not right," he said. "That red hair of yours for instance."

Despite the tension in the kitchen, I laughed, running my palm across the stubble at the back of my head. I'd shaved it off in my teens in sympathy for Mum when she got cancer, then realised I preferred it that way.

Mum's gaze scanned the room as if she were hoping the

kettle or the toaster might bring some sense to the situation. You could still smell the barbecue sauce she'd used to enliven the chops for our evening meal. "Is this about you moving in with Jason?" she said.

Dad cradled the handle of his mug, as if still hesitating to lift it. "He put you up to it?"

What? I thought they liked Jason. Every time he came round ours Dad took him down the allotment to check on the broad beans while Mum rustled up toad in the hole and gooseberry crumble because she said he never ate enough in that bedsit. I cast my mind back to the briefing with the social worker and tried to keep calm by fixing on how weird this must seem from their perspective. "Course not."

Dad glared at his mug: *Best Dad in the world* embossed in snot-green on a muddy-brown background. It had been true when he'd unwrapped it the Christmas I was eleven and it was still true now I was twice that age. I felt such a prick.

Of course Jason hadn't put me up to it, but he'd egged me on. "Look at it this way, Adam," he'd said. "They idolise you. There's going to be one gaping hole in their lives when you leave home. This would give them the chance to go back and pick up on what they had before you came along."

Mum tore off another piece of kitchen roll and dabbed at her cheeks. She was a good-looking woman, even pushing fifty, even with her features pulled out of shape by grief. Had I been a girl I'd have minded more, I think, not sharing her genes. But I might have been unlucky and inherited Dad's bulbous nose instead, and what then? Fascinating the genetic lottery, isn't it? Mum used to think I got my ginger hair from her uncle Cyril.

"It doesn't make sense," said Dad. "How can we not be your real parents?"

"Have we not loved you right, Adam?" said Mum. "Is that what you mean?"

I was almost crying too that Mum should think I'd question their love. Explaining it to Jason had been so straightforward. "No, you've been wonderful parents, a zillion times better than my real ones ever were."

"Who are these real parents then," said Mum, "because I'd really like to meet them. Find out how they managed it since they never spent a minute with you from the day you were born."

Dad made a mock attempt to leave the table. "Maybe I'd better fetch a dictionary because I reckon *real* has changed its meaning since I last looked."

"Thirty-six hours of labour, was that real? Leaning over your cot to check you were still breathing, was that real? Your first smile, your first steps, your first word?" I'd never seen Mum so fierce: she'd gone from Cry-baby to Joan of Arc marshalling her troops.

"False memories," I said. "Implanted."

A look passed between them, the like of which I hadn't seen since I left school. Dad's voice was gentle: "You know we've agreed to disagree about drugs, but you need to tell us if you've taken anything you're not sure about."

Defeated, I drew the leaflet from the back pocket of my jeans and laid it out on the table, not bothering to smooth out the creases. *Telling the Parents* it said along the top, but these weren't any old parents, they were mine. It wasn't right for them to have to discover something so important from a leaflet. But it sure wasn't working coming from me.

I got up and stood at the sink, while they learnt how they'd volunteered for an adoption scheme for severely abused infants. I scraped at the charred frying pan with a spatula while my parents sighed over the poor outcome data for such children in the past. I gazed out at the patch of grass where Dad had taught me to kick a ball and Mum had taught me to catch it, while they read about the radical research programme they'd taken part in more than twenty years before.

"So they thought that if we believed you were our own son right from the start, we'd get on with it better," said Dad. "No sending you back when things got tough."

"He wasn't so terribly difficult," said Mum.

Dad raised an eyebrow. "Which bit? I seem to remember a very rough patch around three and a half."

"That would be when the real memories took over from the implants," I said. "I guess I was one angry and confused little boy with the life I'd had before."

"We got through it though, didn't we?" said Mum. "All those memories of you laughing and playing must've given us the confidence to make it work."

Dad flicked through the leaflet. "All those people throwing off their previous lives and having some experimenter mess with their memories. Getting a whole new identity and not even knowing it. All that disruption to adopt a child."

Mum morphed back into Joan of Arc mode: "I'd give my last breath for him. It's no great hardship to sacrifice my memories."

Dad raised his mug, slurped his tea and grinned, although the drink must have been cold by then. "Aye, it's been worth it, whatever it was we gave up. He's turned out fine. Couldn't wish for better."

"Apart from the red hair." I edged towards them, spreading my arms, ready for the happy-ever-after hug. Fuck, how I loved these two. My mind was leaping ahead, looking forward to telling Jason. I was proud of them, proud of myself. I hadn't ballsed up after all.

Mum cut through all that: "I still don't understand …"

I gave her a goofy smile; I wasn't so hot on the science but now the three of us had the basics we could piece it together between us. We must've seen tons of movies where they plant artificial memories in the hero's brain.

Her voice was all aquiver: "Why did you have to tell us?"

"So you can get your lives back. Now I don't need you anymore you can go back to what you had before. You might have friends you'd like to see again. Brothers and sisters …"

I could have gone on, but Mum's face had taken on an odd purplish tinge as if she might be about to choke, and Dad was handling his mug in a most peculiar way, as if considering bowling it at my head. "Life?" said Mum. "This is my life. You are my life. When you leave to live with Jason being your mother will still be what defines me. How could you be so stupid as to think I'd want anything else?"

They said a few more things after that but it wouldn't be fair to repeat them. I haven't even told Jason half of what came out of their mouths. But that was a few days ago and we're calmer now, and wiser.

I've got an appointment with the social worker tomorrow. I'm hoping she can put me in contact with the scientists who organised the implants. It shouldn't be too hard for them to take away the memory of what I told my parents the other night. Failing that, I reckon I'll have to rewrite the dictionary. Create another definition of real.

# Reflecting Queenie

QUEENIE WOULD NOT have wanted me there, but she could hardly expect Dad to attend her trial alone. So I sat beside him in the public gallery as he held himself as still as his Parkinson's would permit, while the prosecution ripped her personality apart. It was a straightforward case of jealousy, they said, and only Queenie seemed surprised when the jury returned a guilty verdict.

Up until that point, she'd kept herself aloof, not quite focused on anyone, or anything. Now she raised her head towards the gallery and found me. Her fear and confusion beat against my skin, fighting to penetrate my mind. I stayed firm and let it all bounce back to her, as if I were a bat, and she the ball.

I WAS NOT quite three when my mother decided I had special powers. As she told me later, it was the only explanation for the way I seemed to anticipate her every move. She'd be thinking about making an apple pie and before she'd opened her mouth I'd be wrestling the baking bowl out of the cupboard. She'd be wondering how her Gran was getting on and, before she knew it, I'd be pushing a pad of Basildon Bond into her hand.

"How did you know?" she'd ask again and again and, since I hadn't the words to tell her, she concluded I was telepathic.

I WAS FOUR when my baby brother fractured our blissful duet. It didn't matter then if she was thinking about baking or writing a letter, his slightest whimper drew her to him. "What is it?" she crooned. "Are you hungry? Do you want your nappy changing?"

Her sing-song voice embarrassed me. She sounded wrong in the head. As if she were unable to distinguish between a scream of hunger and a summons to clean him up.

Weeks passed before I realised she genuinely couldn't tell the difference. That her ears received each cry in my brother's repertoire in an identical way. I realised that if I didn't call out "He's hungry" or "He's lonely" the moment the baby started to grizzle, we'd never have baked any pies or written any letters again.

My mother would look at me in wonder as the baby latched on to her nipple or gurgled in her arms. "How did you know?"

WITHOUT A SPELL at nursery to acclimatise me to other children, school entered my life with a bang. If I'd thought my baby brother was noisy, it was nothing compared to the playground racket. At first I kept to the edge, intimidated by the terrible uniformity of the other children. I leant against the fence and watched, while I worked out how to survive the confusion, how to remember which blonde-haired blue-eyed little girl was Judith and which was Mandy. Which of my classmates liked Smarties and which preferred Fruit Pastilles. Who walked to school and who travelled by bus.

When the first of the children jabbed me on the chest, I was prepared. "What's my name?" she demanded.

I told her.

She giggled. "How did you know?"

Another sauntered up. "When's my birthday?"

Again, I told her.

"How did you know?"

After that, I was never alone in the playground. The other children could always find a use for my attentiveness. I'd skip along with a gaggle of girls hanging onto my arms. In the early years I suppose it made them feel secure that someone could tell them who they were. Later, their requirements became more sophisticated. *Will I get to star in the Nativity play? Does Pamela really like me or is she pretending so she can play on my bike?* I answered as best I could. I took their questions inside me and reported what I felt. *You're not right for Mary but you'll make a great shepherd. Yes, Pamela likes you but she likes your new bike even more.*

Although in demand, I never took my position for granted. There was always the chance that one day I'd say something inconvenient and be pushed back against the fence. When the teacher wrote on my report, *Myra is a popular girl,* I knew it was provisional. I knew deep down I was no different from the kids who were left to themselves because, when people looked at them, they didn't like what they saw. So I made sure that when my classmates looked at me all they could see was themselves.

When my report described me as good at art, I knew I'd convinced even the grownups there was no more to me than their own reflection. True, my sketches of my friends were well observed. But when I drew myself I could only manage a black outline, an empty space within.

AT BREAKFAST ONE morning, not long after I'd started at high school, my mother left the kitchen abruptly, leaving me to spread marmalade on my brother's toast.

"Sorry about that," she said, when she returned, red-eyed, ten minutes later, to find me sweeping crumbs from the cloth. "Don't know what came over me."

She might not have meant it as a question, but it came across as one to me. The answer seemed to flutter in the lower part of my abdomen. A part of me I'd not paid much attention to before. "You're pregnant."

She shook her head. "You and your premonitions!" And turned away to help my brother find his rugby boots.

We had liver and onions for tea that night. My brother chased his around his plate until my mother lost patience and sent him off to play. She ran the water into the washing-up bowl and passed me the tea towel. I could tell she was on edge; she kept picking up plates I'd already dried and putting them back in the sink. Eventually she came out with it: "How did you know?"

That fluttering again in my abdomen, somewhere below my stomach. In my bowels? In my bladder? It was in the bit of me that the Tampax lady had pointed to on her chart. I blushed.

AS SHE SWELLED, my mother developed a craving for liquorice. Then she'd go mad for cherry pies. Another time it had to be roast potatoes. Even at two in the morning.

My dad worked double shifts to avoid her. My brother could be bribed with a Mars bar to saunter down to the corner shop, but mostly it fell to me to safeguard her sanity. I didn't find it hard. She only had to look at me with a question in her eyes and my stomach would know.

A COUPLE OF months before her due date, my mother was admitted to hospital. Nobody bothered to tell a twelve-year-old what was wrong. When my sister was born she came home again, pretending to be well. When visitors came she held the baby on her lap and smiled, but when they'd gone she'd say, "What's wrong with me? Am I just too old?"

I let my hair hang over my face so she couldn't read my expression. So I wouldn't feel the ache in my budding breast that didn't belong to me.

WHEN QUEENIE CRIED I pulled my hair over my ears but it was never enough to block out the sound. Awaking at night with a pounding heart, I'd lie, sweating, until my mother had put her right. Sometimes, I couldn't bear to wait. My mother would stumble, bleary-eyed, into the baby's room to find me with a blanket around my shoulders, cuddling and cooing.

At first I was afraid to take care of such a tiny thing. Her mewling seemed full of questions; the world contained so much she didn't understand. *What's this hollow feeling in my middle? What's this coldness on my edge? How can I make it go away? What will happen if I can't?*

How do you answer a baby? I did what I had always done, took her pain inside me, felt her hunger in my stomach, her dampness on my buttocks. And because I knew that milk abolishes hunger, and a clean nappy refreshes a baby's skin, her crying no longer scared me. I could answer her with kisses, with the strength of my arms, with the lilt of my voice.

My family joked that Queenie had two mothers. As the cancer gorged on my mother's breast, I became the one my sister preferred. I didn't mind those mornings I couldn't rise in time for school. Scrabbling with simultaneous equations lacked the appeal of resolving my baby sister's existential dilemmas. Why would I want to learn about the whims of the kings and queens of England, when I could play lady-in-waiting to that diminutive royal at home? I made her needs mine, her dreams my own. As she developed through my ministrations, a dash of colour crept into the black outline that defined me.

QUEENIE HAD JUST lost her front teeth, and I'd left school to sweep up at the hairdresser's, when the hospital took my mother for the last time. As I dressed my little sister for the funeral, I wondered where my childhood had gone. It might have been all right if I'd only had Queenie asking, *But where is heaven?* It was the way my brother looked at me. And my dad. Wanting to know why. I couldn't handle four people's grief.

I moved into a squat with some people I met at the bus stop. We covered the walls with murals and made music into the night. Whenever I thought about my family, I'd roll another joint. Nobody asked me to tell them who they were or why they were hurting. Or if they did, I was too stoned to notice.

One day a child with tangled hair and mismatched shoes knocked on the door. I reached for the Rizzlas but Queenie's sadness stopped my hand.

MY BROTHER JOINED the merchant navy. Between raising my sister and keeping house for my father, I trained as a beautician. If I ever felt resentment, I didn't let it show.

That's not to say I wasn't tempted to leave again. Once, a man who smoked Gauloises offered to take me to France where the light was good for painting. Although he may have meant it as a joke. It didn't matter. My sister was beautiful and clever, but she still had lots of questions only I could answer.

When she started dating, I helped her get ready. Choose her outfit. Do her makeup. Made myself available for the debrief. *Did I talk too much? Too little?* So many uncertainties. No right answers. I painted her nails and I listened. Not only to what she said, but what she didn't say. I listened with my whole body. Took it into myself and reflected it back to her. Showed her herself, but with all the blemishes and insecurities filtered out.

QUEENIE WAS NINETEEN when we bumped into an old acquaintance. He'd been married to one of my classmates who had died in a car crash, leaving him with a six-year-old daughter, Blanche. It was Queenie he invited out to dinner. She didn't come home that night to sit with me in the kitchen analysing how the date had gone. Three months later she told me they were engaged. "I know he's the one." No hint of a question. The hollowness in my abdomen was my own.

She dragged me round the shops for a bridesmaid's dress for Blanche.

"Think what you're taking on," I cautioned.

"I love her," she said. "I love them both."

FOR THE FIRST few years, everything seemed fine in my sister's ready-made family. Dad and I didn't see her much but, when we did, we agreed she was happy. Happier than she'd ever been.

As Blanche grew into adolescence, Queenie, not yet thirty, wanted a baby of her own. But her husband disagreed.

She started hanging around the salon again. Popping round home to check on Dad. She poured out tales of altercations with the belligerent teenager, or the girl's increasingly indifferent father.

Queenie lay on the couch as I brushed warm wax over her legs. "Tell me honestly, Myra. Am I good-looking?"

I waited till I'd yanked off the strip of wax and hair. I hated to hurt her. "Of course you are. You're the best-looking woman I know."

"Are you sure? Sometimes I look in the mirror and wonder what he ever saw in me."

DAD TURNED SEVENTY. In the years since my mother died, he'd never gone in for celebrations, but we persuaded him into a small family party. I hadn't seen Blanche for some time and, when she walked into the restaurant all dolled up, I gasped.

"She's beautiful, isn't she?" said Queenie.

"Gorgeous."

Queenie spoke casually, as if it were a joke. "Who do you think is the better-looking, Blanche or me?"

The question weighed on me like her infant cries. "Oh, Queenie."

"Tell me. I won't be offended."

"You're both lovely."

"But who's the prettiest?"

My sister would always be beautiful to me. Yet her stepdaughter had a freshness and sparkle that Queenie, more than twice her age, could not hope to match. Blanche would turn heads whatever I said. I hugged her. "You are, of course."

SOMETHING CHANGED FOR me that day. I began to resent cancelling clients when my sister called at the salon. I no longer cared if her stepdaughter had borrowed a favourite blouse. How her husband returned from work later and later. But I held my feelings within me, for they had nowhere else to go.

For her fifteenth birthday, I offered Blanche a makeover.

Queenie brought her to the salon, looking on as I massaged unguents into her cheeks and buffed up her nails. Afterwards, the girl went off to parade before her friends at the burger bar.

"So what do you think?" said Queenie.

"About what?"

"Who's the most beautiful, Blanche or me?"

I fiddled with a bottle of nail varnish, screwing and unscrewing the cap. "She seems happy with her makeover."

"You're evading the question, Myra."

The rage bubbled inside me, hers melding with mine like depilatory wax. "Grow up, Queenie!"

"I have to know."

I'd given her my teenage years. My work. She gazed into my eyes but still she couldn't see me. "It's Blanche."

The slap made my eyes water.


APART FROM THOSE few weeks in the squat, I never abandoned Queenie. But when she chose to keep away, I wasn't disappointed. My body began to feel my own.

Blanche brought news from home to the salon. How the arguments continued. How Queenie was letting herself go. But the girl was too sweet-natured to fuel the feud between us. If only she'd been less discreet. If only I'd listened better.

Queenie wanted to send the girl to boarding school. I knew Blanche wasn't keen. So when she mentioned the stomach pains I commiserated with her sense of banishment. It never occurred to me to investigate further. Not even when she was rushed to A & E.

I badgered the police to take my statement. "Nobody

knows her like I do."

"So? The poisoning began in October. You last saw your sister in September. This is nothing to do with you."

I drove Dad to the remand centre. When he shuffled back to the car, his Parkinsonian mask reflected nothing of Queenie's state of mind.

"You know, Myra," he said, as we hit the motorway, "I never thought beauty therapy was right for you."

I tightened my grip on the steering wheel. "Oh?"

"Pandering to other people's vanity. Must be rather wearing."

"I'm used to it."

"Didn't you want more for yourself?"

His gaze scorched my cheeks. "What a question!"

Dad stayed quiet so long, I thought he'd nodded off. "You used to love drawing."

"All kids love drawing."

He closed his eyes. It had been a stressful day for a man who wasn't in perfect health.

I drove home, mesmerised by an old man's snoring and the roar of rubber on the road. In the tail lights of the cars ahead I fancied I glimpsed my father's dream. A dream in which a daddy held the mirror while his daughter sketched a detailed image of herself.

# Spinning Signposts

# Heir to the Throne

WHEN THE YOUNG queen died in childbirth, the entire dominion trembled under a cloud of gloom. By night, the king wept alone in his chamber; by day, he stomped around the palace enraged. He seethed at the slightest irregularities – too much salt in the soup, or too little, never mind that he lacked the appetite to eat it – and sentenced the perpetrators to twenty lashes and a night in the dungeon to contemplate their misdeeds. The plaintive lament of a new-born riled him more than anything, so no-one dared remind him of his responsibilities towards his progeny. To grace his offspring with an audience. To bestow a name upon his heir.

Ten years passed and his grief paled sufficiently for him to accept some duties beyond his own well-being. To safeguard the dynasty, he must find a replacement wife. But none of the neighbouring monarchs were willing to trust him with their daughters. He'd lost one queen; who was to say he wouldn't lose another?

He didn't hear the mumblings below stairs that he had an heir already. Although brave in battle, none of his knights had the courage to raise the matter with him personally. Instead, they sent his former wet nurse to petition him. Should the king, in a fit of fury, put her to the sword, she was too old and decrepit to be missed.

When the king saw her shuffle into his chamber, he laughed. "You, old crone? I thought you dead already."

The nurse felt no threat from a man she'd fed for five long years from her own body (an arrangement that had ended only when she'd had the wit to anoint her nipples with a concoction of bitter herbs). With arthritic fingers, she beckoned the king remove his crown. Despite the scratch of his beard against her papery skin, he seemed to her a boy again, and more so when hot tears trickled between her breasts.

"I have committed a grave misdemeanour," he sobbed, when he finally raised his head from her bosom. "I had a child, the fruit of my beloved's womb, and I let him perish. Now I'm doomed to die without an heir."

"Take heart," soothed the nurse. "Your offspring might yet be living."

"Oh, if it were true! I'd devote my entire life to his happiness …" The king paused, puzzled by his nurse's countenance. "Or hers?"

"Theirs."

"Theirs?" At once, the king recalled that multiple births were not uncommon in his wife's family. In fact, she'd been a twin herself.

The nurse explained the queen had birthed a handsome golden-haired son. And a cranky redhead daughter. The boy had been fostered with the queen's own parents, raised as a prince, until the day his father would reclaim him. But the ill-tempered girl had been left in a basket on the moors. The word was a simple shepherd had taken her in.

The king was appalled that his children should be so neglected. "Bring them to me this instant!" he thundered.

"Both of them?" said the nurse. "The golden-haired boy *and* the cranky redhead?"

"Of course," said the king, "if they both be mine."

The nurse explained that, while the prince had spent his entire life preparing for this moment, the girl was unaware of her royal blood. She would need a little time to become acquainted with courtly etiquette.

"Then take me to them," the king insisted. "I'll not disturb them with pomp and pageantry, but go in disguise and see with my own eyes that my babes still live."

And so it was arranged that the king, dressed as a simple yeoman, would ride out to where his son trotted through the woods each morning on a dappled pony. Dressed as a yokel, and on foot, he would observe his daughter tending her sheep on the moors. To his delight, it proved as easy to love the girl, despite her rags and the frown etched on her forehead, as to love the boy, with his neat clothes and regal bearing. He decreed that a room be prepared at the palace for each.

On the appointed day, with tables groaning under a feast of cakes and jellies, the king's children were presented to him for the first time. The boy, immaculate in his velvet suit, knelt and kissed his hand, addressing him as *Your Majesty*. When the girl held back, all assumed she was overwhelmed by the opulence of her surroundings. But when, with a mixture of prompts and prods, she was urged forward, and the king smiled his encouragement despite the unpleasant smell, she refused to kneel before the throne. Instead, she spat at him and, in an accent rough and shrill, declaimed him as her father. "For what father," she cried, "would abandon a child to the elements, to be pecked at by crows and shat upon by foxes?"

The king laughed heartily to conceal his consternation, and his courtiers joined in, and they all took their places at the table. But the girl would not eat, curdling the celebration for everyone, until she was dragged off to the scullery to learn to control her temper.

Fortunately, the king's disappointment in his daughter's character could not corrode his joy in his son's. The boy was cheerful, polite and obedient. The king felt such pleasure in his company that he dismissed the boy's tutor and resolved to educate him himself. Each morning, before breakfast, they would go riding, and then study history, science and mathematics until lunch. The afternoons were devoted to literature and languages, with music and art occupying the early evening hours until dinner. Occasionally, the king would leave the boy with his books to attend to affairs of state but, in general, he delegated the governance to his ministers. He would return to the business of running a country as soon as his son was of an age to play a part.

As for the prince, he knew he must be happy. Every day, every hour of the twelve years he'd lived with his grandparents had been in anticipation of this life. He'd been told that, if he was good, his father would come for him, and he should be continually alert for the happenchance of the king's arrival. He could never climb a tree in case the king's first sight of him would be with dirty hands and torn breeches. He could never leave the estate lest the king's patience be tried awaiting his return. He could never shirk his lessons, linger in bed or sit and daydream by the fire, in case the king considered him idle and undisciplined, unfit to be his heir. Finally ensconced within the palace, the boy's happiness was guaranteed. Yet, alone in the dead of night, he couldn't help thinking that happiness wasn't quite what he'd expected it to be.

WHEN THE NEWS came that his old nurse was ailing, the king was saddened, but resigned. As she too seemed to be. "Now I've seen you reunited with your children, I can die in peace." He ensured she had every comfort and returned his attention to his son. But when the boy also took to his bed with agonising stomach pains, he summoned medical men from across the land. At the same time, he sent for his daughter. Although of royal blood, she was a wild creature; could jealousy have driven her to poison her brother's food? Her place in the scullery afforded ample opportunity.

The king was somewhat relieved when word came back that the girl had fled. With a successor successfully installed in the palace, she was surplus to requirements. He'd offered her a better life; he wasn't to blame that she'd refused it.

Meanwhile, the doctors promised that, once the poison had passed through his system, the boy would recover. The king wondered if perhaps the nurse would too.

Alas, the prince became progressively weaker. The king was distraught. He'd lost his son once through self-absorption; he couldn't bear to lose him again. Perhaps, despite her own poor health, his old nurse could advise him.

In the sickroom, the smell of decay made him gag and swallow his words, so the wrinkled old crone spoke first. "I thought I was ready to die," she said. "But I can't let go until I see you embracing your twins."

How could he confess that his daughter had vanished and his son was too sick to leave his room? But she'd given him an idea. If granting her wish could set an old woman free of life's burden, could something similar release a youngster from the clutches of death? He ran to his son's bedside and asked what he desired.

At first, the boy couldn't understand the question. Although he'd been fed the finest food and dressed in the most gorgeous garments, he couldn't remember ever being asked what he might *want*. The prospect was unnerving, but he couldn't say he didn't know. Not with the king watching him so eagerly, the way he did when he taught him the names of the planets or the Greek for *dissemblance,* obliging the boy to pretend he hadn't learnt such matters from his tutor years before. So he asked for a mango, not ready peeled and cubed and arranged in a cut-glass dish, but a whole ripe mango with juice flowing down his arm the moment he pierced its skin.

Without pausing to consider whether his son's request was suitably princely, the king brought him a mango. As the boy bit through the skin, the juice did indeed gush down his arm. To please his father, the prince grinned, although the stickiness on his arm and hands and cheeks and even on the tip of his nose was most unpleasant, inciting nostalgia for the grandmother who had insisted fruit should be eaten from a bowl with a spoon.

Noting the boy's apparent appreciation, the king asked if there were anything else he fancied (anticipating sending scouts to source guava, papaya and the like). His son, intoxicated by the *idea* of choice, if not the actuality, felt emboldened to ask if he might dig in the garden, another activity outlawed at his grandmother's. The king, taking this to indicate the prince was regaining his strength, ordered a pair of dungarees and a three-quarter size spade to be procured forthwith.

On plunging the spade into the earth, the boy was horrified to find potatoes scattered like pebbles among the worm-infused filth. But his father was beaming, so he smiled and tried to hide his disgust when the vegetables he'd unearthed, albeit thoroughly scrubbed and cooked in butter, were set down on the dining table later that day.

When he'd finished eating, the king asked once again if there was anything he wanted. The prince couldn't offend the king by requesting the return of his tutor, but perhaps he could see his sister. On their initial meeting, he'd been so alarmed by her wilfulness he was glad to see her go. But now the king's devotion overwhelmed him. Although his sister was rough and rude, he might learn from her example how to follow his own desires.

The king could not refuse him. Besides, his daughter's return would pacify his old nurse. So soldiers, knights and explorers sallied forth to find the girl and bring her back. It wasn't difficult; she was where the king had first seen her, high on the moors amongst her sheep.

Once cleansed of the countryside ordure, the girl was escorted to the boy's quarters. When, after a suitable interval, the king summoned the twins to the throne room, the boy arrived alone. His voice seemed weakened by his illness and he kept to the shadows as if afraid. Yet his plea was so audacious, the king almost choked on his pipe. "You want to reign together? Don't you know a boy can't marry his sister, even if they've been raised apart since birth?"

The prince laughed. Never having heard him laugh before, the king's heart leapt.

"We have no desire to marry," said the boy. "Only to have an equal stake in ruling the land."

"That's all very well," said the king. "But the people would revolt if a female took the top job. Even on a half-time basis."

"You don't know that for sure," said the prince. "Besides, if we never appeared together in public it would look as if there was only one of us."

"My subjects might be poor and downtrodden," said the king, "but they're not fools. They can tell the difference between a boy and a girl."

"Can they?" The prince removed his cap to reveal, not the boy's golden curls, but the girl's carrot-coloured mane.

The king recalled his childhood dread of assuming the mantle of monarch. Introduced to the woman who became his queen, it was her brother who had beguiled him. Although he'd learned to love her, it was more as a sister than a wife. He realised, over a decade since his coronation, how lonely it felt at the top. His queen might have been skilled at smiling, waving and wearing a crown, but she hadn't the slightest interest in affairs of state.

Could his children release him from a role conferred not by preference or ability but destiny? Could they overcome the constraints of tradition and rule as one? It seemed they could. As the girl outlined the proposed arrangement, and the boy nodded his assent, the king imagined swapping his robes for a peasant's linen and stepping out to explore the world, communing with whomever he pleased. The girl was brave and smart, the boy amenable; they might be only twelve but they had sufficient nous between them to make it work.

Indeed they did, after a fashion, but the king hadn't particularly shone at the job himself. But, unlike him, they were keen to improve, and grew better at governing as the years went by. As they developed in skill and confidence, there seemed less need for the pretence that the king had but the one heir. No-one complained when they appeared in public together; indeed, their subjects seemed grateful there were two brains to defend the dominion rather than one.

So they all lived happily ever after. Apart from the wet nurse, of course, who, after witnessing the king with an arm on each child's shoulder, died as she had foretold.

# A Dress for the Address

WHEN PATRICK HEADS off for work, and Becky realises I'm the one taking her to school this morning, she launches into a pirouette and plants kisses halfway up my arm. "Can we go by walk? Please, Mummy, pleeeze."

Why not? Anything to atone for not being here tomorrow to help her prepare for Jennifer's party. It gives us more time together if I leave the car in the garage, and the exercise does me good. But it's not only that. Unlike much of her generation, Becky generally prefers to travel on foot. Why hide away in the car when she can turn the street into her personal catwalk? She wants the whole world to appreciate the perfect pink dress she's modelling today.

I never thought I'd have such a *girlie* child. For all I try to interest her in Thomas the Tank Engine and Bob the Builder, Becky insists on pushing baby dolls around in a pram. In Mothercare, I might lead her to racks of denim, but I'm wasting my time, and she knows it. Even when the only dresses available are hand-me-downs from Vanessa's youngest, it's a battle to get my daughter through the door unless she's rigged out in pink. On a day like today, I don't even try to fight it.

Becky prances along the pavement with her hand in mine, absorbing the admiration of her public. Everyone we pass – the neighbours putting out the rubbish bins; the commuters scanning the horizon for the number 42; and especially the lollipop lady in her canary-yellow coveralls – gets co-opted into her fanclub.

Yet, by the time we reach the school gates, she's had her fix and wriggles free to wave to Jennifer, this season's best friend. When I bend to kiss her goodbye, every cell in her body is preparing to be off.

It could be the tears in my eyes that make her hesitate. "Don't worry, Mummy. It's only two sleeps till Thursday, and you'll be home again."

She skips off, a Lothario moving on to the next love affair. Such equanimity in one so young! Such fickleness! Such a contrast to last night, sobbing in Patrick's arms while I opened up PowerPoint on my laptop.

"Don't leave me, Mummy."

"Don't you want Mummy to collect her prize?" said Patrick.

Becky raised her head from the damp patch she'd created on his shirt. "Mummy's getting a prize?"

"Sure," said Patrick. "Bet you can't guess what for."

Becky considered it a moment. "I know. For being the prettiest Mummy in the conf'ence."

I laughed. "Hardly."

"Even better," said Patrick. "It's for being the top scientist this year."

"I want to give Mummy a prize, too." Becky jumped off Patrick's lap and scrabbled in her toybox for her coloured pens and sketchpad. "I'll draw you a lovely picture to take to the conf'ence."

"Okay," I said, "but it's bedtime in ten minutes."

It wasn't, of course. Becky's interpretation of the Carruthers Award ceremony required ten minutes careful attention for the laureate's crown alone. Then there was the regal blue gown, the pass-the-parcel trophy, the ear-to-ear smile. It was nearly nine by the time we got her upstairs, my mother's voice in my head: *You let that child run rings round you.*

BACK HOME, MOONING over Becky's artwork and wondering if I've time for another pot of Earl Grey, I'm as guilty of procrastination as my daughter. I only wish I could borrow Becky's talent in postponing bedtime to delay leaving for the station.

Filling the kettle, I kid myself I'm reluctant to leave my family, but it's nothing so worthy. When I step onto the podium tomorrow, I'll need to look and feel the part. Trouble is, I tell the teapot, no one can predict what outfit will work two hundred miles and twenty-four hours away. Packing for a trip reduces this esteemed professor of physics to one of those post-feminists who can't boil an egg or clean the toilet without reference to some celebrity-endorsed instruction video. Even my five-year-old is more confident about choosing what to wear than I am.

ON THE TRAIN to Blackpool, our family has a compartment to ourselves. Nana and Grampa have the window seats, beside the door that opens straight onto the platform, although neither of them have much use for the view: Nana with her nose in *The People's Friend* and Grampa intent on filling up the ashtray with the leftovers of his Woodbines. Along the bench from Grampa, under the luggage rack where he has stowed the battered suitcase containing me and Vanessa's best frocks, Mummy and Auntie Jean harmonise their knitting needles with the clickety-click of the train. On the opposite bench, going backwards along with Nana and the picnic basket with our salmon-paste sandwiches and mini chocolate Swiss-rolls, we children play with our dolls as I try to ignore the knot in my stomach.

Manoeuvring Vanessa's Sindy into a jaunty air hostess outfit, an arm comes off in my hand and falls to the floor. Even under the eyes of so many grownups, with the odds clearly against me, my first thought is of a cover-up, and I jettison the plastic limb under the seat with a kick of the heel. Not fast enough. Vanessa has already pushed out her bottom lip, Auntie Jean has put down her knitting and scooped her onto her lap, and Nana has lowered her magazine and shaken her head. Before Mummy can speak, I'm down on the floor to rescue the severed limb.

"Get up, get up this minute," says Mummy. "You'll get filthy dirty down there."

Nana snatches the arm and scrunches it into the Sindy's shoulder socket. Mummy spits on a hankie and rubs my knees until they burn. "Can't you play nicely for one minute?"

I glance at Grampa, hoping to meet his gaze but he continues sucking on his cigarette and flicking the ash into the chrome dish attached to the door.

"For heaven's sake," says Mummy, "try and keep yourself clean till after the contest."

I wriggle my bottom to the back of the bench, as far from the grimy floor as possible. I clutch my Tressy. If you press the button on her back, a lock of yellow hair sprouts from the top of her head, making it look as if her hair is growing. I don't press the button.

Vanessa cuddles up to Auntie Jean, as if she is trying to get inside her tummy. When Auntie Jean tickles her, Vanessa giggles. Mummy frowns and counts her stitches. I have heard her tell Daddy that Auntie Jean treats Vanessa like a baby.

Vanessa is the kind of girl mummies can't help cuddling. When she smiles, which is often, she has dimples, as if God couldn't resist dipping his pinky into her cheeks before they were set. Her golden hair is soft and bouncy and you only have to twist it around your finger for it to spring into ringlets as perfect as brandy-snaps. Vanessa never gets into trouble. She doesn't break the arms off other children's dolls and try to hide the evidence. She doesn't crawl on the floor getting filthy-dirty when she needs to keep nice-and-clean. Her mummy doesn't have to rub her knees until they burn.

I DRAG THE wheeled suitcase out from under the bed. So much more convenient than the luggage we had back then. And no need to pack a picnic these days: we'll buy an overpriced Hawaiian chicken wrap on the train and charge it to expenses. But why haven't I upgraded my feelings alongside my suitcase and sandwiches? The prospect of standing before an audience awakens my resentful inner child.

I go to my wardrobe, a cumbersome auction-room purchase from the pecuniary early years of our marriage. The door creaks as it opens; I'm hoping the perfect ensemble will jump out at me.

*Choose me,* calls the grey wool suit that has seen me get my way in many a faculty meeting. I shake my head. You're too formal, too sombre; I'd end up trying to persuade the audience to bump up the physics department's IT budget.

*Choose me,* pleads the Little Black Dress that, with or without the sequinned jacket, has served me well at the Vice-Chancellor's soirees. Not for a speech, however. I can't wear you unless I'm holding a Manhattan with a cherry on a cocktail stick.

*Choose me, then,* cries the calf-length navy pleated skirt that is sometimes partnered with a white shirt on graduation day. No, you'd be mistaken for a school uniform. Besides, you're for when the students are getting prizes, not me.

*Which one will you choose then?* chorus the contents of my wardrobe.

I'm teasing. I'm not as disorganised as I pretend. I

picked out my outfit in my mind four months ago, the day I got the email informing me I'd won the award.

I select two hangers: a slinky silk dress in an abstract pattern of five different shades of green, along with a cropped collarless jacket in a perfectly co-ordinated aquamarine. I pull my jumper over my head and kick off my jeans. The dress cool against my skin, I pull up the zip at the back. I shrug on the jacket and push back the wardrobe door to study the prize-winning outfit in the mirror.

It's not as I expected.

*Who's getting married?* says the shiny green dress.

*Where's the carnation for my buttonhole?* says the colour-coordinated jacket.

I step back from the mirror and look again. I turn sideways and stare at my reflection from over my shoulder. I narrow my eyes so the greens merge as in an impressionist painting. But it makes no difference. No way is this the sartorial statement of a serious scientist at the summit of her career. I rip off the jacket and tear myself out of the dress and stand, wretched, in my bra and knickers.

Taking a deep breath, I lurch back to the wardrobe and rummage through the hangers. There's stuff I haven't worn since before I had Becky, but none of it feels suitable. I peer into the depths once, twice, three times more, as if the strength of my wanting could make the right get-up magically appear. It's useless: I haven't a thing to wear.

This problem needs a whole research team to crack it. But I'm here on my own.

Patrick would have been happy to help, if I'd let him. "What are you going to wear for your talk?" he'd asked last night, after we'd finally got Becky to bed.

"Clothes, of course."

"What clothes?"

"Does it matter? People are interested in what I've got to say, not what I'm wearing. It's not a bloody beauty contest."

WITH A PINK cardboard disc tied with matching ribbon around our wrists, Vanessa and I wait in a line of little girls in party frocks with scratchy layered underskirts. When our number is called, we'll step onto the open-air stage where a man with a microphone will shake our hands and ask us our names. When we've curtsied to all the mummies and aunties and nanas and grampas, we'll get a silk rosebud as a reward.

Some of the younger ones don't know how to curtsy, which makes the audience laugh and the man with the microphone lean down and bend their legs into position, as if they were Blue Peter dolls made out of pipe-cleaners. Vanessa and I practise as we wait in the queue, holding out our skirts and stepping back with the right foot while bending the left knee, and looking up and smiling. Smiling. Even backstage, with no grownups watching, only me and another hundred hopeful Miss Rosebud 1965's, those indentations in Vanessa's cheeks insist this is fun. But I'm a year older than Vanessa and less easily fooled.

"SUE!" HARRY'S PHONE voice is extra buoyant, like he's

swimming with a rubber ring. "Everything okay?"

I glance at the clothes strewn around the room. "There's a bit of a problem."

"I haven't mixed up the train times again, have I?"

For one delicious moment, I realise he thinks I'm already at the station, storming up and down the platform, wondering where he is. "No, it's not till eleven-thirty. But I'm not going to make it."

"Oh?"

"I'm not packed yet." I smile at the incongruity of inviting him over to interrogate my wardrobe, but I couldn't subject any of my senior lecturers to that. "Becky threw a tantrum at the school gates. I couldn't leave her in that state." I'll apologise to my daughter when she's older. When she won't give a fig for what Harry Gormley thinks. "It's put me about an hour behind."

"Should we go for the next train then?"

"No point us both being late. You get the eleven-thirty and I'll follow as soon as I can."

Harry hesitates. He'll have banked on the train journey to bend my ear about departmental restructuring. "If you're sure."

"Absolutely. Someone should represent us at the inaugural address."

The call restores me to my *real* self. I've moved beyond being judged for my curtsying skills. If I can manage Harry, I can manage to select an outfit. After all, nothing could be as bad as my conference debut, delivering a paper in the student section on my final year project. I'd won a prize then, too, but that was no excuse for approaching the rostrum in a third-hand biker's jacket and ripped black jeans clanking with chains, and my hair in spikes, courtesy of two cans of hairspray.

Fashions change and precocious students mature into serious professors. No torn jeans in my wardrobe today. No pink party frocks either. There must be something suitable between those extremes.

What I need, I decide as I slide the hangers back and forth along the rail, is a grading system for the second-bests. It can't be much different to allocating the leftover places on a degree course when the A-level results come out.

Trouble is, some get huffy if they weren't selected first time. *Too formal, am I?* grumbles the grey wool suit. *Too sombre? So don't ask me to bail you out.*

I hesitate before the Little Black Dress. *Too frivolous? Can't imagine me without a cocktail in your hand? You'd better drown your sorrows, because I won't help you.*

*School uniform, indeed! Serve you right if you end up in detention.*

*What do we care if you make a fool of yourself? What do we care about the stupid Carruthers Award?*

THE TRAIN JOURNEY in reverse. The same people a few hours older: Grampa with his ashtray; Nana with her magazine; Auntie Jean with her knitting.

Mummy isn't knitting. She sits with her hands in her lap and her eyes closed and face crumpled like clothes in the ironing basket.

Vanessa plays alone, lining up the dolls on the bench: the Sindy and the Tressy and the Barbie and the one without a name. One by one, she walks them onto the suitcase where they twirl and flirt before an imaginary audience. She presents them with a pink silk flower on a plastic stem as tall as the doll itself. "Congratulations, Miss Rosebud 1965!"

Sitting opposite Grampa at the window, pretending to be engrossed in the sheep and cows passing by, I notice Mummy wince. *It's not a prize, Vanessa*, I want to scream. *We didn't win anything.*

"Congratulations!" says Vanessa to the next doll, as if her mere existence merits a reward.

Looking up from her knitting, Auntie Jean smiles. I've heard Mummy tell Daddy that Auntie Jean isn't very bright. And Vanessa's the same. They don't see beyond the surface of things. They really believe what Nana said, that it wasn't the winning or losing that mattered, it was the fun of taking part.

I don't mind so much for myself. Even as I dreamed of waking up magicked into a beauty-contest winner, I understood my role as companion to Vanessa. But for Vanessa not to be crowned Miss Rosebud, not to sit on a throne in the middle of the stage surrounded by a hundred little girls clutching a pink flower, makes fools of the whole family.

When no-one is looking, I drop my rosebud and flick it under the bench. I picture the pink petals getting filthy-dirty in the dust and grime. Under the seat, neglected, let them wither and die.

"*IN THE PINK*, you said? Round the back of the bus station?"

The taxi driver's irritated, but I didn't design the one-way system. "It was there five years ago."

As we drive down Charnwood Street for the third time, I'm tempted to let him drop me at the station and I'll do the presentation in my nightie with a paper bag on my head. But we turn the corner, and there it is: *In the Pink – Designer Dressing for the Discerning Demoiselle.* Brazen as anything, as if it hasn't played hide and seek for the last ten minutes.

As I walk into the shop, the proprietor looks up from a Mills and Boon: frothy curls dyed Naturally Blonde; purple talons; heavy warpaint. "Sue! What a lovely surprise! How's Patrick? How's my darling Becky?" Vanessa steps out from behind the counter to give me a hug that reeks of roses. "What brings you here? Nothing the matter, I hope?"

In the mirror next to a rail of fussy blouses, I see a ramshackle creature struggling to hold back her tears. Her more decorative cousin proffers a box of tissues in pastel shades. Thankfully, no one else is in the shop.

Vanessa understands my difficulty immediately. She floats along the rails, selecting garments as if flowers for a bouquet. "Something classy, with a bit of an edge. The kind of outfit that's so fabulous you don't even notice it."

Even though she's talking absolute nonsense, I'm relieved to let Vanessa take charge. She drops a pile of glad-rags onto the counter and holds out her final choice. "Try these."

"Beige?" I've never worn beige. So pale, I fear I'd

disappear.

"Ecru," says Vanessa, bustling me into the changing room and hooking three wooden hangers on the door: trousers, jacket and blouse.

When I step out, Vanessa beams. There's still the hint of a dimple. "You look stunning!"

I edge towards the mirror, expecting it to judge me more harshly.

Cheeks flushed with excitement, Vanessa pulls me away. "Not yet. Wait till I get you some shoes."

She darts to the other end of the shop, like Becky off to raid the dressing-up box. What am I doing? I must be desperate to delegate this to my ditzy cousin. Yet, I must confess, the suit feels comfortable. I step to the side and the fabric flows with me, lending my movements an unusual grace.

"Try these." Vanessa leads me to the mirror and drops a pair of strappy sandals at my feet.

The woman who steps into them looks like she means business. She's authoritative but not authoritarian, feminine without being frilly. Surprisingly, ecru is her colour. "Vanessa, you're a genius!"

At the counter, Vanessa wraps my new outfit in tissue paper as if it's a fragile ornament. "You're such a dark horse. Why didn't you tell me you were getting an award? We could've had a family party."

I laugh. I can't imagine my mother and Auntie Jean finding much to celebrate in a prize for physics.

As Vanessa shakes out a pink carrier bag, I put out my hand to stop her. "No need. It can go straight in my case."

"Just as you like." Vanessa lifts my case onto the counter, pushing aside the carrier to make room. It's made of crisp pink card with a handle of woven jute. Attractive in its way: designer-shop carriers are a different species from the flimsy supermarket throwaways. It might be fun to leave my briefcase in my room and carry my notes in something like that. And Becky could use it once the conference is over. "On second thoughts," I say, picking up the bag and placing it on top of the new clothes in my case.

*In the Pink,* I read, in show-off flowery lettering, before Vanessa covers the words with the lid of my case and pulls the zip securely around the rim.

# All the Way from Zokandu

WENDY IS IN the hallway, touching up her make-up, when the letterbox rattles for her attention. From the corner of her eye, she watches a pale-blue airmail envelope parachute to the mat. Her smile crinkles her lipstick; Efuru's letters never fail to brighten her day.

AFTER THE MISCARRIAGE and the collapse of the restaurant in Tenerife, Wendy assumed life could get no worse. But when her husband moved in with the waitress, despair threatened to move in with her. She'd come crawling back to a rented flat ten minutes' walk from her sister's, and a nine-to-five job that stretched to eight-to-six.

She wasn't complaining. *There's always someone worse off than you*, as her mother used to say. Finding herself far worse off than she'd ever imagined had given her the impetus to do something about it. Wendy was saving them both when she decided to sponsor an African child.

She collects the letter franked *Zokandu District 10* en route to the car. The thought of it lodged in her handbag will soothe her through the snarls on the ring road and the infantile demands of her boss.

She files Efuru's letters in shoeboxes at the bottom of her wardrobe. Some days, when she's searching for a blouse that won't make her look too frumpy, it's enough to catch sight of those cardboard boxes with the line drawings of size-five sling-backs on the side. On days dogged by if-only – how her marriage and *Comida Inglesa* might have survived had they appointed a different waitress – she takes out Efuru's letters and spreads them on the bed.

Each is a chapter in a rags-to-riches story: the child in the patched school uniform who becomes head girl; the waif too malnourished to walk three miles to her classroom who's determined to become a nurse. Efuru is an African Cinderella, with Wendy wielding the magic wand. No point breaking into the next instalment until she can give it the attention it deserves.

NO TIME TO catch up on the story at work, with her boss dragging her from one mini-crisis to another, while, in her breaks, her colleagues bend her ear about crises of their own. There's a window in the early evening, whilst the teenaged niece she's supposedly babysitting is upstairs interacting with her keyboard, except that her sister's house is so grubby she feels compelled to don a pair of marigolds and scrub the kitchen cupboards instead.

At last, she's home, reclining on her spotless sofa, free of responsibilities. She pours her tea and selects a gingernut from the biscuit tin. She peels open the airmail envelope.

As she extracts the flimsy blue pages, a strange object, no bigger than the nail on her little finger, drops out from between the leaves. It falls – no, jumps – onto the cushion beside her. A small bug, fiery orange in colour, with a flat and pointed back. Just as she's getting the measure of it, it hurls itself into the tin, leaping from chocolate digestive to custard cream, as if in training for the shield-bug Olympics. Her heart pounding, Wendy grabs the lid and traps it inside.

What the …? Did it hitch a lift in her handbag from her sister's? The house could do with steam cleaning, but Wendy has never considered it a breeding ground for vermin. Such a peculiar insect, it couldn't possibly be local. She definitely saw it shoot out of the envelope along with Efuru's letter. How could it have survived the journey all the way from Zokandu?

While the answer might be contained within the letter, she can't relax to read it with that creature performing calisthenics among her biscuits. It might be carrying malaria. It might have AIDS. If superbugs can thrive even in English hospitals, with all their disinfectants and antiseptics, what kind of horrors might incubate in an African village?

HER HEADLIGHTS PICK out the few cars remaining in the supermarket car park. Wendy drives past them to the recycling dumpsters round the back. There's a green one for green glass, a brown one for brown glass, and a grey container for clear glass. There's a yellow one for plastic and a big blue container for paper (but strictly not for telephone directories or cardboard). Wendy parks at the end of the row beside the dumpster for cast-off clothes and shoes.

It's not that she's got anything against the bug itself, she reasons, as she cradles the biscuit tin in her arms. Just as a weed is merely a misplaced plant, the bug has strayed from its natural territory. It would be a kindness to send it home.

She positions the tin alongside the slot in the charity container, snaps off the lid and pours the contents inside. Along with the faded T-shirts and pilled knitwear and an assortment of biscuits, she's repatriating the bug to a habitat more suited to its needs.

AFTER A BUBBLE bath, Wendy sits propped against her pillows, finally ready to savour Efuru's letter.

*Dear Wendy Auntie.* Wendy has become so fond of this inversion of the usual greeting, she's tried to get her niece to adopt it.

*I could not go to school today because my mother is sick and she needed me to go to the field. I have been here since dawn. Now it is noon, it is too hot to work so I am writing you.* All is revealed: the family fields must be swarming with creepy crawlies on the lookout for an envelope's shade.

*Please do not be cross that I miss school. As soon as my mother is recovered, I will hurry to my lessons.* If only her niece had half Efuru's enthusiasm for her studies.

*I thank you for the photograph. Your home must be as beautiful as Queen Elizabeth's palace. At night I dream I come and visit you. We drink tea and sing songs and laugh together.* Hard to envisage her niece appreciating such low-tech pleasures.

*I am sad that you must work so hard to send money for me*

*to go to school. But also I am very glad that you are so kind …* such a contrast to the grunts with which her niece acknowledged that last birthday gift … *so that I can pass my exams and nurse the sick in my village.* Not only grateful for what she's been given herself, but keen to share her good fortune with others.

*You are always in my thoughts.* Wendy smiles: as you are in mine.

SHE AWAKES IN the dark, sweat trickling between her breasts. In her dream, her flat had become infested with shield bugs. They leapfrogged along the work surfaces, sprang out of cupboards and drawers. They hid at the bottom of the cereal packets to tumble into her breakfast bowl like novelty giveaways. They stowed away in her shampoo and hijacked her hair when she took a shower. When she opened her wardrobe, her clothes were sequinned with orange.

Turning on the bedside lamp, Wendy reaches for Efuru's letter as once she would have reached for her husband's hand.

*Dear Wendy Auntie.* Immediately, her heartbeat steadies.

*I could not go to school today because my mother needed me to work in the field.* Yet the girl ought to have considered the risks of writing a letter out there.

*Please do not be cross that I miss school.* Yet Wendy is cross: she doesn't sponsor Efuru to provide cheap labour for her parents.

*At night I dream I come and visit you.* Wendy lets the page fall to the floor as she remembers how the bugs in her dream had the face of a girl with her hair in cornrows.

Three years of letters: it had never crossed her mind that Efuru might expect more than Wendy's standing order to the charity and the occasional photo. Did the girl genuinely believe she might come and visit? Like the bug in the dream, did Efuru harbour ambitions to go bouncing around her home?

There's always someone worse off than you, but Wendy isn't obliged to redress the balance.

She springs out of bed and pulls on jeans and a sweater. From the wardrobe, she takes out the boxes stuffed with letters from Zokandu. She slips the final instalment into a box with a picture of glittery mules on the side.

There's a pink tinge on the horizon as Wendy drives into the supermarket car park. She pulls up alongside the big blue container designated for wastepaper. They don't accept cardboard boxes, unfortunately, but she can dispose of those in her household rubbish bin when she gets home.

# Elementary Mechanics

ODAYE RETURNS FROM work to a house that is unusually quiet. At this hour, he'd expect to find Vashila chopping vegetables, one eye on the News on the kitchen portable. Or opening a bottle of wine and contemplating the flyer from a local takeaway. He'd expect to hear Pollyanna puffing up and down the scales on her oboe. Or on her mobile, sharing intimacies that couldn't wait until she saw her friends at school the next day. He checked the calendar for some appointment he might have forgotten – a sleepover or a parents' evening or a trip to the hairdresser – but today's entry is blank.

Loosening his tie, he trots upstairs to change. His wife lies on their bed, staring at the ceiling.

"I didn't think you were home." As he bends to kiss her, she seems to flinch. "Another migraine?"

She rolls away onto her side, screening her face with a veil of black-brown hair.

Odaye flings his tie to the floor. "How can I help if you won't tell me what's wrong?"

Vashila shrinks further into herself, wrapping her body around a battered hardback. Odaye hangs up his suit and pulls on a pair of jeans.

A wailing wafts across the landing from their daughter's room. It tugs at his stomach like a funeral chorus from his childhood.

Still in her school uniform, Pollyanna's face is blotchy from crying and there are spots of blood on the pillow under her head. Odaye's gaze darts to the window, but the line-up of teddy bears and makeup containers and unwashed coffee mugs appears undisturbed.

"Oh, Daddy! Why does she hate me so much?"

"Don't say that. She loves you."

"Then why does she have such a crazy way of showing it?"

HE'S KNOWN VASHILA since childhood. They used to race each other through the alleys around her family home, watched by the old men smoking in the doorways of the dark cafés. Although he was a month older, she was always a couple of steps ahead, so that if she should slip between the women examining squashes and aubergines to filch an apricot from a kerbside stall, he would be the one to get caught and cuffed around the head.

In her teens, she had been like Pollyanna: smart and confident and headstrong. Ambitious, telling everyone she was going to be an engineer. Or a ballet dancer. He feared for her even then. She wanted more than was seemly for a girl, even a girl with a wealthy and liberal father. For what kind of father would let his daughter stay in education long enough to become an engineer? What kind of husband would permit his wife to prance across the stage in a skimpy dress? He worried what she'd become once disappointment slapped back her dreams.

Of course he was in love with her. As much as a boy like him was able. But he couldn't tell her, not then. Even if he hadn't been the son of her father's chauffeur, he would never have mentioned it. It wasn't how things were done.

When they took her away he cursed his reticence, his playing by the rules. In his dreams and daydreams his declaration of love would have saved her. Spirited her into his arms, like in one of those European pop songs she and her friends were so fond of.

HE DRIES HIS daughter's eyes with a tissue from the lilac box on her desk. Dabs the blood from her earlobes with pastel-coloured cotton wool balls from the ceramic bowl in the ensuite. He eases the silver hooks through the tiny holes to remove the sparkly earrings she says her mother tried to yank from her ears. He runs her a bubble bath and promises to make her a soft-boiled egg with soldiers.

In the master bedroom, his wife is sleeping. He takes the book from her hands and draws the quilt around her shoulders.

AFTER THE REVOLUTION, it was no longer proper for Vashila's father to employ a man to drive his car. It was no longer possible to withdraw money from the bank to pay his wages. Or his son's school fees.

Vashila's father had sent them both to the international school. From six to fourteen, Odaye learned about a world where the Yanks had all the best lines. He was tolerated by the progeny of diplomats and taught by men and women who believed anyone could be anything: a girl could become an engineer or a ballet dancer, a boy from the slums could marry a girl from a home so vast there was even a separate house for the car. Yet when his father announced it was time to get a job, he was ready. He'd always known his path would diverge from Vashila's. As with any long-expected journey, it was a relief to depart.

Money could be extracted from the bank, it seemed, for Vashila's education. But the school changed. The senior teachers were nudged into alternative employment. Those who resisted woke up in prison to discover they'd committed crimes they'd never heard of. They were replaced by young men and women from the provinces whose only qualification was enthusiasm for the new regime. The diplomats sent their progeny to board at schools in countries where the USA was still considered the centre of the world.

Odaye was apprenticed to a baker. He wondered how lessons in the glory of the revolution would give his friend the skills she needed to become an engineer. Or the grace to dance on her toes.

ODAYE OPENS A bottle of pinot grigio and slumps down on the sofa while he waits for his daughter. He wonders if it would have been easier if she'd been a boy and Vashila the one to stand with a first-aid kit at the ringside while their child wrestled his father's demons. Perhaps not.

He picks up the book he took from his wife. *Elementary Mechanics*. Bound in faded green cloth fraying at the edges, with the spine hanging on by a few grubby threads, it must have passed through several schoolgirls' hands. He flicks through the yellowing pages of line drawings: triangles, pulleys and weights. He skims the invitations to calculate resultant forces and velocity-ratios. There's never been a time when *he* would have been able to do so.

The text blurs so that he couldn't have solved the equations even if he'd understood the formulae. He feels a hand on his shoulder but when he reaches up to meet it, his daughter pulls away.

"So she's shown you the evidence? And now you're going to bollock me too. I know I shouldn't have ripped it, but it's only a book. And she had no right to rummage in my schoolbag."

"Even so, you should look after your things."

Pollyanna flops onto the sofa beside him. "I know. I just wish she wouldn't nag. *Pay attention to your teachers. Do your homework. It's your passport to security.*"

Odaye winces. His daughter mimics his wife's accent perfectly. An accent that was considered near-enough native English at the international school. An accent that everyone assumed would lead Vashila to great things, even if she didn't make it as an engineer. Or a ballet dancer.


HIS HOURS AT the bakery were long and, on some days, he thought he might faint with the heat, but he enjoyed rising early to knead the rubbery white dough. He was too busy to think about Vashila and his old life. But when customers mentioned the student strike at what used to be the international school, his stomach flipped.

They said a female student had raised her hand halfway through a lesson that had once again degenerated into a recitation of revolutionary rhetoric, and challenged the teacher to return to the syllabus. The teacher told the student that, if she didn't like it, she could leave. Which she did. Along with a good three-quarters of the class.

Odaye prayed that Vashila would be among the minority that remained. But, if she had, it could only be because she was no longer the headstrong girl he'd loved as a child.

"What lesson was it?" he asked the customers.

They raised their eyes to the heavens or shook their heads. "What does it matter what the lesson was? They've arrested the ringleader, that's all I know."

Eventually he found someone who could tell him. "Applied mathematics." The foundation of an engineering career.


"SO YOU HAD a fight about the book?"

"Sort of. Well, the book was just the start." Pollyanna bites her bottom lip. "Promise you won't fly off the handle."

His daughter has wrapped her black-brown hair in a lilac towel, tucked in around her ears. She has threaded tiny gold rings through the holes in her ear lobes, all the blood washed away.

He has never hurt her. He never would. "I promise."

VASHILA WAS SEVENTEEN when they sent her to the place where so many of her teachers had been taken a couple of years earlier. Everyone knew that the only exit was to the burial ground next door. Sliding the round flat loaves from the ovens, Odaye concentrated on not burning his hands.

"YOU KNOW *FASHION Idol*?"

"That programme you watch on Thursdays when your mother's working late?"

"The one she hates. Well, they're holding the heats next week at the sports centre and Ms Goldsmith – she's this really laid-back art teacher – said she'd take us if the other teachers agreed. But guess what? It's Wednesday afternoon when I've got extra maths and Mr Patel – he's such an anal retentive – announced today that our class can't go. Too close to the exams and all that bollocks."

Imagining her mother's reaction, Odaye strains to appear sympathetic.

"Do you know what I said to that?" Pollyanna's eyes sparkle. "I said, Mr Patel, that's an abuse of our human rights, and if you won't let us go to the *Fashion Idol* heats, I'm not coming to class. I'm going on strike."

Odaye looks at his hands, still strong from the years of kneading dough from three in the morning. Stares at the elegant wine glass they hold by the stem.

His daughter punches his arm. "Don't you think that's cool?"

WHEN THE RUMOURS filtered through that there was a route from prison other than in a box, Odaye began to knead the dough with extra vigour. They claimed the route wasn't open to everyone. Certainly not to middle-aged teachers. Nor to men of any age. When he saw a young woman shrouded in black walking two paces behind one of the brutish prison guards, Odaye averted his eyes.

"HOW OLD ARE you?"

"You know how old I am. Nearly fourteen. Dad, don't look at me like that. You're making me nervous."

Odaye reaches out for her hand. "Did your mother tell you about the time she organised a school strike?"

"Mum? But that's brilliant. What happened?"

"It was during the revolution. She was a bit older than you. Seventeen. They sent her to prison."

Pollyanna gasps. "Wow! You mean it was illegal? *Super*cool."

IN THE CITY, life went on. The bakery continued to produce the round flat bread that people ate with the squashes and aubergines sold at the market. As long as they didn't dwell upon the starvation and the beatings, the hoodings and the electric shocks, the executions mock and real, those outside the prison walls could keep going from day to day. The greater freedoms they had once enjoyed were best forgotten. So when people saw a pretty girl shuffling along the street in the company of a man who earned his luxuries attaching electrodes to the genitals of their former neighbours, they didn't rejoice in a survivor. They saw a daughter who had relinquished her virginity without her father's permission, and spat at her.

ODAYE LETS GO of her hand. Is it an indication of their triumph or failure as parents that Pollyanna thinks prison would be an adventure? That they've shielded her so completely from their own nightmares she doesn't know her own mother. Just as they don't know her. With Vashila's almond eyes and black-brown hair, with her courage and her sassiness, he'd thought he had the measure of his daughter. Lounging on the sofa in her western clothes and hair wrapped in a towel-turban, Pollyanna is more attuned to fashion and reality TV than the terrors that drove her parents to seek asylum far from the alleys where they used to play. He gets up.

"Are you going to make me my egg?"

"What?"

"Dad, you promised to do me a boiled egg with soldiers."

Odaye laughs. "You're too old for that."

Pollyanna pushes out her bottom lip.

Does the child consider that endearing? "If you want an egg you can make your own. I'm going to check on your mother."


HE SAW VASHILA once. She was with the man they called The Butcher and she was no longer as pretty as she'd been. She waddled two paces behind him, a chain linking her wrist to his, her other hand on her swollen belly. He called out to her, but softly. She didn't raise her eyes from the dusty street.

The bomb in the central square changed everything. It splattered bits of The Butcher over the walls of the mosque.

The shockwaves set off contractions for which neither Vashila nor The Butcher's baby were prepared.

This wasn't quite enough to inspire him to follow the precepts of those over-optimistic teachers at the international school and work towards a future where he and Vashila could be together. But the bomb brought the revolutionary guards to the bakery. Accusing the owner of counter-revolutionary activities, they smashed the brick ovens with a sledgehammer. Odaye was left without a job, and the fear they'd come for him next. So he combed the alleys and squares in search of Vashila. He found her hiding in the latrine behind The Butcher's house, battling the rats for the body of her stillborn child.

Two years it took them to reach Britain. Another three years before they were granted permission to stay. A couple more before they felt safe enough to have a child of their own.

Many a time, sweltering under blankets in the back of a truck or waiting, at a border encampment, for the moment to cross, he'd thought to ask Vashila about the school strike and its consequences. To fill in the gaps between the day he left school and when he tracked her down, half-mad with grief. He'd thought about it, but he'd looked at her face closed up with pain and told himself, Later. When she's ready.


HE WATCHES HER sleeping, black-brown hair strewn across the pillow, eyes darting left and right behind closed lids. Roughly, he shakes her awake. She whimpers like a wounded animal. Then she recognises him and smiles.

"Tell me what happened."

Vashila pulls herself up to lean against the headboard. "I lost my temper. You know how it is. I'll take her to buy her some new earrings at the weekend."

"I don't mean tonight."

"What then?"

"I'm talking twenty-odd years ago. In prison." He almost spits. "And with that man. The Butcher."

"Don't ask me about that, Odaye. It was so long ago. Another country. Another life."

His hands are in fists. Hands that pummelled the dough as if it were The Butcher's face. "You've never spoken about it."

Vashila's lip trembles. "You've never asked."

Odaye waits. From downstairs he hears the lament of his daughter's oboe. He fancies he sees his wife's body stir in response. Easing her shoulders. Pointing her toes. He waits for the girl who thought she could be anything to lead the way. For the boy who followed her through the alleys to catch her up.

# Flexible Rostering

H E HAS VERY little time. Only a small window in which to do this thing. Even with the new flexitime system, he must be back at his desk by half-past two.

*We've tried it before*, he'd wanted to tell Marcus. *Flexible rostering doesn't work in a building society.* But he wouldn't have listened. Eddie knows there's nothing he can do to divert his boss from his mission to action all that theory from his MBA.

Striding down Ellington Street, his jacket slung casually over his shoulder and his tie freed from his collar, other concerns take over. Soon his parents will need his help to move from the terraced cottage where he was born, into a place where someone else will cook their meat and two veg and collect their pensions from the Post Office. But first this other thing: his son, halfway through college, in need of a dad to point the way to the next stage, a dad who understands his world.

Kids in uniform, their ties off-duty like his own, litter the street. The rusting railings around the schoolyard cannot contain them. A row of girls, arms linked in a sluggish *passagiata* across the pavement, force him into the gutter. Boys push and punch each other all the way to the fish and chip shop. They're laughing, but every time a fist collides with an arm or a torso, Eddie winces. Ought a grown-up put a stop to such behaviour? The kids smoking on the sidelines, marking his progress like cowboys outside the saloon eyeing the stranger who has just ridden into town, convince him not to intervene.

Things were so much more orderly in the old days, when this was Middlethorpe Grammar, and he and Gordon Welch spent lunchtimes at the chess club, or as monitors in the canteen. Gordon Welch. Adjacent desks from eleven to sixteen; enough time to get to know a person, one might think. Yet he'd never really known Gordon, as it turned out. Not known him at all. But he'd never thought there was anything *to* know.

What did it mean to know a person, anyway? As long as there was someone to nod to in the pub, and see you safely home if you'd had a pint or three too many, you didn't ask yourself how well you knew them. It was enough to have someone reliable to look after the rings on your wedding day, to be godparents for your kid, to put a hand on your shoulder at your wife's funeral and say *Sorry, mate*. That was what it meant to have friends.

Until now: taking an extended lunch break to visit Gordon Welch and find out more about him than he'd ever known, more than he'd ever wanted to know. And not even knowing why he was doing it. To deepen his friendship with Gordon? To help his own son?

THE SMELL OF beer, like sweaty socks, accosts him from the Red Lion at the top of Ellington Street. This was where it had all started, six months or so ago.

After the brewery performed major surgery on the Traveller's Rest, dressing it up in a parody of the Olde English Pub, Eddie had been forced into the seedier part of town for a proper place to drink, a man's pub. He'd been pleased to find his old schoolmate propping up the bar in the Red Lion. Gordon seemed pleased to see him too, after all these years. They had no trouble picking up their friendship again. Neither of them saw the need to fill in the forty year gap with details. Friendship was a present-tense business.

Gordon was a regular at the Red Lion; he lived just round the corner on Botany Terrace. He introduced Eddie to his friends, Clive and John. Soon Eddie was a regular, too. The Red Lion became his local, even if it was a bit of a trek from home.

Sometimes, worn out by Marcus' textbook enthusiasm, Eddie would call in at the Red Lion straight from work. He'd phone home and tell the lad to get his own tea, and ask the landlord to microwave a pie. He'd have downed a few pints and be in a conversational mood by the time the others joined him at the table opposite the dartboard.

Three weeks ago, it wasn't just management according to Marcus the Magnificent that urged him towards the Red Lion after work. Something had been niggling him, and he wanted advice from men he could trust.

It began with a casual question from a woman who came in to the building society to deposit a cheque. An old friend of Grace's, who always took an interest in the lad. *How's the course going? When are we going to see him on the telly? Has he got a girlfriend yet?*

Women notice things. If Grace were alive she would have taken care of this. But Eddie had friends at the Red Lion who could help compensate for Anthony's lack of a mother.

He took a deep breath. "The lad never brings any girls home."

"He's shy," said John. "He'll let you meet them soon enough."

"But I don't think he sees anyone. He's on that computer all night long. Or playing his violin."

"They mature at different rates," said Clive. "He'll be all right."

"But I don't think he's interested in girls at all."

"Don't worry," said Clive. "He's still young. Our Rob didn't have a girlfriend till he was twenty-six, but he's fair made up for it. Three kids, three mothers. Count yourself lucky."

Gordon glanced across at the bar, then at the half-full glasses on the table. "Might as well get the beers in while it's quiet."

"Right," said John, as Gordon sloped off towards the bar.

Eddie took a swig of his beer, letting the drink talk for him, "I think he might be a poofter."

John got up. "Got to go for a slash."

Clive glared. "How can you say that word?"

The shame made Eddie backtrack. "No, you're right. He's probably a late developer."

Clive's cheeks blazed. "I said, what you doing saying poofter?"

Eddie felt eleven years old again, kitted out in his grammar school uniform, the kids in the street sneering. Thinking his superior education should give him the words to win them over, but unable to find them. "There's no harm in it, Clive. It's just how some people are."

"I fuckin' know that, you bigoted old arsehole."

"What's your problem then?"

"Your fuckin' language, that's what. The word is gay."

"Okay, sorry. I didn't mean to offend you."

"It's not me you've offended, is it?"

Eddie sighed. Maybe the Red Lion wasn't really the pub for him. He had to admit, it was a hassle getting the bus in and out of town just for a pint. "Isn't it?"

Clive gave Eddie a filthy look, then, Janus-faced, beamed at Gordon, approaching their table with two pints of beer. He turned pointedly back to Eddie signalling with raised eyebrows and a slight jerk of the head, their friend, now on his way back to the bar to collect the other two pints. "What are you, a fuckin' retard? I thought you two were at school together."

Eddie watched Gordon set down the other two pints and take his seat. Then, as John returned to the table, leaned back against the leatherette banquette, leaving the other three to an analysis of Saturday's match. Gordon lined up the beer mats to demonstrate some point about a missed penalty. Clive kept protesting, moving the mats to a different position. "Didn't you see the bleeding match?"

It was the kind of conversation that left Eddie yearning to go and chat with the women about shopping and bingo. But there was no such conversation he could gatecrash that evening. Nothing to distract him from the shocking revelation about the guy who'd sat next to him for five years at school. That's if he'd understood Clive correctly.

Gordon looked ordinary enough. Rough workman's hands, strong enough to tackle any job, unlike Eddie's slim fingers fit only for leafing through bank notes. Beefy chest, clad in black T-shirt and denim jeans and jacket. Ruddy complexion, unfussy haircut, no sign of pampering with creams and unguents. A proper man, as far as Eddie could see. Gordon looked up from his simulation of the football match and met Eddie's gaze. Eddie blushed, like he hadn't done in years. And Gordon, rather than looking angry or embarrassed, winked.

THAT WAS THREE weeks ago. Now Eddie stands outside Gordon's house on Botany Terrace, still not quite sure whether this is for real. Pressing the door bell, he smooths down his hair as he would to take his stint on the counter at work. He stares at the red front door and half hopes Gordon won't be home.

The door swings back and there's Gordon, dressed in jeans and a plain blue shirt and looking, well, ordinary. That he has not been transformed into someone whose off-duty attire includes mascara and a frilly housecoat, is both a relief and a concern. Eddie still isn't sure they have the same idea of what this meeting is about.

Gordon takes Eddie's jacket and leads him down the hallway to the back of the house. Below a poster urging visitors to Gordon's small dining room to Make Trade Fair, a table is set for two. There's a mixed salad in a wooden bowl and new potatoes in a crystal dish. Eddie shudders when he sees the quiche.

"You shouldn't have gone to so much trouble," he says.

"Aren't you hungry?" says Gordon.

"It's just that I wasn't expecting ..."

Gordon smiles. "So what were you expecting?"

Eddie has always felt awkward at this stage, even with a woman, unsure of the polite progression from fully clothed on the sofa to naked on the bed. What a relief it had been to be married and not have that embarrassment anymore. "I thought we might go upstairs."

WITH HIS EYES closed, Eddie can just about convince himself it is Pamela Anderson who is inducing these sensations in his body, her luscious lips that have coaxed his penis from a flaccid slug to the vibrant focus of his being. The rhythm rocks him like the tide, so that he can almost believe himself on the beach with her, all big blonde hair and bronzed cleavage.

Almost. It's not only the incongruity of being in Gordon Welch's bedroom, with a dull ache in his wrists from balancing his buttocks on the edge of the bed that threatens his fantasy. It's hard to stay with the lapping waves, the distant calls of athletic twenty-somethings playing beach volleyball, when there are other voices, like interference on a poorly-tuned radio. How could Botany Terrace be so busy on a Monday afternoon? It looked the kind of street where everyone is either out at work or watching daytime television with the curtains drawn. Yet now it sounds as if all the householders are congregating on the pavement outside Gordon's door. It's as if they've time-travelled to the terraces of his childhood, where the kids played hopscotch on the pavements, the men stood around smoking while the women were down on their hands and knees scrubbing the front steps.

Gordon's bedroom is suddenly infused with brightness. Eddie opens his eyes to a circle of light drifting across the wallpaper, exposing the dust on the top of Gordon's chest of drawers before disappearing through the window. Kneeling on the floor beside the bed, his head between Eddie's thighs, Gordon seems unaware of the intrusion.

Sliding his backside further onto the bed, Eddie pulls himself out. Gordon rocks back onto his ankles. It reminds Eddie of a book they read at school, where Julia and Winston believe their lovemaking to be an act of rebellion, only to discover they've fallen into the authorities' trap. Gordon wipes his mouth. "I thought you were enjoying it."

Eddie creeps over to the window and peers out from behind the curtain. "Fucking hell!" He grabs his y-fronts from the floor and starts to get dressed. "There's a load of people with cameras out there." He jiggles awkwardly into his trousers, as if he hadn't been doing it every day for more than half a century. "Someone's put a ladder up to the window. That must be how they shone that light in here.

They're having a look in next door now. Is there a back way out?"

Gordon puts an arm around Eddie's shoulder. "It's okay, mate. They're not interested in us."

Eddie ducks away and scrambles on the floor for his socks. "Oh yeah?"

"Don't tell me you thought the press were onto you?"

Eddie shoves a pile of Gordon's clothes off a bentwood chair and sits down to tie his shoelaces. "What are they here for, then?"

"I imagine it's about the guy next door." Gordon saunters over to the window, glances casually down at the street and turns back to face him. "There's a group of Iranians live next-door, asylum seekers mostly. One guy went on hunger strike and sewed up his eyelids, lips and ears. You must have read about it in the papers."

Eddie rarely bothers with the papers. They're always so depressing. "Sounds a bit sensational for Middlethorpe."

Gordon shrugs. "Sometimes people need to be shocked out of their complacency. I'm sorry they gave you such a fright."

Eddie feels overdressed now in his grey wool suit trousers, shiny black laceups, shirt and tie. Yet he'd feel even more foolish if he were to start undressing again. All he wants is to complete the ensemble with his jacket and return to where things are more predictable. "It's nothing." They hover around the bed, studying the grey and red geometric pattern of the duvet cover. Two middle-aged men in a bedroom farce.

"We could still have lunch," says Gordon.

"I'm needed at work."

"YOU'RE BACK EARLY!"

Eddie slips his jacket onto the back of his chair and settles down in front of the computer. "Yeah, I didn't need as long as I thought I would."

"That's the beauty of sexual rogering," says Marcus. "You can come and go as you please." Eddie's chest is a wet rag being squeezed dry. Now he knows for sure that, on the staffroom noticeboard, amongst the photocopied announcements of a colleague's new baby, the notices of courses on Customer Care, the reminders of the withdrawal of the Silver Saver Account, there must be a digitally enhanced photograph of the Assistant Manager being pleasured by his old schoolfriend. And yet Marcus doesn't look as if he is in possession of such a powerful weapon. Sure, he has that patronising air of schoolboy-turned-teacher that has had Eddie itching for his carriage clock ever since the youngster was promoted above him. But this is no more humiliating than those times he takes Eddie to one side to spell out in grandmother-sucking-eggs detail the latest directive from Head Office. Daring to look up into his boss's baby-blue eyes, Eddie sees Marcus looking down benignly, as if Eddie is a pet dog he has given a bone. With his cropped hair, his cartoon-character socks, his body building regime at Gymfastic, Marcus could well be one of them. Maybe this is Marcus' way of welcoming Eddie to the club.

"Is it? I'm afraid I'm new to this game."

Marcus' face goes as blank as the passbook of a defunct

account. "I thought you said you'd tried flexitime before."

Flexible rostering. Sexual rogering. It doesn't even sound the same. Never mind worrying about his parents going senile, maybe it's time for Eddie to bow out. "Yes, of course, what am I saying?" Better to be thought a doddering old fool than a sodomite. Better to pander to Marcus' ego than be exposed as a queer. "It's just that we didn't do it properly before. It didn't have a chance. Not like your system."

Marcus smiles. "Good to have your support, Eddie. I'd be lost without you."


THERE'S NO MESSAGE in his inbox offering to swap a set of negatives for £100,000 in used notes. There are no new photographs of any description pinned to the staffroom noticeboard. The absence of incriminating evidence reduces Eddie's anxiety enough to see him through the afternoon. But for proof that Gordon's lunch had not been bait for a plot to humiliate him, he must wait for the evening news.

In the front room at home he opens a can of beer and switches on the television. The runner-up of *The Weakest Link* expresses her relief at avoiding the Walk of Shame. Eddie thinks he knows how that feels.

He hears a key turning in the front door. Anthony slouches into the room. Eddie strains his lips into a welcoming smile. "Good day?"

The lad shrugs. "I've got something to tell you."

"Great," says Eddie, turning his attention back to the TV. "Get yourself a beer if you like. I'm just going to catch the news."

Anthony hovers at the living room door. "You won't

like it."

As the jingle counts down to the six o'clock news, Eddie swings round to face his son, standing red-faced with one hand on the door handle. Poor kid, he doesn't know he's chosen the worst possible moment to make his confession. Eddie will have to find some way of helping him through it. At least after this afternoon he's a bit more prepared. From deep in his bowels he summons up an easy-going-parent laugh. "Come and sit down." He pats the seat of the sofa beside him. "I'm not such an ogre, am I?"

Anthony lets go of the door knob, but doesn't venture any further into the room. He makes his announcement to the faded Axminster. "I've packed in college."

Eddie jumps up, spraying beer down his tie. "What?"

Anthony meets his gaze. His voice is quiet but determined. "I've given up my course." Eddie braces himself to go storming down to the college to demand his son's reinstatement. "They've thrown you out?"

"No, I chucked it in myself."

"Why would you do that?"

Anthony comes closer. "It was doing my head in."

Eddie has to look up to meet his gaze. When did the lad get so tall? "I thought you were enjoying it. It was what you always wanted."

"It was what *you* wanted. I wasn't fussed either way."

Eddie had anticipated a difficult encounter, but he hadn't been prepared for this. "I don't understand."

Anthony clenches his fists. "Performing Arts. It's all pointless pratting about."

"How can you say that? There are good jobs in the

entertainment industry." Better than the boring building society, any day.

"There are crap jobs in the entertainment industry. Unless you're mega-talented. Or mega-lucky. Or prepared to audition in the gents' toilets."

Eddie's heart thunders in his chest. But they're back on track. This is what he has been waiting for, preparing for, dreading. "There's no shame…"

"For fuck's sake, Dad. Can't you listen to me, for once? I want to do something useful."

Eddie shrinks before his son. He scans the room for inspiration, pausing at a framed photograph of Grace on the sideboard. She looks back at him reproachfully.

Anthony gestures towards the television. He too sounds deflated. "So, he's given up his hunger strike."

On the screen a man rests his head on a pillow. Stitches, like barbed wire, have concertinaed his ears into tiny flaps. Furious red bobbles mark the point where the needle has been forced through his skin, like a health-warning to the young about the dangers of body piercing. A nurse wearing surgical gloves snips at the thread clamping his eyelids together. Gordon's asylum seeker. Eddie turns from the scene in disgust. "You knew about this?"

"Of course. It's the most important thing that's ever happened in Middlethorpe."

Eddie catches his breath. "You were there?" With the press, shining a light into Gordon's bedroom?

"No. I've been following it on the Internet. But I should have been there. I should have got involved."

"You want to be a reporter?"

"Hell no! I don't want to *write* about all the shit going on in the world. I want to do something about it."

Eddie might as well have sewn his own lips together. His ears too, since his son's words make no sense. What can he do with a kid prepared to sacrifice a career in the footlights for some masochistic foreigner, a kid inspired more by a nauseating publicity stunt than an uplifting stage-show? Stupid to think there was anything he could do to make life easier for the lad. It's as if he's deliberately chosen the hard route.

Staring at this stranger, his son, Eddie is surprised to find his thoughts returning to Gordon. Not the here-and-now Gordon of the grey-and-red duvet cover and the quiche mouldering on the dining-room table, but a younger chap from when the teenager was newly invented. Gordon with his canvas knapsack slung over his shoulder, trying to persuade Eddie to accompany him to the student protests in Paris. Of course, Eddie had declined. He was afraid of jeopardising his job at the building society. He was afraid of eye-stinging tear-gas.

It's as if the stitches have been snipped from his own eyelids. Perhaps his son hoped to move beyond such fears. "Why did that guy sew his face up? Seems weird to me."

"It's the asylum laws. He wanted to show they make a person feel like they don't matter. Like they've no voice." Anthony stops. "But you'll know this?"

"I never took much notice of politics." Eddie glances around the room again. How shabby it looks. How outdated, barely altered since Grace died. All the photographs on the sideboard are of the long-ago three of them, his hair without a trace of grey, Anthony never more than six years old. "Maybe you can teach me why it matters." He feels an urge to hug the lad, like when he was a toddler. But that might be overdoing it. Before he can take the risk, the landline's ring cuts the connection between them.

Anthony picks it up and passes it to his father. "Someone called Gordon."

Too late to have Anthony pretend he's not in, he asks the lad to go and put a couple of pizzas in the oven. Yet he feels even more exposed with the boy out of the room.

"I just wanted to check you're okay," says Gordon. "You saw the news?"

What can he say? He's made such a mess of things. But he can't keep hiding behind his son. "I'm glad you rang, Gordon. I wanted to apologise." If Anthony can head off in an entirely new direction, perhaps Eddie can too. "And to ask if we could rearrange that lunch." He's always been fond of Gordon. Why not relax, follow his instincts, and see how far that friendship can go?

# Spring Cleaning

"RIGHT," SAYS MY mother, as we drive out of the hospital car park. "Now's our chance to get to work on that bungalow."

Even with both eyes fixed on the road, she must notice my alarm, because she takes her left hand off the wheel and places it on my knee and says, in that wheedling what-do-I-ever-ask-of-you tone, "Come on, Emma. If we do it together we'll have that place bottomed in no time."

Home from Uni for the Easter holidays, I'm supposed to be churning out an essay on the English civil war. I'm supposed to be searching for a McJob to tame my overdraft, or hanging out in the pub with friends I haven't seen since Christmas. Unfortunately, what I'm *supposed* to be doing is of no consequence to my mother. Set against one of her projects, any plans of mine turn out to be as flimsy as cobwebs.

To be fair, when we get back to the bungalow, I do see

her point. Without Gran enthroned on her armchair in front of the telly, I can't help but notice the state of the place, and it isn't good. Without Gran to commandeer the visitor's attention with her chronicles of the doings of the neighbours, wrapped up in the latest from the soaps and her memories of war-time evacuation, the dust and grime and piles of rubbish are right in your face. A week on the ward, the nurse said, if all goes to plan. What harm can it do if we tidy up while she's away?

Over the next couple of hours, curtains and nets are taken down and bunged in the washing machine. Rugs are suspended over the washing line and the dust beaten out of them like an exorcism of evil spirits. Used tissues and rogue buttons are needled out of their hiding places and chucked in the bin. A drawer full of out of date money-off coupons is similarly disposed of. A treasury of ornaments is swept off the mantelpiece and submerged in a basin of soapy water.

The exercise is not without its casualties. A china shepherdess, inscribed 'A Souvenir of Devon', tumbles onto the marble fireplace and loses her head. Before I can say Superglue, Mum has her consigned to the bin.

Rooting for rubbish under the cushions of the settee, Mum's fingers encounter a mouldering plum, squidgy as an eyeball, that spouts its remaining putrid juice right up her sleeve as soon as she tries to pick it up. But she appears undaunted. Indeed, the incident feeds her determination to do battle with the dirt.

When she comes back from rinsing her blouse I'm lounging in Gran's chair, engrossed in a *Woman's Weekly* from before I was born.

"Since when were you interested in knitting patterns and baking?"

"It's Social History," I say. "My subject."

"It's a fire hazard," she says, and packs me off with a box of old newspapers and magazines to the recycling point down the road.

When I get back, I hear a funny scratching sound coming from the front room. I wonder if I'll have time for a cup of tea before Mum sends me back out on a quest for mousetraps. And then I spot my mother, down on her knees, fretting at Gran's country-cottage wallpaper with a scraper.

"Cleaning!" I say. "You said we were just cleaning."

"Oh, don't make such a fuss," says Mum. "It won't take long to paper the lounge. Think how pleased your gran will be when she sees it."

I'm not convinced, but years of being dragged into Mum's hypermanic missions have instilled in me the virtue of resignation. "What do you want me to do?"

"Tell you what." Mum sponges a section of wallpaper and sits back on her heels and smiles at me, like she's about to give me a present. She pushes a stray lock of hair behind her ear with a hand peppered white by the decomposing wallpaper. "Why don't you go and choose the paper? Something bright and cheery."

At least that's easier than stripping wallpaper and sanding down skirting boards, I think, as I drive Mum's car to the out-of-town DIY emporium.

Once inside, I'm not so sure. Stumbling down the colossal aisles, the odour of sawn wood renders me nauseated, rather than raring to get on with honing up my home-improvement skills. The muzak – wouldn't it have to be my mother's theme song, *I'm Every Woman* – seems to mock rather than empower me.

Too much choice can be worse than too little. Geometric figures, flora and fauna, minimalist brushstrokes all but invisible to the naked eye. Lilacs and blues, reds and pinks, yellows, browns, greens. Hard enough to pick the right one for yourself, never mind for another person.

One and a bit semesters of a history degree has shown me that, under conditions of uncertainty, it makes sense to plump for what's worked in the past. Yet no matter how many times I inspect the ranks of wallpaper, there's no sign of vintage country-cottage. I've no option but to pick out a new design. If only I'd spent less time attending lectures and more time watching makeover programmes on cable, I'd be better equipped for the task. I imagine a woman with a cheesy smile extolling the virtues of decorating a room to reflect the occupant's personality. Reasonable advice, perhaps, but I'm not sure Gran has a personality, apart from Neighbourhood Gossip.

I close my eyes and try to conjure up an image of Gran sitting in state with her brand-new hip in a transformed front room. She'll have new stories to tell, about handsome young doctors and angelic nurses and crazy hospital routines. I picture her now, holding forth, while daughters and granddaughters bring her cups of strong tea and sandwiches with the crusts cut off. Prattling away with her false teeth shunting around in her mouth independently of her gums, looking like a character in an old film where the sound is out of sync with the action. In my mind, I try freezing the frame, zooming in on the walls, trying to discover what background would fit with this scene. But it doesn't work. I can sense the presence of my gran – that's easy enough – but the walls are just a nondescript grey.

But then it hits me: isn't that the point? I have to laugh at myself. Here am I, agonizing about getting it right when Gran is unlikely to give a monkey's what the place looks like. Of course, I know who my gran is: a woman more interested in exercising her vocal chords than keeping house. A woman who cares more about interacting with people than the detail of her surroundings. Gran would still be Gran whatever we put on the walls. I open my eyes and grab half a dozen rolls from the first rack I see. Empress Narcissus it says on the wrapper next to the bar code. Quite appropriate, I reckon.

When I get back to the bungalow Mum's already stripped two walls and is ankle deep in concertinas of damp paper. She grabs the bag and peeps inside. "Daffodils! Just right for Easter. Your gran will be pleased."

MUM DECIDES I should stay over at the bungalow to help Gran get used to her new hip. "It's not as if you're doing anything at home," she says.

I suppose I can not do my essay just as easily here as at my parents'. Just as easily fail to find a McJob or catch up with friends at Gran's as at home.

So I'm waiting in Gran's spruced-up front room while Mum goes to collect her from hospital. The sun streaming through the windows dances on the yellow flowers on the wall. I've bought a bunch of real daffodils and planted them in a vase on the mantelpiece, among the freshly laundered knick-knacks. A room to come home to.

Gran hobbles in on two sticks. Mum hovers at her side, ready to catch her if she totters.

"Well, what do you think?" says Mum, grinning like a Cheshire cat.

Gran looks bewildered, like she's stumbled into a neighbour's bungalow by mistake, like she's been away from home for a year rather than a week and forgotten where everything is. "Oh sweet Jesus! Let me sit down."

She looks old. All my life Gran has been old, but this is different. That was the old of experience, of ancient sagas that acquire a deeper meaning with each retelling. This is the old of technophobia, of assumptions way past their sell-by date. The old that, if you remove the familiar landmarks, gets hopelessly lost.

"Isn't it great?" says Mum. "Daffodils. So cheerful."

She helps Gran into her old armchair, now jazzed up with a new cushion, the colour of jaundice. "Emma wanted to brighten the place up for you. Wasn't that sweet of her?"

Gran twists awkwardly to look at me. From the expression on her face she could be holding up a mirror to mine. Betrayal.

"Oh yes, *Changing Rooms*," she says, after a long pause. "I used to watch that on the telly."

That ought to be enough for anyone, but Mum doesn't do restraint. "But do you like it?"

Gran sighs. Her words seem stuck inside her, as if the hospital has treated her for verbal diarrhoea instead of an arthritic hip. When she finally speaks, her voice is tiny. "It's lovely."

Passionless. Passive. Past it. It doesn't sound like Gran at all. Against the vibrancy of the clean and bright daffodil room, all Gran's colour seems to have been drained away, leaving her a nondescript grey.

# What Time It Sunset?

I T'S THE RATTLE of the teacup in its saucer that wakes you. Your father stands beside your bed, dressed for work. "Bad news, poppet. Emergency at the hospital. Victoria is going to have to take you to the airport."

The rage sets your throat ablaze and you flounder around for some cold words to douse the flames. "I don't drink tea," you say. "I thought you'd know how caffeine buggers up your system." But you take the cup from him and let him kiss your cheek. Tonight you'll be back in your own room with Marilyn Manson watching over you from the posters on the black-emulsioned walls.

VICTORIA SNATCHES YOUR ticket and thrusts it at the check-in steward. "Could she have a window seat, please?"

"An aisle seat," you insist. "I like to stretch my legs." Hasn't she noticed how tall you've grown this past year? How you still don't know where to put all that extra body?

Probably not: too busy pushing her tongue down your father's throat.

She gives you a mournful look. "Don't you want a window seat? The view would help pass the time."

"Yeah. Eleven hours of staring at clouds. Bliss!"

Undaunted, she offers to buy you things: a giant Toblerone; a cheery pink paperback; a T-shirt embroidered with a dancing dragon.

"Put your purse away," you say. "It'll be half the price at the duty-free."

"Come to the café, then. There's loads of time till your flight."

"Not if I've to queue for an hour at Security. Someone might try to smuggle a lethal nail file onboard."

That gets her off your back. Victoria wouldn't want to stymie a security check. "I'd better say goodbye, then." At least she knows better than to try to kiss you.

"Bye."

You walk to the barrier.

"Have a good flight. See you next summer."

You show your boarding pass. You don't look back.

YOU WERE RIGHT about the queue for Security. People shuffle along, sliding their overweight hand-luggage ahead of them. An airport official ushers a couple of children to the front: Unaccompanied Minors. A brother and sister, probably; they remind you of you, years ago, in the days before Victoria. Buoyed up by the special attention, terrified lest a link in the chain of minders should come loose, and you'd be abandoned at the next gate. You blink hard so as not to mess your eyeliner, and fill your mind with memories of Victoria's pathetic attempts to befriend you over the holiday, memories that cool your throat as smoothly as vanilla milk-shake.

THE WINDOW SEAT is occupied by a bearded man in a white crochet skullcap and a grey tunic that covers his legs. The shy smile he flashes you as you dump your backpack on the seat reignites the furnace in your throat.

You open the overhead locker and fumble about for somewhere to put your backpack. He puts down his book and gets up. "I help you." But the stewardess beats him to it, and he shrugs and sits back down.

"The flight's not full today," says the stewardess as she closes the locker. "You can move seats after takeoff if you like. Plenty of space at the back."

You glare at her. "I'm perfectly comfortable here, thank you very much."

She blushes and scurries away. It feels good until you realise you're stuck with the bearded guy in the dress all the way to Heathrow.

DURING TAKEOFF HE stares out the window, checking his watch as if to ensure things are going to plan. He has all the makings of a terrorist. Not that you care: it would be an appropriate ending to a disastrous holiday for you to be blown to pieces over the Himalayas.

Once you're airborne, you tear your headphones from their wrapper and fiddle with the controls on your armrest until you find the least nerdy channel. You settle down with a Sudoku.

There's something deadly about a long-haul flight. You don't fear for your safety, the way Victoria does; indeed, a whiff of danger would spice it up. It's the in-betweenness that does you, that feeling of being nowhere at all. Your senses defeated by the interminable drone of the engine, the artificial light, the sour air, the miniscule meals that taste of plastic. The only way to handle it is to give up all pretence of control. Let the emptiness engulf you.

Once you allow yourself to slip into the void, it isn't so bad. The injustice that fed the fire in your throat fades away. You don't have to fight anymore. It's like the anaesthetic when you had your appendix out last year.

YOU'VE JUST LOWERED your table for lunch when he decides he wants out. You step into the aisle and he pushes past, a striped towel in his hand. You think perhaps he doesn't know there'll be a whole stack of paper towels in the cubicle. You wonder if paper towels are one of the many things his religion forbids.

He doesn't return until you're halfway through dessert: a doll's-house portion of lemon mousse reminiscent of washing-up suds. "Excuse please."

It's easy to show him how inconvenient it is for you to interrupt your meal and let him through.

"Sorry, sorry," as he squeezes past, the words a soothing balm to your throat.

You see now he's much younger than you thought: twenty, maybe. Not much older than you. It was the long beard that deceived you. You wonder if he was ever an

Unaccompanied Minor.

You pretend not to watch as he folds away his towel in the holdall under his seat. You feel bad now that you didn't collect his meal tray for him earlier. You offer him your salad in its hermetically sealed packet, along with the sachet of French dressing. He smiles and shakes his head. You notice the gap between his two front teeth.

AFTER LUNCH THEY dim the lights for the movie. You've seen it before, but it's in the nature of air travel to be bored out of your head, so you flip the switch on your armrest to channel 2 and watch it again. He doesn't watch though. He turns on his reading light and studies his book. It's one of those books you read backwards like Manga, only without pictures and a text like curly mirror-writing. You decide it's cool to sit beside someone who can decipher those squiggles.

THE MOVIE'S BUILDING up to its climax when he's agitating to be out again. "Excuse please. Sorry, sorry." His rolled-up towel in hand.

You could pretend to be so engrossed in the fate of Leonardo DiCaprio that you haven't noticed your neighbour has a bladder problem. You doubt he has enough English to insist. But it gives you some satisfaction to stand in the aisle, blocking the view of the screen for the people in the row behind.

"Thank you. Sorry."

You're readjusting your headset when you realise he's got a point. The queue is always shortest while people are watching the movie.

You squeeze your feet into your trainers and saunter down the aisle. There's only an elderly woman waiting at the toilet door. You can't see him. He must be inside, drying his hands on his stripy towel.

A man and a woman sidle up behind you, holding hands. The toilet door opens. It's not him, just a little boy over-dressed in jacket and tie. Your neighbour must have taken a walk to one of the other toilets. Stretching his legs to ward off thrombosis.

No he hasn't. He's there by the emergency exit, kneeling on his towel and rocking forward till his forehead kisses the floor. The people in the seats nearby stare at the screen, self-consciously ignoring his salaaming.

You must have shared a long-haul flight with hundreds of Muslims since your father discovered his mission to tend the sick in countries as far away from you and Mum as he could get. Strange how you've never before encountered one of them praying. Even though everybody knows Muslims have to pray a zillion times a day.

The woman behind taps you on the shoulder. "It's free now."

You squeeze into the toilet cubicle and reapply your black eyeliner.

AS USUAL, THE tedium gets to you sometime around the middle of the second movie. Still too many hassles till you're home: the final meal; the landing; the long wait at the luggage carousel; the drive from the airport with Mum contorting herself to ask about the holiday without ever mentioning your father or his paramour. The fire of your throat has subsided, leaving a dull ache and that deadly fatigue that comes from an absence of all the things that make you feel like a person: good music; texting your friends; somewhere to go beyond the loo.

Your Muslim also seems unsettled. He raises the blind and peeps out into the clouds. He consults his watch. You hope it won't be long before he detonates his bomb and puts an end to it.

He catches you watching him. "Please, what time it sunset?"

You laugh. Of course you've noticed before how, towards the end of the second movie, the sky begins to blush, then bruise. But to label such a phenomenon sunset, and to try to pin it down to a specific time, up here in this no-man's-land, seems to you ridiculous. Sunset and time belong on the earth's surface: your father's cue for a first G&T, Mum's for the evening news. You can't have a sunset unless you are somewhere.

Your Muslim looks hurt. But determined. You admire that.

"You know or you not know?"

"I not know. I mean, I don't know."

"I ask stewardess."

You feel strangely protective. "She'll think you're a nutter. Look out the window and watch. You can't time it exactly."

"I must exactly."

"Tough titties! You can't always get what you want. We know what time we set off and we know what time we'll land, but for the bit in the middle, who can say?" You're not sure if he's following you. "Why's it matter to you so much, anyway?"

He raises the blind. A pale light floats in. He lowers the blind abruptly. "I must pray. Before sunset."

You unclip your seatbelt, ready to move yet again to let him out. "Then go. Who's stopping you?"

He stays in his seat. "Before sunset. But not too before."

You swallow your laughter. "That's tricky." How would you survive the deadness of air travel if you still had to stick to your on-the-earth routines? There's a certain freedom in abandoning yourself to nothingness. You're not sure how you'd manage a flight if you couldn't let go. "How do you usually judge it?"

He shakes his head. "It first time I flight."

You feel your throat hotting up again. Then you remember those two children in the care of the airport official at Security. They'd never manage to negotiate their way from one world to another without someone to show them the way. You lean across him and push up the blind. There's a faint tinge of pink in the distance. "If we both keep watch we might manage it."

He smiles. "Thank you."

"What's your name?"

"Yusuf," he says. "What your?"

# Forging a New Path

# Fat Footprints

WHEN THE HEAT had dissipated somewhat, Selina and Sam went for a stroll to work up an appetite for dinner. At that hour, abandoned by all but the most stubborn souvenir sellers and tourists, the beach seemed their exclusive domain. Sauntering hand in hand, as waves roared across the reef and pale crabs scuttled off to bury themselves in the sand, they relished the freedom to go barefoot for one last day.

After a while, they turned to measure the distance they had strayed from the thatch-roofed chalet that had been their home for the past ten days. Selina gasped. Day-glo pink fringed the horizon, but it wasn't the overture to another splendid sunset that caught her attention. "Look at our footprints. They're enormous."

Sam squatted to check that the bloated indentations were not merely a trick of the light. "Freaky!"

Selina gazed back over the meandering path their feet

had traced along the beach. Each print seemed double its usual size. "What makes them go like that?"

"Must be something about the type of sand," said Sam.

"But sand is just sand."

"Well, actually ..." Sam slipped into what Selina's mother termed his Pompous Englishman voice. "Sand is constructed of grains of silica bonded together by water. The composition varies with the proportion of water and coarseness of the sand. The particles must have expanded under pressure, making our feet appear bigger than they are."

"But *his* are like a baby's!" Selina pointed out a homebound hawker, a basket of trinkets balanced on his head. Depressions, like dimples, mapped his route from one palm-shaded lounger to another. "How can sand stretch some prints and shrink others?"

"I'm sure there's a simple explanation."

"Fat footprints. Makes me feel a slob."

"You could diet."

"No chance. Not when there's lobster for dinner."


SHUFFLING ALONG THE check-in queue the next day, they found consolation in the prospect of their next trip.

"We've got another week's leave to use before the end of the year," said Selina. "How about Goa?"

"Why not?" said Sam. "If we can grab some cheap flights."

"I'll check online when we get back." Selina leafed through her passport. "Strange we haven't been already." She flicked past the pages of skewed immigration stamps to the identification details at the back. Her image, fusing her father's sharp nose and full lips with her mother's blue-black hair and slanting eyes, evoked a smile. "My ancestors would have had tiny footprints."

Sam lifted his gaze from the visa collection in his own passport. "What?"

"The Chinese bound women's feet to stop them growing." Selina recalled a pair of embroidered slippers she had seen in a museum in Shanghai. It was hard to believe they weren't designed for a doll. "It was considered erotic."

Sam nudged their trolley forward. "It was barbaric. Lucky for you civilisation's moved on."

THEIR HOMETOWN STREETS were decked with snow. Even in the fleeces they'd excavated from their luggage, they shivered as they dashed from the taxi to their door. But Selina wasn't so intent on escaping the cold she didn't notice the ridged imprints of their trainers, swollen to twice the normal size. "So it doesn't only happen with sand," she said, but Sam was too busy stoking the central heating boiler to respond.

HER MOTHER WANTED to hear about passion-fruit cocktails, beach barbecues and shoals of rainbow fish, but Selina manoeuvred the conversation around to Chinese traditions. Perhaps she had a great-grandmother whose infant feet had been fashioned to fit those dainty slippers?

Her mother cackled. "You think *your* ancestors were free to lounge around all day? Peasants had to work and for that they needed feet they could walk on."

SELINA DIDN'T RELISH the thought, but a diet would be preferable to being dogged by ugly footprints. When the snow melted she drove to the supermarket to stock up on low-calorie ready-meals.

Returning the trolley to the collection point after loading up the car, she felt lighter already. But turning back to her treasured white convertible, she startled. Four broad lines of tyre-tread ran from her wheels right across the car park. As if she'd parked in a muddy field.

TO AVOID HER car's fat footprints, Selina resolved to cycle to work. Sam thought she was mad. "It'll take you hours."

Selina set the alarm. "That's okay. I need the exercise."

Overtaking cars and buses, the journey was exhilarating. She arrived smug and sweaty, and had availed herself of the staff shower and tackled half her inbox by the time her colleagues emerged from the snarls of rush-hour traffic.

Her muscles ached for the first few days, but she hardly noticed. She was too excited by the discovery that her bicycle tyres left no mark.

NOR WERE THERE any footprints when she stepped onto the bathroom scales to monitor the progress of her diet. After dropping three kilos, her favourite trousers sagged at the waist. Sam suggested she wore a belt but she needed a whole new wardrobe.

Her mother didn't need persuading to accompany her to the shopping mall. She loved the colour-coded car parks, the up escalators and the down escalators, the bright lights that made it like New Year the whole year round. She loved the sanitised allusions to the traditional high-street: the signposts; the mock market stalls peddling baskets of dried flowers; the electric brazier roasting chestnuts she had no inclination to taste. She loved being able to wander from one shop to another with no weather to intervene.

Her mother held the bags while Selina grappled with buttons and zips. Each time she stepped out from the changing room, her mother would nod and smile. "Very beautiful. You buy it." Until Selina was tempted by a drill trouser suit with a stand-up collar. Her mother shuddered. "Horrible. Like Chairman Mao."

At lunch in the food court, Selina reflected on how different this was from the world her mother was born into. Yet her knowledge of that world was vague. Her mother had never been forthcoming about the past. Selina found it difficult to imagine the well-groomed woman wolfing down her pseudo-Mexican meal ever having worn a Mao suit.

"Mum, when you were my age …"

"I was never your age. I was born old."

"Be serious! I want to know what it was like. Growing up without …" Selina stumbled for the words, "… without *things*. Not even allowed to choose what to wear."

Her mother scooped up another forkful of chilli from the Styrofoam plate. "Why worry about such long-ago times? You should be happy. All these new clothes."

ALONG WITH THE clothes, Selina bought bicycle saddlebags. The following afternoon, after chaining her bike to the railing beside the supermarket entrance, she picked up a basket and meandered down the aisles. It was time to get serious about her diet. Fresh fruit and vegetables would be healthier than the ready-meals she'd been relying on.

Feeling virtuous, Selina loaded the produce onto the conveyor belt. Baby sweetcorn and mangetout peas. Peppers and courgettes. Apples, bananas and pears. Itching to get home to prepare her meal, she hoped there would be room for all her purchases in her panniers.

She glanced around idly as she waited for the person ahead to pay. Although the checkout area was busy, no one came to stand behind her. A woman with a trolley-load of tins and toilet rolls approached and veered off to join another queue. Nervously, Selina eyed the floor. Dirty fat footprints led all the way from the fruit and vegetable section to her size-four trainers.

Red-faced, she paid for her shopping and hurried out. Despite the weight of her shopping bags, she tried to tread lightly, but the footprints pursued her. She was almost in tears as she fumbled to release her bicycle lock. It didn't make sense. Regardless of her dieting and exercising, her footprints remained fat.

BACK HOME, SAM looked up from his new laptop. "Did it say if we need a visa? I can't find anything about it here."

"Did what say?"

"The site where you booked the flights for Goa."

"I haven't booked any flights."

"You're such a scatterbrain." He jabbed at the keyboard. "It's only a month away. We'll be lucky to get anything now."

Selina sighed. "I don't want to go."

"But it was your idea."

"I don't feel like it now."

Sam transmogrified into Pompous Englishman. "I suppose a woman's entitled to change her mind. Where *do* you feel like going?"

"I don't want to go anywhere. I'm too fat to go on holiday."

"That's crazy. Are you on your period or something?"

SELINA WONDERED IF she *was* going crazy. Who but a madwoman would believe she was being stalked by her footprints? Yet she wasn't the only one who'd seen them: Sam on the beach; the shoppers at the checkout.

It was less their existence than the lack of logic that threatened to send her over the edge. Her strappy Jimmy Choos left a larger print than her clumpy Wellingtons. Her attempts to shed weight lifting weights at the gym would be mocked by the obesity of the prints that followed her home. After a particularly humiliating evening almost fainting in the sauna because she didn't dare leave her seat, Selina decided drastic action was needed. She would give up her car.

Her mother was horrified. "It's like selling a kidney."

Sam was horrified. "It's throwing away your independence."

Selina was horrified herself. She used to love revving down country lanes in the summer with the top down. Driving the car to its new home, she wept so much she could have done with windscreen wipers for her eyes. But walking home in the rain there wasn't a shadow of a footprint on the pavement.

SHOPPING STILL MADE her nervous. Before leaving the house, she'd scrutinise her reflection in the wardrobe mirror. Looking supermodel slim in Lycra wouldn't necessarily prevent a sooty trail of footprints pursuing her down the aisles.

Each trip to the supermarket was like a commando raid. She'd park her bike round the back, grab a few packets of fruit and vegetables, and dart out. She didn't always come home with what she'd intended, but she discovered a hinterland of retail of which she was previously unaware.

At the back of the superstore, where the shelf stackers took their smoke breaks, were a row of bright-blue dumpsters. Spotting staff disgorge cardboard boxes into them, her curiosity was piqued. As soon as the staff returned to their posts, Selina leant her bike against the dumpster, and lifted the lid. Inside, it was like a well-stocked but disorganised larder, crammed with packets of food. Exactly the kind of produce she'd planned to buy: baby sweetcorn and mangetout peas from Kenya; peppers and courgettes from Israel; bananas from Costa Rica; apples and pears all the way from New Zealand. Pristine in its wrapping, the food looked fresh, albeit with use-by dates for the previous day.

"It's stealing," said Sam later.

"Recycling," Selina corrected. "It was only going to waste."

"I can't see the point of economising," he said. "It's not as if you're saving up for anything. You won't even go on holiday."

Selina couldn't see the point herself. Or couldn't put it into words that would convince Sam. "It just seems the right thing to do."

"It's not normal," said Sam. "Do you think you could be depressed?"

IT WAS TRUE she'd lost interest in the activities that had defined her. Was she still the same person without her enthusiasm for travel and shopping, or even the gym? While her increasing bank balance brought no particular pleasure, she resisted being diagnosed as depressed.

Then it struck her that, if she wasn't *spending* money, she didn't need so much coming in. She asked her boss if she could go part-time.

For the Pompous Englishman, this was further evidence of derangement. "What will you do when you can't afford the next generation phone?"

"I'll do without, along with most of the world's population."

Sam sniffed. "People use mobiles everywhere. Even in the heart of rural China. Ask your mother."

"My mother's as bad as you. Always after the latest gadget."

"Anyway," said Sam, "you'll be bored at home on your own."

"No I won't. I'll take up dressmaking. Clear a bit of lawn and grow my own veg. Sit in the sun and read."

"You'll have no money for books."

"I'll use the library."

Pompous Englishman stroked his screen.

THE FAINTER HER footprints, the more Selina fretted that she and Sam were drifting apart. "We don't want the same things anymore," she told her mother. She found him too frivolous; he complained she'd become obsessed.

"You need a holiday," said her mother. "Time together with no-one else around."

Selina shook her head. "I get a panic attack even contemplating boarding a plane."

"It *is* possible to have a holiday in your own country. Remember we took you to Scotland when you were small?"

Cosy evenings in their simple log cabin, her father telling stories by candlelight as they warmed their toes around fire: the memory made her feel safe and loved even now. With days exploring rock pools and building sandcastles, she hadn't missed running water or TV.

SAM REFUSED TO spend an entire day getting there. He'd hire a car at the airport; Selina had to do the four-hundred-mile bus trip alone.

On arrival at their cabin, she found the door locked and a hire car parked alongside. Calling Sam's name, her voice was swallowed by the breeze.

She couldn't let their relationship end this way. Abandoned by Pompous Englishman at an out-of-season holiday home. Selfish Englishman, not caring enough to hang around to greet her, to run her a hot bath.

Dumping her backpack on the veranda, she followed a trail of muddy fat footprints across a field towards the beach.

Despite her snatched sleep on the overnighter, she no longer felt tired. Twenty-four hours apart and she'd really missed Sam; missed his smell, his touch, his pompous English voice. She ran, placing her feet in the oversized prints. The mud gave way to sand as the path curled through clumps of marram grass, pricking her legs through her jeans.

Cresting a dune, she paused to catch her breath. Below, the cinnamon sand arced around the bay. Apart from the sanderlings pattering along the spume, the beach appeared deserted. Then she saw him, far in the distance, a lone figure strolling by the water's edge. She was tempted to race across the beach to wrap her arms around him, but how could she let her prints defile the surface of the sand?

But she couldn't remain where she was, her feet forming roots in the dunes. Her mother's voice echoed in her head, insisting progress was an unstoppable tide.

Squinting against the low sun, she watched Sam's footprints disappear where the water met the sand. Each step carved a crater, but each wave lapped it clean.

Not daring to hope too much, she descended to the beach and slipped off her shoes and socks. Tentatively, she placed her feet in Sam's podgy footprints, sucked up the fat through her bare soles as if channelling the power of the waves.

# I Want Doesn't Get

I WANTED CHEESECAKE and a chocolate fountain but I didn't want to pop the button on my best black skirt. I wanted a bronze plaque on a bench beside the bowling green and souvenir service sheets on embossed paper with a photo at the front.

I wanted a poem in the paper but my sister thought it sentimental and swapped it for prose. I wanted rosewood with brass handles but she insisted plywood would suffice. I wanted lilies but my sister didn't want the smell.

I wanted a spa with a grand conservatory but my sister booked the function room at the local pub. I wanted "Abide With Me" but my sister can't abide it. I don't want an argument but I'm sick of being overruled.

*I want doesn't get* our mother used to say, so I tucked my wants away while awaiting my reward. I watched my sister *get*, and plenty, so why did I miss out?

I would've wanted to go to college if I'd got the grades. I

would've wanted a white wedding if anyone had proposed. I would've wanted to travel if I wasn't so timid. I would've wanted my own life if Mum hadn't wanted me in hers.

I want a glass of sherry but I'm drinking tea. I don't want to be trapped in a corner by my mother's friends from church. I want someone to ask how I'm feeling as if they want to know. I want to be born again in my sister's skin.

I want her to forget where she left her handbag. I want her not to notice her keys have gone astray. We both know she can't get into her penthouse apartment without them. She can't unlock her brand-new coupé.

I want her not to guess where I hid them. But I want doesn't always get. So I'm learning to generate my own getting. It can't be difficult; my sister's done it all her life.

I don't care whether *she* learns anything in the process. I don't care if she finds her keys or not. But she'll have to dig deep to retrieve them. Because I wanted to bury them within the folds of our mother's shroud.

# My Beautiful Smile

I'M WALKING PAST the plate glass windows of the Wellcome Foundation when they hit me with it. Above the roar of the traffic along Euston Road, cocky as a novelty ring-tone: "Cheer up! It might never happen."

I don't flinch. I know what they're after and they're not going to get it. I keep my head down and walk on. Make out I haven't heard.

If I had a pound for every time I've had that said to me ... I could pay for the operation in cash.

I wish I had the guts to march back and smack them in the mouth. Instead, I do my mindfulness meditation as I walk along, listing everything I see that's grey. My boots, my scarf, my leggings. Tarmac, pavement, sky. You know where you are with neutrals. My second favourite colour is beige.

The ash falling from the cigarettes of the lads outside the Wellcome. My treacherous handbag. My hoodie. Roll on the day my hair goes grey like my mum's.

It would never have happened if she'd let me borrow her car. Shielded by a screen, letting the lights take care of my non-verbals. As gallant as a curtsy going: "After you!" Or as sour as a clenched fist and a scowl: "I was here first!" Snug behind the wheel, I marvel at the vehicle's virtuosity.

But Mum doesn't trust me to drive in central London, so this week and last I came down by train. I told her I was meeting a friend at the National Portrait Gallery. When she wrinkled her nose, I said it was a girl I'd met on the chat room. Mine must be the only mother in the world who wishes her daughter would spend more time online.

It wasn't so bad on the train. Both times I bagsied a seat on my own, with the back of the seat in front like a barricade. Unfortunately the Tube wasn't so cosy. That's why I decided to walk from St Pancras this time. It's not a great trek to Harley Street. But I hadn't bargained for the men on their smoke break.

It was too wet to walk when I came for my assessment. I took the Bakerloo line two stops to Great Portland Street. At first, it was fine. Grey faces turned in on themselves. Ears plugged into iPods or lost in the music of the train. Eyes fixated on newsprint or thin air. No one giving a monkey's about anyone else. Until a woman flopped onto the seat opposite at Euston Square.

She'd just made it on board before the doors closed. She wriggled into place, burning for some acknowledgement of her achievement. I kept my head down, intent upon a crease in the grey leather of my bag. I had my iPhone inside, but I didn't think I'd get a signal. Besides, I've moved on from Instagram, Facebook and Twitter. Those emoticons so beloved of my mother make me want to scream.

As the train slowed down for the station, I stood up and shuffled into the aisle. That's when I did the stupid thing: noticed the woman opposite had a handbag identical to mine.

Of course, she noticed my noticing. It was the connection she'd been after from the moment she sat down. To underline the point, she cocked her head, raised her bag and grinned.

A lorry driver, seeing another truck approaching, will flash his lights. But I wasn't in the car and all I had to offer was a blank stare.

THE CLINIC WAS done out in beige, although they'd probably call it oatmeal. But the decor made the prodding and the prying somewhat easier to bear.

Once the tests were over, the doctor pronounced his verdict. "We can't give you a smile you can turn on and off. You can't activate a muscle if there isn't an existing nerve. But we can tighten you up around the mouth. Still a fixed expression, but you wouldn't look so glum."

It was what I'd expected. Even so, the emptiness doubled inside me.

He widened his eyes. "If you decide to go ahead, we'll do some mock-ups on the computer first. There's a degree of choice over how big a smile you end up with."

I knew exactly the smile I wanted. I'd been scrawling red crayon over photos of myself since I was four years old. But I'd been around hospitals enough to know how to play the game. "That sounds great."

"Right. Have a think about it and let me know next week."

"Why wait till next week? I've already made up my mind."

The doctor patted my hand. "Most people appreciate some time to think it over."

"I've been thinking it over my entire life."

"Then one more week won't make much difference." He twitched his cheek muscles. "Go home and talk it through with your parents."

"I don't need their permission." My date of birth was on all the paperwork. "I'm not a child!"

He arched his eyebrows. "Of course not. But they could help you weigh up the advantages and disadvantages."

"Disadvantages?"

He narrowed his eyes. "A smile you can never switch off. Looking cheerful when you're feeling sad."

"I'm willing to take that risk." I could have explained about the woman on the Tube. Yet, with his flexible face, the doctor had as much chance of seeing it my way as my parents. "At least I'd get it right half the time."

His jaw dropped slightly. "I'm going to arrange an appointment for you to see our counsellor."

"I don't need therapy."

He pursed his lips. "I can't operate until I'm convinced you've worked this through."

"I've got to be vetted? When I'm paying?"

"It's in the practice guidelines."

I pointed at my face with both hands. "What the hell does a do-gooding counsellor know about living with this?"

The doctor pulled back the corners of his mouth. "You'd be surprised."

THE COUNSELLOR SMILES as she collects me from the waiting area. Smiles as she directs me to a comfy chair.

I've been meaning to play it cool, but before I know it I've launched into the story of the handbag woman on the Tube. "People keep pushing for a reaction."

"You didn't like having something in common? Or that she wanted you to acknowledge it?"

Her questions niggle. I change the subject, jabbering on about the smokers outside the Wellcome Foundation. "You'd think after twenty-three years I'd have learnt to avert my face."

She smiles. "Why did you look at them?"

"I didn't fancy them if that's what you're thinking."

"Not at all," she says. "I was thinking of something more fundamental."

There's a tickle in my chest as I remember. "I thought it was amusing. The incongruity, you know. Three men smoking outside this flashy centre for health care research."

Again, she smiles. "You wanted to share the joke?"

"But I just looked gormless."

"You couldn't share the moment because you couldn't smile."

"Exactly!" This is going okay. "Which is why I've got to have the surgery. To come across as a human being."

The counsellor doesn't speak. Her smile says it all.

"If I had a pound for every time my mum's told me I'm fine as I am ... I know my parents love me, but it isn't enough." I think again about the handbag woman. "You never get used to it. You'd expect, when it's something you're born with, it would seem normal to you, even if others find it odd. But I hate it. The reaction from strangers most of all. They seek out my face and it's just a mask. It makes them uncomfortable, and they retaliate. Come out with something to bounce the bad feeling back to me." I take a tissue from a box on the low table. "No one ever says, *Oh poor you, it must be so hard having Moebius.* It's always, *Cheer up! It might never happen.*"

She watches me, still smiling. "It's so isolating."

I'm impressed she's caught on so quickly. And a little scared. Even my parents struggle to understand. "When I was a baby, it took a while to get a diagnosis. They thought I had a learning disability." I stop, startled by a new idea. Not even an idea, but a feeling. Not quite a feeling, but a space. An emptiness, a hole, a lack. I grope for the words to explain it. "My parents ... when I couldn't give them what they expected ... what they needed ... they must have felt as scared and confused as the strangers I pass in the street." I don't bother with the tissues, I let the tears dribble. I'm hardly aware of the counsellor now, sitting across from me as I confront who I am. And who I've been. The infant whose mother frowns when I need her to smile, pouts when I need her to delight in me. "I've felt so lonely. My whole sodding life."

I stare at the oatmeal walls, wailing for what I never knew I'd missed. It's going to take more than a surgical smile to fix that.

After a while, I run out of tears. I don't know what I

think anymore, don't know what I feel. But something's shifted. Lurking at the bottom of that deep dark hole, there's an extra piece of me. I look up at the counsellor. It doesn't matter that I can't produce a smile.

She's sitting exactly as before, back straight, legs slightly apart, hands resting in her lap. And she's smiling, her face a mask of eternal pleasantness.

"Oh my God!" My hand goes to my mouth, although I've no expression to hide. If I were in the car, I'd be tempted to flash my headlights.

Or maybe not. It strikes me that in all my years of longing, I've never questioned what constitutes a smile.

She tilts her head, still wearing that inane grin. "Yes?"

I pick up my bag. There's nothing more this place can give me. Not now I can plunge into the hollowness inside me, and touch the edges of my beautiful smile.

# Doctoring

ARTHUR JEKYLL WAS a doctor. Of course he was, how could he be otherwise, when both his parents, and their parents before them, had been doctors? What other options did he have when all the terrors and comforts of his formative years had been accompanied by a heavy dose of familial doctoring?

The general consensus at the hospital was that Arthur was a good doctor: one who could soothe the most fretful patient with the kiss of his stethoscope. Nurses abandoned all hope of a social life for the chance to work alongside him, happy to negotiate their attendance at weddings and school sports days around Dr Jekyll's duty roster. Managers were emboldened to kick off their shoes and turn away from their computers to contemplate the flowerbeds in the car-park after reviewing his monthly stats.

Arthur strode the hospital corridors with the air of a man who was fulfilling his destiny. And doing it well.

Smiling. Until one of those viruses that do the rounds each winter wormed its way through his defences and he had to take a few days off sick.

So what? Doctors get sick like anyone else. Even those, like Arthur, with doctoring antibodies circulating in their bloodstream since infancy. And it was only your bog-standard flu: unpleasant and debilitating but no big deal for a not-too-unfit man of forty-three. A few days in his pyjamas watching mindless sitcoms should have seen to it. Should have.

Battling his aching limbs between sheets soggy with sweat, the thought came to Arthur that he was tired of doctoring. This thought surprised and unnerved him but, once it was out, he could hardly unthink it. The more he thought, the more he realised that he hated doctoring, and everything about it. He hated the patients who would piss on him and shit on him until he had exorcised the pestilence from their bodies. He hated his retinue of puppy-eyed students who sucked like leeches on his every word and gesture. He hated the bureaucrats who could flip from friend to fuehrer at the drop of a Department of Health directive. "I want out," he told his wife when she brought him his scrambled eggs on toast. "I'll do anything: deliver the mail, sweep the streets. I just can't go back to that job."

Sheila made sympathetic noises as she wiped his brow with a flannel. But even if she worked full-time it wouldn't be enough to pay the mortgage and keep their two kids in pizzas and videogames. "Let's discuss it when you're better," she said.

For all his delirium, Arthur knew he couldn't *get* better

until the doctoring problem was sorted. So Sheila came up with a compromise: Arthur would keep his job but, every other weekend, instead of carrying out his duties as husband and father, he would do his own thing. It didn't matter what, as long as it took his mind off doctoring and didn't entail breaking faith with his marriage vows. Sheila would look after the kids.

Arthur spent the last day of his sick-leave musing on how he'd use this gift. Any hobbies had long been cast aside to make space for studying, interminable hours on-call and, later, changing the occasional nappy. So it was not without anxiety, and some embarrassment, that he kissed Sheila and the kids goodbye on the first Friday evening of his part-time new life. But the farther he drove away from their neat suburban house the lighter he began to feel. The burden of his responsibilities slipped off him with each mile of tarmac. His weekend in an anonymous Travelodge under an assumed name – his associations to Mr Hyde were of a damp wooden hut from which men with binoculars could spy on the wildlife, rather than the dangerous alter ego of his namesake in the story – was as relaxing as a holiday in some tropical paradise. Until that weekend, Arthur had not known the meaning of the word bliss. Nothing could match the feeling it gave him: not his graduation; not his wedding; nor even the birth of his two beautiful children. It was like a shot of morphine, without the disturbing side-effects.

His excursions were soon incorporated into the family routine. On alternate Friday evenings, Arthur drove off in the Mercedes, bummed around, and came home again forty-eight hours later. He didn't go anywhere in particular, just any place where no one knew him as Dr Jekyll. First he stayed in cheap hotels, then in youth hostel dormitories, and then – inspired by an unusually warm and dry summer – he slept out in the open, with a large bin-bag to ward off the morning dew. This wasn't about saving money; more seeking out a lifestyle as different as possible to that bequeathed to him by his parents and grandparents. He parked the car in some out of the way place and set off walking with little thought about where he'd end up. As he grew more confident, he added amusing challenges: surviving all weekend on whatever money he could make busking (not much); posing as a deaf-mute who didn't know sign language (serenely isolating); avoiding all objects and places beginning with D (an intellectual version of not stepping on the cracks in the pavement).

Sheila saw their marriage strengthen and the children blossom as Arthur became more contented. She conspired in protecting this other life: scouring the charity shops for I'm-not-a-doctor clothing; absolving him from the responsibility of phoning home; and concocting clever cover-stories lest friends or family should try to make contact while he was incognito.

Furthermore, his unconventional mini-breaks seemed to make Arthur an even better doctor, were that possible. He might have arrived home on a Sunday evening looking and smelling like a bath-phobic down-and-out, but at eight o'clock the next morning he'd be sporting his white coat and stethoscope with extra conviction. Having found the perfect balance between freedom and responsibility, his work became a joy.

When the post of Medical Director fell vacant, colleagues queued to encourage Arthur to apply. And why not? He was popular, and possessed the necessary experience and qualifications. He submitted his application without a word to Sheila. He wanted his promotion to surprise her, a vindication of his unorthodox hobby. And, on the slight chance of his not being offered the post, her ignorance would shield her from disappointment.

The interview was scheduled for nine o'clock on a Monday morning. The old Arthur would have spent the weekend doing a dry-run with a colleague, and swotting over the latest policy documents from the Department of Health. But the new Arthur believed a clean break the best preparation, a retreat into his other identity in order to return completely refreshed.

On Friday evening he set off down the motorway as usual, Woody Guthrie on the CD player, and nothing about his person to identify him as Dr Jekyll, would-be Medical Director. After sleeping on the back seat of the Mercedes in a secluded coastal car-park, he hid his keys among a pile of rocks and set off walking at first light.

As he tramped the cliff-top paths in the drizzle, he waited for the usual sense of euphoria to engulf him. It didn't happen. He'd successfully sloughed off Dr Jekyll but neither the chorus of seagulls nor the whisper of the waves could conjure the spirit of his alter ego from his hiding place. But he wasn't overly downhearted. He'd spent enough weekends avoiding Dr Jekyll to have faith in their capacity to revitalise him, regardless of how actively Mr Hyde might play a part.

Arthur spent a restless Saturday night under the inadequate protection of a municipal bandstand dreaming of the candlewick bedspreads and Full English Breakfasts of his childhood holiday B&Bs. Awaking cold and hungry, with a throbbing above his right temple presaging a headache, he had little enthusiasm for rambling the next day. He decided to take a train to a station near where he'd left the car to be home in time to help the kids with their homework and scan the job description before tomorrow's interview.

It didn't worry Arthur that he had no money for a ticket. Small trains rarely had a guard at weekends. Were he to encounter one, he would say he'd lost his wallet. He recalled a colleague's tale of this very situation en route to a conference in Brighton. The guard had simply taken his name and address and he'd paid when his wallet turned up in the laundry basket a few days later.

Boarding the train, Arthur sat beside a woman in a shiny raincoat. She sniffed the air and promptly squeezed in beside a pregnant teenager across the aisle. Arthur shrugged and settled into the fuggy warmth of the carriage. He was looking forward to seeing Sheila and the kids again.

He didn't realise he'd fallen asleep until he felt someone shaking him by the shoulder. "Ticket please."

Arthur explained he didn't have a ticket, nor his wallet, but would happily leave his name and address.

The guard frowned. "I wasn't born yesterday."

Still half asleep, Arthur struggled to make the transition back to the rule-bound world of Dr Jekyll. "Pardon?"

"How would I know it was the right address?"

Feigning absorption in their newspapers, their babies or

limp sandwiches from the station buffet, the other passengers listened in.

"I'd give you my word," said Arthur.

The guard rolled his eyes. "How do I know you even have an address?"

"No fixed abode, more like," said his ex-neighbour, the shiny-raincoat woman.

"Look, you can trust me, I'm a doctor."

People laughed. Well, it was a bit of a cliché.

"And I'm the Prime Minister," said the guard.

A woman twisted around from the seat ahead. She smiled at Arthur with tangerine-painted lips. "Show him some ID."

Arthur slapped at his second-hand fisherman's jacket and dirty ill-fitting trousers, trying to conjure up some doctor-documentation from imaginary pockets. "I don't have any." It was a pity he'd left his car keys behind, although the guard may not have been reassured by the tramp's access to a Mercedes.

The train slowed as it approached the station.

"Listen, sir," said the guard, "let's have no more fuss. You get off here and we'll say no more about it."

Arthur glanced out of the window as the station sign came into view. Still two more stops before the one he wanted. He grabbed his rucksack, while the woman from the seat in front nodded in encouragement. But when he tried to stand, his head pounded and a wave of nausea overwhelmed him. Even if he were to stumble off the train, it would be an arduous trek to his car in this state. "You could phone my wife. She'd vouch for me."

The guard sighed. "Wait there." As the train came to a halt, the guard left to oversee the passengers getting on and off. He returned as the train started up again. "Where's your phone, then?"

"I haven't got one."

The friendly woman with the orange lipstick passed Arthur her mobile. Struggling to focus, he keyed in his home number.

The guard snatched the phone from him. "I'll do the talking." A pause, while passengers rustled newspapers, jiggled babies and chewed. "Ah, good afternoon, Mrs ...?" He scowled at Arthur.

"Jekyll."

"Dr Jekyll, that's a good one." The locals hadn't seen such entertainment since the Punch and Judy tents graced the sands. "Mrs Jekyll? I'm sorry to bother you but I'm trying to locate your husband. Is he at home this afternoon? ... Dr Jekyll's away at a conference, you say?" The guard nodded at Arthur's friend with the tangerine lips. "Flying into Heathrow late tonight? ... From the Seychelles?" He raised his eyebrows in the direction of the shiny-raincoat woman. "I wish I had his job! ... No thanks, no need to leave a message. ... Goodbye, Mrs Jekyll and thank you."

The woman with orange lipstick shook her head as she took the phone from the guard. "He needs help. You can't put him off the train in that condition."

"Don't worry," said the guard. "I'll radio ahead to the next station. Get the police to deal with him."

As the guard scuttled off, Arthur reassured himself that

the police would have more important matters to attend to than an off-duty doctor boarding a train without the means to purchase a ticket. When the shiny-raincoat woman met his gaze, he felt brave enough to wink at her.

She turned away with the kind of face his children made when Sheila had allowed some unpalatable food – olives, maybe, or unadulterated vegetables – to encroach upon their end of the dining table. Arthur was amused to realise that, to his fellow-passengers, Dr Jekyll was a far less credible character than Mr Hyde.

Tangerine Lips responded to his laughter with an expression of concern. "If I were you, I'd get my story straight before the next station. The police won't take kindly to your playing games."

"Impersonating a doctor," Shiny Raincoat told Pregnant Teenager. "That's against the law."

Arthur tried to summon up his memories of half-watched police dramas to envisage the probable fate of a smelly vagrant posing as a doctor to avoid paying his fare. Surely the worst that could happen would be a night in the cells deprived of his belt and bootlaces. He'd use his one phone call to apologise to Sheila for not being around to see the kids to bed.

All of which would be fine, were it not for the appointment panel assembling in the boardroom eighty miles away before the police would have sent him on his way. If he could get a message to them, they might reschedule. After all, his interview was merely a formality.

The stumbling block was the single phone call; he'd have to ask Sheila to forward his apologies to the panel. He hated to dump more problems on her. He hated to spoil the surprise.

The train began to decelerate. "Any sign of the police on the platform?" Shiny Raincoat asked her neighbour.

Arthur felt her disapproval nagging at his temples. He wondered whether being escorted from the train by the police would amount to a criminal record. Were that the case, it wouldn't be only his promotion at risk, but his entire career. He couldn't afford a night in the cells; he'd have to rise above his shabby clothes and convince them of his bona fides.

"Four of them," said Pregnant Teenager, pressing her face against the window as the train approached the station. "No escape."

Arthur thought how lucky he was to have a supportive wife. But, like anyone, she'd have her limits. Might she be less tolerant of his alternative lifestyle once she saw it could jeopardise their livelihood? No one would blame Sheila were she to cancel his weekend leave.

Under his second-hand lumberjack shirt, Arthur felt sweat trickle down his back. Because of the irresponsible Mr Hyde, his professional life was in peril. But without him, the ambitious Dr Jekyll might expire from a doctoring overdose.

The train came to a halt. Tangerine Lips turned around. "You've got to cooperate," she said. "Tell them your real name and everything will be all right."

Arthur wanted to believe her. Life would be a lot less complicated with just the one name. Perhaps the time had come to jettison his superfluous identity.

A policeman entered the carriage and immediately

picked out the troublesome tramp from among the passengers. He strolled down the carriage towards Mr Hyde, looking stern.

Arthur sat back in his seat, almost euphoric as he waited for the constable. And for release from his baneful doctoring.

# No Hard Feelings

EMILY WOULD NOT have followed that path if she'd known it would lead to the graveyard. All those dead people lovingly remembered; all those people who might have been right bastards when they were alive.

A cleft between shoulder-high stinging nettles, it had looked so promising when she'd stumbled upon it on the way home from the day centre. She'd imagined it snaking through field and forest to a runaway's secret den. She'd imagined a skinny teen offering her a mug of muddy tea brewed in a treacle tin in exchange for not betraying his whereabouts. Instead she'd pitched up in a churchyard barely a hundred metres from the main road.

Once there, she felt obliged to wander around the graves, acting as if this had been her destination, although there were only birds around to judge her. Besides, she had a couple of hours to kill before teatime: she might as well be bored here as in her room.

She knew the feelings she was meant to have in such places. Didn't she recite a thesaurus worth of synonyms for sadness every week? The counsellors were nice enough, but hypocritical. *Claim your feelings*, they said. *Embrace your emotions!* As if feelings were groceries waiting to be bagged at the supermarket checkout. But as soon as anyone showed a smidgen of genuine agitation, they freaked out. *Calm down! Take deep breaths!* And if that didn't douse the flames of rampaging sentiment, they went knocking on the psychiatrist's office door.

Emily took note of their insincerity, because she was a hypocrite too. She filled in her charts, circling the words for the emotions she might have experienced that day, had she known how to feel. There were no words in the English language for what Emily had seen, no answering echo in another's soul. But she was smart enough to lay claim to the feelings that would pay for her room and board at the hostel. Whenever her review was scheduled, she threw in a *despondent* and an *anguished* to safeguard her place.

Wandering between the graves, she rubbed at her forearms. Even though she'd pushed down her sleeves to negotiate the nettles, her skin stung. On her inner arm, tiny red welts had sprung up among the network of scars, like station stops on a rail map. Pain was the sole authentic feeling Emily knew.

Worn letters on mildewed stones, and weeds growing through the gravel: she'd stumbled upon the old part of the cemetery. Cracked urns atop graves sunken at the belly and edged with shattered stones, like the rubbled remains of an earthquake. Then, smack between a Percy and a Gladys, she found herself or, at least, her namesake, an Emily Blyth who'd died fifty years and a day before she herself was born.

She'd have a story to tell that evening at the hostel. Curtains drawn, a candle at her chin, she'd spook them, or have them quake with laughter. *And then a hand reached out and grabbed me by the ankle.* Terror was a feeling she'd circle sometimes on her chart.

A dog barked. Emily turned to see a woman walk a poodle towards a gap in the hedge. She thought to warn her about the nettles but other words spilled from her lips. "I've found my own grave!"

The woman seemed to shiver as she hurried out of sight. Emily didn't need a checklist to decipher whether it was from fear of a ghost or disgust at her dishevelled state. At least she had no need to worry about dirtying her jeans as she made a daybed of Emily Blyth's grave; headstone as a backrest, legs stretched out in front. Laughing, she clawed a clutch of soil and stones to rub between her fingers.

From her pocket, she took a printed sheet and a pencil. Resting the paper on her leg, she began to circle a random selection of phoney feelings. And stopped. She didn't want to lie anymore. She didn't have to. Something had changed inside her.

She'd been dead inside, like a ghost, like her namesake, and it was only with the numbness in retreat that she could claim it. For as long as she could remember she'd been this way and now, like a storybook granny picking up her dirty socks and apple cores and scrunched up tissues, old Emily Blyth had taken her deadness from her. She couldn't say what she was without it. It wasn't anything on her printed sheet.

She wouldn't share her story with the girls at the hostel. She wouldn't tell the counsellors she was ready to move on. Not-dead-inside was a treasure too precious to reveal to another living soul. But that didn't matter, now she had a grave to visit. Next time she'd borrow a trowel from the day centre and tidy Emily Blyth's plot.

# Sensitive Skin

SOMEONE TOUCHED HER once. The shock sent her spine into spasm and the heat raised a welt on her skin. For weeks it festered, raw and oozing pus. When even a gossamer-thin garment inflamed it, she hid, naked, indoors.

When she healed, she threaded her coat with thorns and laced her shoes with razor wire. Safe in her prickly carapace, she ventured far from home. Enchanted by new tastes and textures, she forgot her former fears. The wounded wretch became a bold adventuress, with curiosity her only guide.

In a foreign land, she met a man whose gentle words and loving gaze revived her withered heart. Each time they met affection deepened until she led him upstairs to her bed. She let him kiss her, bade him undress her, but he refused to stay.

No-one could touch her now. No lover wrap her in a warm embrace. No friend or foe would dare come near her. The spiky coat of confidence had melded with her skin.

# Rebekah's Foreskin

"**M**UMMY MUMMY MUMMY, look what I can do, Mummy!"

I turn, splashing bubbles onto the bath mat, poised to express wonder at my three-year-old's latest accomplishment.

Dressed in nothing but his Mickey Mouse socks, his grin accentuated by a smear of ketchup, Reuben makes a stage of the doorframe. Taking his infant penis between finger and thumb, he twists it like a corkscrew. He holds it in position and awaits my applause.

My golden-haired boy looks at me and waits. Some Victorian prude has taken command of my face and he sees, once again, that Mummy isn't pleased. He lets go of his penis as if it were dog poo and rubs his hand against his thigh.

I shake my head, willing my features into a more accepting pose. "Come on, Treasure. Let's get you in the bath."

I don't want him growing up with a complex.

FROM THE BEGINNING, I'd assumed Dave was Jewish in the way I was Church of England: religion a label for parents to bestow on their children before we were old enough to protest. Later, it came to represent order and security when ticking the boxes on official forms.

Dave didn't wear a skullcap or plead exemption from Saturday trips to the supermarket. I'd assumed he managed his religion like I managed my curly hair and myopia: part of my persona that was beyond argument. An integral part, a part that might require certain adjustments – like hair straighteners and glasses or contact lenses – but beyond that, easily forgotten. Relative to questions of party politics, credit-card usage and putting the lid back on the toothpaste, I'd assumed that the box we ticked under religion would have little impact on our relationship.

When we visited his parents in Hendon, the part of Dave that linked him to his tick-box was more apparent. Yet this didn't seem qualitatively different from his wondering if my family had shares in *Specsavers*. But better. Loads better. While my parents would welcome in the weekend slumped in front of the television with a takeaway, Rebekah, Dave's mother, would set silver candlesticks on the dining table alongside the braided challah bread. Simon, his father, would pour sweet wine and bless us all with incantations that carried a six thousand-year-old pedigree.

If marrying Dave meant more of this, I wasn't grumbling. Having studied anthropology, I respected the social function of ritual. On that basis, Dave's tick-box trumped mine. While his puberty had been broadcast with a bar mitzvah, mine had earned me a discrete portion of the bathroom shelf to stow my tampons.

I'd assumed we could treat our backgrounds like a pick-and-mix: selecting the best from each and filling the gaps with rituals of our own creation. So there was no conflict between church and synagogue messing up our wedding plans. I walked down the aisle in a smart hotel, posing for photos in the grounds while the staff worked to convert the wedding chapel into a banqueting hall. Our parents joked about the countdown to their first grandchild in a quiet, understated manner. Both sides too busy with their own lives to have any pretensions on ours.

Going for the scan, we were nervous. At that stage, it was hard to believe our baby was real. Unlike many of our friends, who'd tried for years, I'd conceived easily. Too easily, perhaps. Were we ready to become parents?

"So is it a boy or girl?" Dave asked, once assured all the vital organs were in place. I'd assumed, like me, he'd have no preference. But it would help to know. The thing growing inside me would feel more human if it had a gender.

When the technician pointed out the squiggle between the baby's legs, it struck me I'd been mistaken in some of my assumptions. Still, Dave made a show of hiding his disappointment.

Afterwards, he drove me back to work. He parked outside and switched off the engine. "You know my mother will want him circumcised?"

"Don't be daft." I laughed, dashing off to show my colleagues the blurred Polaroid of the creature that was to become our son.

ONCE WE KNEW that we needed to consult the blue book rather than the pink, I was ready to discuss what we were going to call our baby. "How about Isaiah? Jacob? Or Reuben?" Those Old Testament names had been fashionable for some years, and I liked the idea of maintaining a link with his Jewish heritage.

Dave had other matters to discuss. "What about getting him circumcised?"

He'd just cooked dinner: spinach ravioli in tomato sauce. He had a glass of merlot. I had soda and lime. "You don't really want to, do you?"

"It's what Jews do."

"Can't we wait till he's born to think about it?"

"We need to decide in advance. It's done on the eighth day."

I felt the foetus wriggle in my belly. "So young."

"My mother keeps asking."

"Rebekah? What's it got to do with her?"

Dave's fork clattered onto the table, splattering the beechwood laminate with pasta sauce. "She's going to be his grandmother."

"We're his parents."

Dave drained his glass. Poured himself another. "Family means something in our culture."

I looked longingly at the wine bottle as I sipped my soda and lime. "You never used to have a culture."

I DREW HIS penis into my mouth, stroked the tip with my

tongue the way he liked. It would be stupid to say I'd never noticed Dave was circumcised. Like saying he'd never noticed the way my hair sprang into curls in the rain. But sex was different with every partner. And the same. The presence or absence of a foreskin was just one of a range of factors shaping the experience. And I'd never approached my love-life with a checklist. Perhaps my husband thought I should.

Afterwards, we held hands as we lay, half dozing. "You want him to look like you, is that it?"

"Never had any complaints."

"But surgery at eight days old!"

"I wouldn't call it surgery."

"What then?"

"I don't know. Tradition, maybe. I wish I could make you understand."

I squeezed his hand. "We could find out a bit more about it."

"I'll ask my mother."


REBEKAH PHONED. "WE'VE not seen you for a while. Why not come over for Shabbat?"

"We'd love to but we've got so much on. Including clearing out the spare room for the nursery."

"Dave tells me you're going to get the baby circumcised. I can't tell you how pleased I am. Simon, too. It's so important for a boy to know where he comes from."

"Well, yes, but ..."

"You're not going to change your mind again?" Her tone embraced a lifetime of Jewish-mother jokes and nothing of the easy-going woman who came to our wedding. "I thought you respected our culture. You know, when Dave said he was marrying out …"

I stroked my belly. "It's the process. I don't know enough about it."

"It's quite natural. Every baby boy has it done."

"But what if ours didn't? You wouldn't mind too much?"

A long silence, oozing with self-righteousness.

"Rebekah?"

A stifled sob. "Let's not think about that right now."

"Dave said they don't use anaesthetic."

"Of course not. Far too risky at such a young age."

"Won't it hurt him?" My voice came out so small I had to repeat myself.

Rebekah laughed. "Is that what you've been making such a fuss about? It's just a little snip. Do you think I'd have had my boys circumcised if it was going to hurt? He won't feel a thing."

I blushed at discussing my husband's penis with his mother. How did she know it didn't hurt? Even fish, caught on the line, feel pain.


THESE DAYS, WITH the internet, there's no excuse for not knowing. I googled circumcision, and there it all was. Guidance on postoperative care for men and boys undergoing treatment for a tight foreskin, and international campaigns against female genital mutilation. Adverts for clinics competing on price, and manifestoes from so-called survivors seeking retribution. My eyes stung.

I could've refined my search, but my pregnancy had reached the stage where my back ached if I sat too long at the computer, and the juxtaposition of genitals with surgery made me queasy. And the skirting board in the nursery was still unpainted.

It remained unpainted when I went into labour. Thirty-six hours of pain and confusion. At first, I was afraid the baby would die. Later, I was afraid I would. In the end, I prayed for us both to die. Until he took his first cry and the ordeal was over.

My parents and Dave's parents came to the hospital to hold him and to smell him and to kiss and admire him, while I flopped on the pillows, exhausted.

On the eighth day, we strapped Reuben into his car seat and drove to the synagogue. They seemed to think it strange it was just three of us. With Reuben in his arms, Dave followed the mohel into the room. I stayed outside curled up against the sound of my son's wailing. Then we got back in the car and drove home.

For a couple of weeks, until the wound was healed, I couldn't bear to look. Dave had to bath him and change his nappy. I said it would help him bond with the baby.

It looks fine now, of course, and there's no evidence of ill effects. He's a normal healthy little boy who enjoys doing gymnastics with his penis. Playing with his plastic boats in a bubble bath with his mother looking on.

While I'm patting him dry, the landline rings.

Reuben wriggles on my lap. "Phone, Mummy."

"Daddy's downstairs. He'll see to it."

Later, when Reuben's asleep and Dave's dishing up the

risotto, I ask who called.

"My mother. She wants us to come over this Friday."

"I presume you told her we can't?"

"We can't? But we haven't been for weeks."

"Didn't you check the calendar? Reuben's been invited to a party."

Dave carries the plates to the table. "Another one! He's got more of a social life than we have. Couldn't he give this one a miss?"

"No he couldn't. It's really important for an only child to socialise with other kids."

Dave shrugs. "Have it your own way."

I will.

They say you're not fully grown up until you're a parent. I don't know about that, but I do know you're not a proper parent until you've had to fight for your child.

# Into The Light

# Getting to Grips with Liathach

J AMES WAS SURPRISED when I mentioned I might have a hen party. He knew I was too sensible to get plastered in some East European capital with an L-plate pinned to my back. But I fancied summoning my female friends for some ritual bonding. Once I was married, I wouldn't have such a compelling excuse.

Most of my friends were outdoor types. They had the boots, the backpacks, the rainproof coats. But I wasn't sure they'd have the stamina for Liathach. I wasn't sure I would myself.

"Does it have to be Lee-a-thack?" said James. "There are hundreds of other Monroes to choose from."

Years ago, my dad had said it the way James did, his Sassenach tongue challenged by the Scottish 'ch'. But I'd found an audio file on the internet. "It's pronounced Lee-aaarrrchhh. And, yes, it does."

The internet also described the mountain as formidable.

Could it really be formidable if I'd conquered it at twelve? I poured myself a glass of chianti, and phoned my dad.

He assumed I'd called about the wedding. "Look, Lisa, I'd be delighted to be there on any terms. But I'd understand completely if you didn't want me to give you away."

My eyes prickled. I was touched by his ready acceptance of his relegation in my affections. But I knew I'd start blubbing if I tried to put it into words. "We're not bothering with all that pomp. Too archaic."

"I thought you might have asked Zach. You used to be so close."

Did we? But his reference to my brother provided the perfect preface to what I really wanted to talk about. "Remember that half-term camping in Torridon? Mum had stuff on at work and it was just us three?" I didn't add that before the school year was out he'd run off to start a new family.

"Of course I remember. I wrote a story about it."

Twenty years of estrangement had left gaping cavities where knowledge of my father should have been. "You're a writer?"

"It's just a hobby. I'm not very good."

"Even so." I was twelve again, and he was the kindest, cleverest, handsomest man in the world. "Can I read it?"

He hesitated, said he'd have to tidy it up before emailing it over, but he sounded pleased. It wasn't until I'd switched off the phone that I realised I hadn't asked whether he thought Liathach would be too formidable for a bunch of thirty-somethings more accustomed to the gentler peaks of the Yorkshire Dales.

I STAYED UP late that night, refreshing my inbox every twenty minutes in the hope of his name flashing up on my screen. We hadn't established how much time he'd need to tidy up his story but, whether as much as a month or as little as an hour, it exceeded my fragile patience. Underneath the grown woman on the brink of marriage was a preteen girl yearning to have her father all to herself.

Sunlight shimmering on the lochs, crags scratching the skyline, endless days basking in his attention. I'd happily trade the romance of Paris, the wonder of the pyramids, the thrill of a safari for another taste of that Torridon trip. And to know that *he* hadn't forgotten. That, on the contrary, he'd treasured it so much he'd written a story about it. Perhaps he hadn't exited our lives quite as casually as I'd assumed.

His story arrived when I least expected it. Although already late for work, I couldn't resist clicking on the attachment.

*Lisa loved being in the mountains …*

Oh, Dad, how I've missed you! All these wasted years thinking you didn't care.

*… but, since reaching her teens, she especially relished being in the mountains with her brother, free from parental control.*

What? I scrolled down the page, speed-reading for a glimpse of my dad. But he'd written himself out of the story, his only role to deliver his son and daughter to Mrs McTavish who'd keep a motherly watch over them in the B&B. To compound the insult, he'd made me complicit in my own abandonment, the Lisa-character asking for a weekend away without her parents for her fourteenth birthday treat.

I unbuttoned my coat. I couldn't go to work with tears streaming down my cheeks. I told myself it was make-believe but, if it was, why had he given his teenage characters his real children's names? The details he *had* altered only intensified his betrayal. *His* Lisa was a couple of years older than I'd been, with a boyfriend back home, whereas the girl who'd scrambled up Liathach was more into horses and hiking than burgeoning romance. My dad had created a fantasy of his leaving; one in which his departure dovetailed perfectly with his children's push for lives of their own.


"WE DON'T HAVE to get married, do we?"

James looked aghast.

"I mean, we're happy living together. Why tinker with something that isn't broken?"

"What's got into you, Lisa?"

I couldn't tell him how suspicion had poisoned my heart. Marriage had no meaning when a man could up sticks without warning to begin again with someone new.

I'd made a feeble stab at admitting my disappointment to my dad. Emailing to thank him for the story, I'd expressed surprise it didn't contain more of him. His reply was apologetic, if a little defensive, but it missed the point. *I've a long way to go before I'll reach Saki's standard,* he said.

I'd have to find my sparkle again, or it would be James who wanted to cancel our nuptials. "I could do with getting away for a break. Somewhere remote."

"Liathach with the girls?"

"I've gone off that idea. I'm considering a retreat."

WE CLUSTERED AROUND the table, pens and pencils poised. My fellow students terrified me with their talk of point of view and muscular verbs. Even the spotty teenager, who turned crimson if anyone as much as looked at her, proved zealous on the page. I didn't dare admit I hadn't written a story since Year Six.

Our tutor was a soft-spoken man in his sixties whose wild hair and grizzled beard brought to mind King Lear. But he was no doddering old fool. He guided us through the basics of character, conflict, the killer first line. I didn't believe I could concoct any of them, but he inspired me to have a bash. "Just go for it, Lisa. You can't go wrong if you write from the soul."

On the final evening, we were due to read aloud the stories we'd composed during the week. As my turn approached, my stomach churned. I almost tripped over my feet as I made my way to the front. Stumbling through the opening paragraphs, my hands holding the paper shook so much I could hardly see the text. I looked up, ready to apologise and flee from the room. But, serious or smiling, the other students appeared engrossed. The tutor had the look of a father taking pride in his daughter's tentative first steps.

I inhaled deeply and read on. "*Does it have to be Lee-a-thack?* said James." A murmur of satisfaction spread through the room.

A shiver rippled through me, but it wasn't from nerves. I didn't have to climb a mountain to lay claim to this story and I could pronounce Liathach however I chose.

# Albarello di Sarzana

I T WASN'T THE best party I've ever had. Forty-odd sweaty bodies crammed into the boardroom to toast my expulsion (sorry, my early retirement with generous benefits package) with a glass of cheap sherry and a lukewarm mini-samosa. A witty speech detailing the parallels between my rise through the ranks and the steady increase in our market share, deftly glossing over the last three years since He Who Must Be Obeyed started meddling with my systems. A bouquet of enormous lilies and the lavender envelope containing the holiday gift vouchers. All those soon-to-be-former colleagues anxious to see how I would deal with it.

How did I deal with it? Professionally, of course: I kept a rictus smile and spoke the lines that could have come straight from one of He Who Must Be Obeyed's operational policies.

*I'll be thinking of you all when I'm drinking rum cocktails in the Caribbean,* with an ironical laugh to show that nothing would be further from my mind. The work-weary fifty-somethings were too busy calculating the months till they too could be standing here thanking colleagues for support and friendship over the years to recognise that a holiday loses its meaning when you won't be returning to your desk.

*Times change. My job wasn't needed anymore. And they made me an offer I couldn't refuse,* with a coy flick of the hair to acknowledge every woman has her price. The mid-career forty-somethings were too absorbed in auditing their own ambitions to ask whether a pension were sufficient compensation for exile from the buzz of the workplace.

*Four grandchildren, actually. It'll be wonderful to have more time for them,* with a faraway look in my eyes. The guilt-ridden thirty-somethings gobbled up the nibbles like they were their toddlers' leftovers, without pausing to wonder whether escorting an infant to playgroup could ever be as fulfilling as acclimatising an awkward school leaver to office politics.

It was all going swimmingly until Lydia stepped up and thrust a pot-plant at me.

More interested in fashion and pop music than knuckling down to work, Lydia was the last person I would have expected to bring me a personal gift. She'd hardly made eye contact since her disciplinary hearing six months before. I put down my glass and held the grubby thing away from my suit, while I tried to figure out whether it was a joke.

"I've really appreciated working with you." The girl's voice quavered. "I know you don't think much of me, but you've always been fair, and it's disgraceful how they're treating you. After all you've done for the company."

I ordered my chin to stop wobbling. No way could Lydia make me bow out with smudged mascara. I cleared my throat. "That's very sweet of you." I glanced at the plant. It wasn't terribly attractive: three pale green leaves the size of coasters and no sign of a flower. Careful not to soil my fingers, I inspected the hand-written plastic label stuck into the compost. "Al-bar-ello di Sar-zana. What a mouthful! Some kind of geranium, is it?"

Lydia laughed. "A courgette. I grew it myself from seed."

"A courgette?"

"You mentioned at the Christmas meal it was your favourite vegetable. I thought you might like to grow some yourself."

"Thank you, Lydia." Even after thirty-five years with the same company, one can still be taken by surprise. "I'll put it on my kitchen window sill and think of you when I'm doing the dishes."

Lydia shook her head. "You won't get any courgettes that way. You'll need to plant it in the garden."

My cheeks relaxed as I found myself smiling genuinely for the first time that day. The girl looked so pleased with her offering. I didn't have the heart to tell her I don't have a garden.

WHEN AN OVERLY-INDULGENT parent wakes up on Boxing Day to the realisation they've given a puppy to a child too squeamish to change a litter tray, they can farm the creature out to the Cat and Dog Shelter. Similarly, I reasoned, a woman with an aversion to the slightest speck of dirt under her fingernails who finds herself unexpectedly in possession of a nascent vegetable should dispatch it promptly to the nearest allotments. A specimen with so grand a name could hardly be thrown in the wheelie bin, and I appreciated having some business to attend to, beyond a trip to the hairdresser's, on my first weekday morning as one of the nation's retired.

It took a fair amount of shouting to attract the attention of the old man in a scruffy boiler suit pottering about near the entrance to the allotments. He laughed when I told him why I'd come. Unlocking the wooden gate, he ushered me inside.

My heels sank into the path as he led me between rows of greenery. There were cabbages anchored to the ground, and peas clambering over twigs, along with other vegetation I didn't recognise. But even I could pick out the plethora of thriving courgette plants, each an enlarged replica of Lydia's gift. No one would be able to give Albarello the attention it deserved in this place. It would be like dumping a baby in a Romanian orphanage.

The man stopped at the edge of a plot without a single edible plant among the forget-me-nots and thistles. "Why not grow it yourself?"

"Oh, no, I don't know the first thing about gardening."

The man scanned my crimson suit and now mud-splattered office shoes. "You could learn. There's plenty of folk here to help you."

"I'd be no good at it," I said, but even to me, my protest sounded half-hearted. I've never been one to turn down a challenge. "Surely someone else could make better use of it."

The man chuckled. "If only! We're overrun with vacant

plots at the moment. You'd be doing us a favour if you took it on."

I remembered the holiday vouchers in the lavender envelope. I was supposed to be trading them in for my dream trip. "I doubt I'll have the time."

"Just put in what you can manage. No need to clear the whole plot. We can cover the rest with an old carpet to smother the weeds."

Sheltered from the traffic by a hawthorn hedge, the site was as peaceful as a Caribbean hideaway. Those regimented rows of vegetables had a certain appeal. It could make perfect retirement project. But would those healthy outdoor types entrust so much land to someone who still half believed that vegetables were hatched wrapped in clingfilm on supermarket shelves? "Let me take it on probation. One season at a time."

"The whole site's on probation. The council's been wanting to close us down for months. It's prime building land, you see."

"I've nothing to lose then, have I?"

"Welcome to the club." The man offered me his hand. "Frank Earnshaw, allotment society chairman."

I had to give him Lydia's plant before I could shake his hand. Either that or tuck it under my arm and get my suit dirty. "Daphne Wright."

Frank examined the label. "Albarello di Sarzana. Good variety. Let me get my spade and I'll plant it for you."

IT RAINED FOR the rest of the week. I divided my time between the library, swotting up on the mysteries of horticulture, and the garden centres, wishing my colleagues had bequeathed me the cash rather than holiday vouchers when I came to pay for my wellies and an assortment of tools. I almost bought my first pair of jeans in twenty years, but I refused to take my new hobby that far. Nevertheless, by the time the sun came out again on the Saturday, I was itching to get down to the allotment to see how much Albarello had grown.

I could have cried. There was less of him than when Frank had so carefully placed him in the ground.

A young woman in faded dungarees sauntered over. "I'm Martha." She indicated a tawny-haired boy of around seven. "And this is Thomas. Need any help?"

I balked at being the new starter who had to be shown the ropes. But somebody had to diagnose the problem with Albarello or I'd have to keep buying courgettes from Sainsbury's.

Thomas crouched down and examined the leaves. "Slugs," he said, triumphantly.

He held out his finger to show me the culprit, a slimy black apostrophe with a fierce orange underbelly. I stepped back. "Urgh, it's disgusting."

His mother laughed. "You'll have to get used to slugs if you want to be a gardener."

Frank hadn't warned me of this. "What can I do? They'll murder my poor plant."

"Some people use slug pellets," said Martha, "but that's no good if you want to go organic. You can set beer traps, or put a barrier around the plants with something dry, like eggshells, or bran. Or," she ruffled her son's hair, "you can get a small boy to pick them off."

Thomas looked from his mother to Albarello, bright-eyed as if he'd been offered a bucket of ice cream. "Can I, Mummy?"

"If it's okay with Daphne."

"Be my guest."

"Gruesome creatures, aren't they?" said Martha as the boy ran off.

I didn't ask whether she meant slugs or children.

WHILE THOMAS ATTENDED to the slugs, I made a start on the weeds. The soil was heavy after the rain and digging left me breathless. Separating the roots from the mud proved a messy process, and I cursed when I broke one of my nails, but I felt some satisfaction in applying myself to the job. The allotment site was like an open-plan office, everyone beavering away at our individual workstations, each a small but crucial cog in the enterprise as a whole. My back ached but I was proud to have cleared a corner of the plot by the time Martha summoned Thomas for lunch.

But she wasn't pleased. "What have you done?"

The child and I looked up, warily. Martha snatched the fork from my hand. It turned out I was the one in breach of policy. "You can't dig when the ground's waterlogged. You'll ruin the soil."

I'd never thought of soil as a delicate thing in need of protection. In my few previous encounters with the stuff, my sole objective had been to prevent it fouling my clothes. "Sorry."

Martha looked me up and down, like an officer inspecting the troops. Once she'd found one thing to criticise, everything about me was open to scrutiny. "Are you sure you're comfortable in a skirt? Don't you feel restricted?"

In the office, *I'd* policed the dress code. "I don't have the figure for trousers." My laugh sounded false, even to me.

IT WAS A mistake not to take a break after finishing work. I'd let Frank bamboozle me into taking on the allotment, not because I wanted it, but for fear of being left with nothing to do.

I abandoned Albarello to the slugs and went off to visit friends. *Retirement's a huge adjustment,* they said. *You need to stop and think before launching into something new.*

I couldn't think at the allotment, with Martha finding fault with my performance. It was time to cash in my holiday vouchers and get as far away as I could. But it wouldn't be right to book my ticket until I'd told Frank I was giving up my plot.

It was a quiet Monday morning when I unlocked the gate with my own key for only the second time. When Frank wasn't at his plot near the entrance, I strolled down towards my own. But I couldn't find it. No sign of the weed-infested patch with a single sickly courgette in the corner. Someone else's plot had replaced it, properly planted up with green things, including an entire row of courgettes.

I hadn't heard Frank creep up behind me. "So, what do you think? Martha thought you could use some extra help."

"This is my patch? And Martha arranged for the makeover?"

"You don't mind, do you?"

It was as well-stocked and orderly as the stationery

cupboard at work. Of course this was my garden: there was Albarello in the corner, twice the size as when Lydia gave him to me, and with a yellow trumpet-shaped flower blooming in the middle. Mind? "It's wonderful."

I HAD PEAS and runner beans and lettuce and parsley. I had spinach and beetroot and fennel and leeks. I even had outdoor tomatoes, both yellow and red. And, of course, I had courgettes. All I had to do was keep them weeded and watered until harvest time.

The grandchildren had to share my attention with the slugs. My holiday was put on hold. With a sun-lounger beside the water-butt, I didn't need the Caribbean.

Although I was there nearly every day, fussing over my darlings, my visits never seemed to coincide with Martha's. We finally met up on the day I picked my first courgette. Pale-green flecked with yellow, it wasn't much thicker than a whiteboard pen, but it was mine. I dashed over to show Martha. "Isn't it perfect?"

She was sitting with Thomas on her lap, and he was crying. I hoped she hadn't been on at him the way she'd snapped at me.

"I've just told him the news," said Martha. "He's devastated. We've no garden at home and the flat's tiny. He hates being cooped up indoors."

"You're giving up your allotment?"

Martha gave me that new-girl-in-the-office look. "Oh, Daphne, haven't you heard? The council's selling the site to a property developer. We'll all have to leave."

"They can't do that. We'll have to fight it."

"We've been trying for months. It's hopeless."

"I wouldn't have thought you'd accept defeat so easily."

Martha sighed. "I've done my best but I haven't the time. And Frank's lovely, but he's so disorganised. I'm afraid it's a lost cause."

"That's not good enough."

Martha looked startled. My voice sounded equally strange to me. Sharp as a hoe slicing through weeds. The voice of authority, the voice I used to have before He Who Must Be Obeyed poured scorn on my work. "Leave it to me. Anything's possible if you approach it systematically."

I BROKE INTO my savings to buy a new laptop and spent a rainy weekend setting up a spreadsheet with the names of the allotment holders down one side and the jobs that needed doing along the top. Organising a petition. Setting up a Facebook page. Getting the editor of the local rag on board. I emailed it to Frank shortly before midnight on Sunday. I wasn't concerned the next morning that he hadn't got back to me. But I was rather irritated at waiting an entire week for his reply: *Sorry, Daphne, I don't check my emails very often. And I can't open the document. Was it important?*

I could have kicked myself for the time I'd wasted. Nothing for it but to go on a splurge of stationery shopping and set up a makeshift office among the broken tools and sacks of leaf mould in the communal shed. Down came the tattered month-by-month planting schedules. Up went the sheets of lining paper with the lists of deadlines and things to do.

At first I had to approach each allotment holder

individually and persuade them to play their part. Although I had no sanctions to fall back on, it wasn't vastly different from management: making everyone feel valued, that their contribution mattered and that together we could achieve great things. After a while, I could have sat in my office – a.k.a. mission control – and had them come to me, but that would be aping He Who Must Be Obeyed. After that initial push to get them motivated, the project belonged to everyone equally. Even the kids.

In fact, my proudest moment came when Thomas showed me his designs for promotional badges and cards. My proudest, but also my most shameful, when I asked Martha if she planned to get them printed. As if a single mother had cash to spare! But I was quick to redeem myself. "Why don't I see if I can get the garden centre to sponsor them? It's in their interest, after all."


IT WAS THE best party any of us had ever had. Forty-odd allotment holders in their old clothes, tucking into organic potatoes baked in the embers of the bonfire and toasting each other with plastic tumblers of home-made rhubarb wine. Thomas and three of my grandchildren chasing each other along the grass paths.

I'd just attended my first open-air AGM and, if that weren't enough, Frank had reported that the council had postponed the decision to sell the site.

"It's all down to Daphne." Frank raised his tumbler for a toast. "Thanks for saving us from the bulldozers."

"Someone had to bring you lot into order," I said. "Anyway, the fight's not over yet. I want every one of you at the council chambers next Wednesday."

Frank laughed. "Bully!"

"You don't know the half of it," said a woman behind me.

I spun round. "Lydia!"

"Good to see you, Daphne." She gave me a hug. "You're looking well."

"Thanks. But what brings you here? Checking up on the courgette you gave me?"

"Didn't you know? I share the plot with Martha. But I've not been able to get here much these last few months. Too busy studying for my degree."

"A degree?"

"Don't look so shocked. You're the one who pushed me to take my career more seriously. Anyway, you've hardly been sitting with your feet up yourself. What about your holiday?"

"I've given vouchers to my daughters. I don't like being away from here too long. Someone needs to monitor the council's shenanigans, and I've big plans for my plot. I want to plant some fruit trees. And dig a pond to lure frogs to come and eat the slugs." I'd bought a pad of graph paper and sketched out where it was all to go.

"Spoken like a proper gardener." Frank grinned, holding out a plastic washing-up bowl filled with apples.

"Thanks." I took an apple at random from the bowl and bit into it, without a thought as to whether it had been washed.

"I reckon you've served your probation," said Frank. "Don't you?"

# Four Hail Marys

MARY IS ON her way to the new sandwich shop on Saint Michael's Road, ruminating on the relative merits of coronation chicken versus tuna mayo, when she spots Graham lolloping down the street towards her. At least it looks like him. She can't be certain at this distance, but who else still wears his thinning grey hair hanging loose to his shoulders? He doesn't seem to have noticed her, probably plugged into his smartphone and off in a time-warp with the Rolling Stones, but she isn't going to hang around to check. She has a moment's grace to backtrack and take refuge in the churchyard.

Once there, however, she feels lost. Foolish. There's nowhere to hide among the flattened gravestones and, if Graham should catch her skulking there, it would be all too obvious she's trying to avoid him. Without stopping to think, she darts up the path to the porch and rattles the door handle.

Amazingly, the church is unlocked. Hard to imagine what kind of service would be going on at a quarter to one on a weekday, but there being *anything* is almost enough to restore her faith in God.

Mary creeps inside. It smells of damp and incense, with a parsimonious chill to the air. Three ranks of wooden pews are lined up to face a trio of altars flanked by stone statues stemming from a more elemental age. The gloom is kept at bay by little more than a bank of candles alongside the minor altar on the right, and the borrowed light from the outside world that, filtered through the stained-glass windows, casts watercolour shadows on the flagstone floor. Hugging her coat around her, Mary inches forward.

The meagre congregation kneels a few rows back from the candle-lit altar: a trinity of women with white hair frothed up like meringue. No sign of an officiating priest. Perhaps the women are waiting for the service to begin. Mary slips into a pew in the middle section half a dozen rows further back, to watch, and wait with them.

She doesn't kneel. The wooden bench looks uncomfortable enough. Her stomach rumbles and she promises it she'll only stay a moment. Just long enough to see what happens. Just long enough to ensure Graham is safely out of the way.

A door creaks. Her gaze follows the sound to a wood-panelled cubicle jutting out from the right-hand wall below a stained-glass image of a half-naked saint shot through with arrows. A woman in a green quilted jacket steps out and hobbles towards the pews in the middle section. One of the meringue-haired women gets up to replace her in the cubicle.

Mary smiles. The women aren't waiting for someone to come and lead the prayers from the altar. Each has come for her own private service: the holy sacrament of confession. An old woman and a priest with only a shrouded partition between them. She confiding her transgressions, he granting absolution. Mary appreciates the attraction.

But, oh, the agony of waiting. Mary remembers it well. The shuffling along the queue of kneelers, rehearsing over and over the sins she would parade before the priest when her turn came. The awful list of a whole month's misdemeanours clogging her mouth with a sour taste of guilt. The searing shame of giving them voice, even if only to gentle Father Harrison who was the type to crack a joke midway through his Sunday sermons in compassion for the children who struggled to sit still so long. The fear that this time he would decree her offences too serious, would slide back the grille between them and announce that God could not forgive. A dread too awful to share even with the friend who knelt beside her.

Extracting a chain of crimson beads from her pocket, the quilted-jacket woman kneels down a couple of rows in front of Mary. Her right hand zooms from her forehead to her chest to her left shoulder to her right and then down again. She palpates a bead between finger and thumb as her lips shape the prayers.

The rosary. Mary spools back through thirty years of godlessness in an attempt to recall its strange mathematics. Ten *Hail Marys* topped and tailed with an *Our Father* and a *Glory Be* to make a Decade. Five Decades to make a

Mystery. One Mystery to a set of beads. She can't say how many Mysteries for a full-blown rosary. She'd never got that far.

She watches now as the woman fingers her sacred beads. She imagines tapping her on the shoulder and whispering *What did you get?*

Kneeling side-by-side, their sun-blonde hair covered with black lace mantillas, Mary would nudge Bernadette. "What did you get?"

Bernadette always finished first. Just the one *Our Father* and a couple of *Glory Be*s. In comparison, Mary felt the weight of her punishment. From behind the veiled partition, Father Harrison boomed, "And for your penance, say four *Hail Mary*s." Always the same: four *Hail Mary*s. HailMary-fullofgrace theLordiswiththee blessedartthouamongwomen andblessedisthefruitofthywombJesus. HolyMaryMotherof-God prayforussinners nowandatthehourofourdeath Amen. Even rattling them off like a tongue twister, it seemed to take an eternity.

The quilted-jacket woman continues to work through her beads. So many trespasses to atone for. Yet the woman looks so innocent in her cosy jacket, her tweed kilt and her sensible brown shoes. So ordinary.

The four *Hail Mary*s used to bother her. She wondered if more was expected of a Mary. She was called after the mother of God, a girl could go no higher, whereas Bernadette was only a saint. But how, when he couldn't see her face, did the priest know her name?

She wondered if it were because her misdeeds were so much more heinous than her friend's. "Bless me, Father, for

I have sinned. It has been four weeks since my last confession and these are my sins. I have been quarrelling, telling lies, disobedient …"

Decades on, Mary shivers. This litany of wrongdoing, unaltered from one month to the next; how was it that they never questioned what it was all for?

"So what?" said Bernie, when she told her what she had done. "Everybody slips off the rails once in a while. Don't beat yourself up about it."

The quilted-jacket woman makes the sign of the cross and returns the beads to her pocket. She struggles arthritically to her feet.

Once a month on a Saturday afternoon, she and Bernadette made their confessions. Each month Mary fretted that Father Harrison would tell her that God could not pardon her. So there was a wonderful sense of release when it was over, of stepping out into the sunshine with her soul scrubbed clean. To go forth and swap her pocket money for Sherbet Lemons and Pineapple Chunks to guzzle on the swings. To have a few blessed hours without the stain of quarrelling, telling lies and disobedience blotting out the light of God's love.

The quilted-jacket woman moves into the aisle. She genuflects, crosses herself again and turns. Despite the wrinkles, her face has a beatific glow. She limps past Mary's pew towards the exit.

Mary stares at the space the woman has vacated: the wooden pew, the padded kneeler, the scattered hymnbooks. The emptiness. She imagines the woman coming back, taking her arm and leading her across to join the queue of repentant sinners below where Saint Sebastian's torment is glorified in stained glass. The quilted-jacket woman would kneel with her, offering encouraging platitudes to see her through the wait. She would promise her redemption if only she could bring herself to confess.

The ache of her buttocks on the hard seat brings her back to reality. How could she tell the priest what she has done? The only words she has for the confessional are those of a child. Her slipping off the rails with Graham, as Bernie put it, requires an adult vocabulary. The seventh commandment: Thou shalt not commit adultery. Wedged between Thou shalt not kill and Thou shalt not steal, hers is far too serious an infringement to shrug off with four *Hail Marys*.

"An eye for an eye," said Bernie. "You were only playing Nick at his own game."

"Two wrongs don't make a right," said Mary. Her husband's cavalier approach to his marriage vows is no excuse for her own behaviour. It gives her little comfort that Nick is in no position to judge her; nor can he provide her with the absolution she craves. Nor have these priests, using their rituals as an alibi for all kinds of dubious behaviour, the power to assuage her guilt. There is nothing to be gained from throwing herself on the mercy of a man. And yet she needs something. Her sin grows cancerous inside her.

One of the meringue-heads emerges from the cubicle and lumbers towards the minor altar on the right. Beside the bank of burning candles she drops some coins through a slot in the wall. She takes a fresh candle from a wooden box and, with a shaking hand, lights the wick from one of the flames.

She places her candle at the front of the metal rack and drops to her knees before the altar.

Despite what Bernie might think, Mary has sinned. She made a promise to Nick and she broke it. Yet no man has the right to convict her, no man the authority to set her free. No God, either.

She is tired of having to dodge Graham at lunchtimes. She is going to have to confront him, tell him it was once and never again. But she can hardly bear to look at him. The thought of his *Casino Royale* duvet cover and the leaky tube of haemorrhoid ointment on his bathroom shelf fills her with disgust.

If she were going to break the seventh commandment, why couldn't she have done so with someone she actually fancied? It was so wasteful, so unnecessary, like defaulting on a diet with sugar-saturated chocolate-flavour confectionery when she might have had the seventy-percent-cocoa-solids real thing. A miniscule pleasure for a mountain of regret.

Mary falls to her knees. She's thinking of the four *Hail Mary*s. She's thinking how a child never thought to ask what the words might mean.

No man can condemn her, no man exonerate. No God, either.

She bends forward, rests her forehead on her clasped hands as she used to years ago. She has done wrong, but it is time to move on. Time to find a way of relating to Graham as simply a work colleague. Time to have a heart-to-heart with Nick about whether there's a future they can share.

She raises her head, squares up to the altars, the stone statues, the stained glass. "Hail Mary," she says to herself.

She does not need a priest to prescribe her means of atonement.

"Hail Mary," she whispers, calmer already.

There is no God, but there is Mary. "Hail Mary," she says aloud. In the quiet of the church, her voice sounds brash. Brazen. Beautiful.

No man can. No God. Only she. Alone. Accuse, acquit, move on. "Hail Mary," she shouts, godless in the echoey church.

The meringue-heads turn round. They seem surprised to see Mary kneeling there but they soon recover, and bestow on her their holiest smiles.

# In Search of Mr Right

ONCE UPON A time, on a High Street not so very far from here, a fresh-faced young virgin looked up from the record counter at Woolworth's, straight into the beautiful chestnut-brown eyes of Mr Right. Flustered, colouring to the tips of her dainty little ears, she looked down again immediately and began flicking through the albums in the W rack and, when she looked up, he had gone.

Yet the image of his perfection was imprinted on her mind. She had to see him again. Over the next few days and weeks and months, she searched for him in all the likely places. But her efforts were fruitless. Roaming through the record shops, she had several sightings of shaggy Afghan coats, but none on the back of Mr Right. Loitering with a raspberry milk-shake in yet another coffee-bar, she was afforded multiple glimpses of men with flowing golden curls, but none adorning the head of her prince charming.

At that point, she could have given up on life, taken to her bed in despair, but, being a practical kind of girl, she decided to cut her losses and accept an invitation to see *Tommy* at the flicks with Mr Good-enough. A meal at the Wimpy followed soon after. Before she knew it, she was back on the High Street discussing wedding bouquets at the florist's. Then, after the proper interval, inquiring about remedies for colic and nappy-rash at Boots. Later, with the kids settled at school, she had a desk at Prospect Residentials, popping out at lunchtimes to pick up some groceries from the Co-op.

She loved her husband, her children, even her job; never mind that it placed her lower, in the eyes of the general public, than politicians and traffic wardens. A proper fairy-tale ending. I should be happy.

Why, then, thirty-odd years on, are my dreams still haunted by a man I thought the spit of Roger Daltrey? Why is each waking moment filled with thoughts of how life might have been had I had the courage to engage him in a deep-and-meaningful conversation about the relative merits of *Pictures of Lily* over *Substitute* when I had the chance? I'm not eating, I'm not sleeping, and sex is merely going through the motions. My fingernails are chewed down to the stumps and I've given up watching my soaps because I can no longer follow the storyline.

"Tell me what you want," says Husband. "I can change." He even suggests sessions at Relate.

How can I expect him to turn back the clock to when I was younger than Daughter is now, and twice as naive, to a time before cassettes, CDs and YouTube? How can I blame

Mr Good-enough for going bald and podgy on me, for falling asleep before the end of the Six O'clock News? That's real life.

"File for divorce if you're not happy," says Best Friend. "The kids are grown up. You're due some excitement." She's never forgiven Husband for turning down an offer to go bungee jumping as a foursome.

"I couldn't," I say. "He'd never get over it."

But will *I* get over it? What will become of me if I can't expunge the thought of Mr Right from my mind?

Like the desperate teenager I once was, I seek him everywhere. Each time I go to assess a new property, each time I take a customer for a viewing, I'm scrutinising the faces of middle-aged men, looking for some hint that, if I were to close my eyes and kiss their leathery cheeks, their hair would grow and their trousers would flare at the ankles and magic them into my handsome prince.

One day, off to view a property on Castle Street, the gas board is digging up the road and I have to find a different route. An unseasonal fog has settled on the town, and I lose my bearings. That's when I come across the little record shop on the corner that I'd swear wasn't there when I was last in the neighbourhood. *The Slipped Disc*, it says above the window, in funky pink and yellow lettering. I can't resist.

The tinkling of a cow-bell as I push open the door. A waft of sandalwood from the joss-sticks burning on the counter. Rank upon rank of vinyl. It's like stepping into a film-set of the early Seventies.

A man looks up from one of the racks and meets my gaze. The hair, although now quite grey, hangs to his shoulders in luxuriant curls. There's no mistaking those rich brown eyes. He smiles, as if he's been expecting me. As if he, too, has felt something missing all these years. "Is it …?"

"Yes?" I can hardly catch my breath.

He laughs, shakes his head. "Sorry, I'm waiting for the estate agent." He runs his hand through his wavy hair. "Every time somebody walks into the shop my heart misses a beat."

"But I'm an estate agent." I feel as if I've walked into someone else's dream.

"I was expecting a man."

My lip trembles as Mr Right reveals himself as Mr Chauvinist. Never mind the Seventies; this guy is a throwback to the days before women had the vote! Yet I've been equally ridiculous: building my hopes around someone I've never even spoken to.

He flicks through a desk diary. "Mr King, I was told. But it doesn't matter. I assume he's given you all the details."

"Oh, I see. You're dealing with King's Commercials. I'm across the road at Prospect Residentials." They do shops, we do houses; it's a matter of specialisation, not gender. Perhaps there's hope for us yet. "I was on my way to Castle Street and got lost with the fog and the roadworks. And then I noticed your shop. What a coincidence you were waiting for an estate agent as well."

"Isn't it?" He steps towards me. "Although I'd call it serendipity." He blushes, like a teenager plucking up the courage to propose to his girlfriend. "May I ask you something?"

I hold my breath, half close my eyes.

"You needn't tell me if it's a trade secret. But there's something that's been bugging me since I rang Mr King. Is it true estate agents sometimes give you a valuation a bit on the low side? Maybe they've got a friend who's going to snap it up on the cheap before it goes on the market?"

This wasn't in the script. The smell of sandalwood is making me light-headed.

Mr Right steps to the side, leans his belly against the rack of records. "Sorry, I shouldn't have asked. You must get fed up with stories about crooked estate agents. It's because I'm nervous about selling up. I've got so attached to this place."

No sign of customers. "Business not good then?"

He shrugs. "Not too dreadful. But it's my wife. Wants to move nearer her parents."

His wife! Obstacles keep springing up between us, like a thorny thicket on the path to the enchanted palace. Stupid to expect him to be my knight in shining armour, galloping across continents to rescue me from my turret.

I've got to take charge of my own destiny before I die of a broken heart. I can't let the opportunity pass me by. "Are you sure you're going to leave this place? It must be a fantastic job." Even princesses have to fight for their happy-ever-afters.

We stare into each other's eyes with absolute understanding. Then he looks away and flicks through the albums in the rack before him, his fingers hesitating over The Who's *Live at Leeds*.

"It was okay," I say, "but I preferred *Quadrophenia* myself."

"THAT IS GROSS," says Daughter. "I'll die of embarrassment! Didn't you even think of us?"

"Go for it," says Best Friend. "Life is for living."

"Why not?" says Husband. "A change of career might be exactly what you need."

"How dare you?" says Eric Knight. "I had my eye on that shop for a friend."

"That's really cool," says Son. "Vinyl is in for a revival."

I kept the corny name, despite Daughter's protests. Business isn't great, despite Son's optimism. Nevertheless, I'm happy running *The Slipped Disc*; how could I not be when I can play my favourite music all day long? As Best Friend says, when she pops in for coffee, with Husband's promotion and the children having left home, work isn't only about money now.

The shop's fun but that's not the whole story. The real magic comes at closing time. That's when I look up and meet the eyes of Mr Good-enough across the record counter. Still bald, still liable to fall asleep in front of the television, still too boring to go bungee jumping, but, after all these years, the man for me. He leans across the ranks of vinyl and kisses me. Then I get my coat, lock up the shop, and let Husband drive me off into the sunset.

# The Witch's Funeral

D OREEN WAS TAKEN aback when the man from the
Co-op leant into his briefcase and produced a leather-
backed desk diary. Did he use a computer with his younger
clientele, she wondered, or was this a truly democratic
affectation?

He wasn't much of a man, quite dwarfed by Arnold's
armchair, as he leafed through his book to April. Like a lath,
he was, from the narrow lapels of his grey jacket to his lips so
thin they stayed hidden as he moved his mouth to speak:
"There's a window on the twenty-second."

Even his voice lacked substance, making her pause, ever
so briefly, to ask herself if he were real. Of course he was,
she'd watched him scuff his shoes on the doormat not half
an hour before. It was the situation. As the wraith-like man
from the Co-op had explained already, everything seemed so
fuzzy because it hadn't yet hit her.

As if to underline his point, her mind snapped back to

last night's dream. She'd been dancing with Arnold, a dance like no other in their fifty-three years of marriage. For one thing, they'd never mastered the foxtrot, and, for another, they were dancing at his funeral, and that was beyond the pale.

"I was hoping for something sooner," she said.

"There's space on the seventeenth of course..." The man from the Co-op crossed one leg over the other knee, exposing a rib of puce-coloured sock. How unfortunate that the only lively thing about him should clash so lividly with the fireside rug. She knew she shouldn't have let him take Arnold's seat.

"The seventeenth then."

His face stayed fixed in a mask of compassion. "You do realise that's the day of the ceremony at St Paul's? Not many round here would want their final send-off to compete with Baroness Thatcher's."

Who was this creature to dictate what was and wasn't right for Arnold? He was draining her strength with his fake gentility. She needed him out, gone, skedaddled, with his reedy voice and outdated paper systems. "The witch is dead. She can't harm us now."

"YOU COULDN'T HAVE held back one more day till I got here?"

Doreen hated to see Barry disappointed, so she looked out the kitchen window to the tiny lawn where he used to kick a ball around as a boy. The jaundiced grass was mottled with brown, hunkered flat by the snow that had lingered into the start of April, but now that Spring had finally arrived Arnold would want to get the mower out, except that Arnold was lying in state at the Co-op.

Barry couldn't let it drop: "The whole point of me coming was to help you."

She turned round, forced a smile. After all, the boy had lost his dad. Of course, he wasn't a boy anymore, yet he still had no idea, *no idea,* of a mother's drive to push. She'd protected him, let him stay a child when there was no money coming in save the strike pay. With the men patrolling the picket line, the women had had no choice but to roll up their sleeves and revamp the Welfare as a soup kitchen. Nearly thirty years on, the smell of sweating onions still brought back that sense of panic and camaraderie. No, she couldn't have held back one more day. "You can help. There's loads still needs doing."

She turned on the cold tap and a jet of water spluttered into the kettle. Barry would want a cup of tea after his long drive.

"Maybes I could start by swapping the date of the funeral."

She scrabbled behind tins of baked beans and rice pud for a packet of the double chocolate chip cookies she kept for visitors. "What was that?"

She'd had to step behind him to fetch the biscuits and it seemed that in the ten minutes he'd been in the house, his bald patch had stretched wider across his crown. Now he spun around to face her: "Can you not sit still for a minute?"

"I'm mashing you a brew."

"I said I didn't want anything. I had a meal on the motorway."

Doreen knew her feelings were all wrong at the moment. Barry was angry with her over nothing and she should have been angry back. Or, if not angry, tearful and upset. Widows were supposed to cry and she'd been stowing a tissue up her sleeve since it happened, but she was still waiting. Now a cartoon image of Barry loomed before her: a giant-sized boy sitting cross-legged on the motorway, stuffing his cheeks with a burger, as cars zoomed by.

Before she could disgrace herself by giggling, her mind flipped to last night's dream. They were dancing again, she and Arnold. The jive this time, which they'd definitely tried at least once in their time together. They seemed to be doing rather well, as far as Doreen could judge, but the dream came with a voice-over which made her cringe. A man's voice that might have been Arnold's, or perhaps his dad's, harping on about jungle music.

The kettle brought the water to a boil and turned itself off with a click. "You could manage a cuppa," said Doreen.

Barry shook his head. "Let's get this stuff sorted first. Where's the number for the undertaker's?"

JANET POPPED ROUND to see if she wanted to go to the bingo.

"I hardly dare show my face," said Doreen.

"Folks are surprised, that's all. Him being a staunch union man."

Doreen filled the kettle at the sink. She got out the china teapot and the matching cups and saucers. Janet reached for the teabags, but Doreen flapped her away. For a moment, the women were on the verge of fighting for custody of a carton of own-brand tea, until Janet stepped aside.

She shrugged off her coat and draped it over the back of a chair. "Barry out somewhere?"

Doreen ripped open the packet of double chocolate chip cookies and arranged them on a china plate. "He said he needed to speak to the florist."

"I suppose he's glad the funeral's Wednesday. He wouldn't be able to take too long off that job of his."

Doreen poured the water into the teapot. So people blamed Barry for the date of the funeral; they'd always resented a clever lad. Surely now she'd find her anger and leap to his defence. Or find the tears as yet unshed. She loved her son, as she loved her husband, yet all she wanted to do was laugh. She must be going doolally.

She set down the teapot on the table. "No, he didn't want his dad's send-off to clash with Maggie Thatcher's. He was right narked I wouldn't change it."

"Why wouldn't you?"

"Why should I take a scrap of notice of that bitch?"

Janet frowned. She had a fleck of lipstick on her front tooth and her roots desperately needed retouching. Doreen felt a stab of anger so fierce it was almost pleasant as she patted her own lacquered head, the result of a long-standing hair appointment Barry had insisted she keep. How could Janet get away with being so slovenly when she still had a man to warm her bed?

"You can't pretend she didn't exist," said Janet.

The rage deserted her, leaving her more hollowed-out than before. It was like watching a good film on the telly and falling asleep before the end. Sleep: that was half the problem, she couldn't settle and when she did, she wasn't terribly impressed with the programme. Last night's show had been more stomping than dancing; if the dreams didn't stop after the funeral she was thinking of asking the doctor for a tonic. She sighed. "All that was finished for us yonks ago. We lost. She won. That's all there is to it."

"Fair dos, but you don't have to rub everyone's noses in it."

"Arnold didn't choose when to have his heart attack."

Janet's hand fluttered around the teapot before dropping to her lap. "Of course not." Her lips were pursed, as if to muzzle so much more.

Doreen had noticed a similar reining-in with Barry. He must have been furious when she wouldn't let him switch Arnold's funeral slot, yet no one could get properly cross with a grieving widow. She wished they would, but even this was more honest than the man from the Co-op's manufactured sympathy.

Janet could hold back no longer. She grabbed the teapot and poured. "I just hope you don't regret it."

BARRY HAD ONE of those cocky phones that lay on the table like an old-fashioned cigarette case. When he picked it up, Doreen didn't know if he wanted to check the weather forecast, play solitaire or merely wish his wife and daughter goodnight.

"This'll cheer you up," he said.

It was Saturday evening and Barry had cooked chilli con carne. Doreen had said it was delicious, although it was already sparking queer sensations in her stomach. She'd been all set to clear the table and launch into the washing-up, but she stayed put, not bothering to mention she had no notion of cheer and uncheer, and pretended to be curious about what might emerge from his phone. Yet *The Wizard of Oz* soundtrack came as a genuine surprise.

Barry waited for the ditty to end, like it was church music, a hymn he might have wanted at the funeral. It couldn't have lasted more than a minute. "*Ding Dong the Witch Is Dead.* Everybody's downloading it. They're hoping it'll top the charts tomorrow."

She remembered him watching the film as a boy, hiding behind the sofa like the cowardly lion. "But why?"

"I would've thought it was obvious."

Last night's dream had featured Apaches with painted faces and feathered headdresses hooting as they circled a campfire in the desert. Was that what was disturbing her sleep: a childish wish to dance on the woman's grave? "Old people kick the bucket sooner or later, even an old war horse like Thatcher. It's not exactly good triumphs over evil."

Barry shoved his phone in his pocket. "They're spending ten million pounds on a bloody state funeral while Dad gets dispatched at the local crem. Winners and losers, clear as day. Aren't you pleased there's a protest?"

She'd managed to shield him from the worst of the 80s, often going without so he'd have shoes for school. Even before the strike, even if the pits had stayed open, Doreen would have wanted a less confined life for her son. Yet in saving him, she'd also lost him and, although he'd never come out straight and said it, Arnold had felt it more keenly than she had.

While their neighbours had been too stunned even to tend their wounds, their clever boy went gadding off to university and from there to the City, whatever that meant. Doreen would bet her life Barry had never voted Tory, yet he'd been ever so cosy with Thatcher's natural heirs, New Labour. *He can talk the talk, that un*, Arnold used to say, after one of Barry's regular lectures on whatever variety of inequality was in vogue at the time. But they always had the sense that if he were ever to be taken at his word, if he were to be stripped of his two-bathroom house and his BMW, he'd go to pieces. He'd been looking a lot happier since Labour returned to the opposition benches.

She brought to mind the wicked witch in the film, green-faced below a big black hat, with a pointy nose and chin. "That jolly little ditty is what passes for protest these days?"

THE NIGHT BEFORE the funeral, Barry and his wife booked into a hotel, while Jade spread her things around what used to be her dad's bedroom. Doreen felt more comfortable sharing her home with her granddaughter although, approaching midnight, neither seemed inclined to retire. Jade had the never-ending task of updating herself on Facebook, and Doreen was dreading the next instalment of her dancing dream. She put down the magazine she'd been pretending to read and went to make them both a mug of cocoa.

Returning to the lounge, she found Jade sprawled over the photo album, picking through pictures of her granddad.

"Hey, Nan, have you got a scanner?"

The girl was clad entirely in black, from her clumpy lace-up boots to her powdered eyelids and varnished fingernails. There'd been an argument earlier that day when Barry had said that goth attire was unsuitable for a funeral and she'd have to wear the business-like skirt-suit her mother brought for her, but Doreen thought her layers of sullen lace and velvet made her seem yet more sweet and lovable. "What do you think?"

"Pity. Tiffany's making a poster for the anti-Thatcher march tomorrow ..." Doreen must have been wearing one of her old-lady looks, as Jade continued: "You know, a collage of people who've been harmed by her policies."

For all Doreen knew, Tiffany was as likely to be a singer with a girl-band as one of her granddaughter's schoolfriends. But that wasn't what had triggered her perplexed expression. "There's going to be a march?"

"Didn't you watch the news?"

Doreen had a strange sensation, as if her heart had been in the freezer and was beginning to defrost. "Shall we go?"

"It's in London, Nan. There's nothing going on here and, even if there was, we couldn't go, cos of Grandad's funeral."

"Spineless, the lot of them," said Doreen.

"Why do you say that?"

"What's the point of protesting in London? That's not where the damage was done."

"Dad did kind of say people were thinking of doing something local. But you'd booked the Welfare for the funeral shindig."

Arnold had always been suspicious of the freezer. Thawed-out food was never the same. Doreen didn't know how she would be when she warmed up and lost her numbness, but she wouldn't sit around moping. She no longer feared her dancing dreams.

EVEN SO, DOREEN felt rather sad when she pictured Barry and his wife arriving at the empty house that morning, although not so sad she needed to use the tissue lodged up her sleeve. She consoled herself with the thought that, after the hotel breakfast, he wouldn't be wanting a cup of tea.

Jade looked quite at home among the women at the trestle table, despite the difference in age and style. Watching her wipe a smear of poster paint from her cheek, Doreen remembered they'd sent Barry a text around two a.m. telling him to come straight to the Welfare. Jade had assured her he'd check his phone first thing, even on the morning of his father's funeral.

It hadn't been a problem rousing the women, no-one past seventy expected to sleep through the night. Doreen glided between the hall, now serving as production line for posters and banners, and the kitchen, steamy with bubbling cauldrons of soup. She wasn't sure if she were overseeing the operation or merely an observer, watching it unfold around her like a dream.

But the buzz of women at work was no mere fantasy: the crushing loss simmering to a purposeful rage. Her husband was dead and she was angry, and, while she couldn't pin that on the woman in blue from Grantham, the death of the community was another matter. Barry might balk at her wearing red for her husband's funeral, but she could hardly wait to see the crack in the face of the man from the Co-op when they all started dancing and waving their banners.

Her most recent dream had provided the blueprint: a South African funeral from apartheid days. The mourners were dancing, shouting, singing, wailing; tingling with an inner power no government could take away. A dignified protest a million miles from that puerile ding-dong ring tone. Arnold would've loved it.

# Acknowledgements

Thanks to Sara-Jayne Slack for encouraging me to assemble a short story collection and for stellar editing to substantially improve upon the original submission to Inspired Quill.

Composed between 2004 and 2018, previous incarnations of some of these stories have appeared in various literary magazines and websites in the UK, USA and Sweden, including *Allas, Alliterati, Amarillo Bay, Apt, Baltimore Review, Blue Lake Review, Bunbury, Cantaraville, eFiction, Far Off Places, Fiction on the Web, Fictive Dream, Firefly, Foliate Oak, Gold Dust, Greatest Uncommon Denominator, Halfway Down The Stairs, Lincolnshire Echo, Metazen, Open Pen, Pygmy Giant, QWF Magazine, Red Fez, Rose & Thorn, Short-Story Me, Spelk Fiction, Still Crazy, Storgy, Stories for Homes, The Honest Ulsterman, The Journeyman, The Yellow Room* and *Zouch*.

"After Icarus" won the 2007 All Write competition; "Reflecting Queenie" won the December 2012 Creative Writing Ink competition; and "Tobacco and Testosterone" won the 2016 Ilkley Literature Festival short story competition. "How's Your Sister", "My Beautiful Smile" and "Shaggy Dog Story" were also placed in competitions (Southport Writers 2007, Writers' Bureau 2010 and Ashby Writers Mary Gornall Memorial 2007).

I'm indebted to all the editors, judges, friends, family and other readers who have, in various ways, supported my penchant for short fiction.

# About the Author

Anne Goodwin's debut novel, *Sugar and Snails* was shortlisted for the 2016 Polari First Book Prize. Her second novel, *Underneath,* was published in 2017. Alongside her identity as a writer, she'll admit to being a sociable introvert; recovering psychologist; voracious reader; slug slayer; struggling soprano; and tramper of moors.

Find the author via her website:

annegoodwin.weebly.com

Or tweet at her: @Annecdotist

# More From This Author

## Sugar and Snails

The past lingers on, etched beneath our skin …

At fifteen, Diana Dodsworth took the opportunity to radically alter the trajectory of her life, and escape the constraints of her small-town existence. Thirty years on, she can't help scratching at her teenage decision like a scabbed wound.

To safeguard her secret, she's kept other people at a distance… until Simon Jenkins sweeps in on a cloud of promise and possibility. But his work is taking him to Cairo, and he expects Di to fly out for a visit. She daren't return to the city that changed her life; nor can she tell Simon the reason why.

Sugar and Snails takes the reader on a poignant journey from Diana's misfit childhood, through tortured adolescence to a triumphant mid-life coming-of-age that challenges preconceptions about bridging the gap between who we are and who we feel we ought to be.

**\*\*Shortlisted for the Polari Debut Novel Award, 2016\*\***

## Underneath

*He never intended to be a jailer …*

After years of travelling, responsible to no-one but himself, Steve has resolved to settle down. He gets a job, buys a house and persuades Liesel to move in with him.

Life's perfect, until Liesel delivers her ultimatum: if he won't agree to start a family, she'll have to leave. He can't bear to lose her, but how can he face the prospect of fatherhood when he has no idea what being a father means? If he could somehow make her stay, he wouldn't have to choose … and it would be a shame not to make use of the cellar.

Will this be the solution to his problems, or the catalyst for his own unravelling?

Both titles available from all major online and offline outlets.

Lightning Source UK Ltd.
Milton Keynes UK
UKHW011515071121
393540UK00001B/80